BLACKBIRDS

ALSO BY CHUCK WENDIG

THE MIRIAM BLACK SERIES
#2: *Mockingbird*
#3: *The Cormorant*
#4: *Thunderbird* (coming soon)

Zerøes
The Blue Blazes
Double Dead
Gods and Monsters: Unclean Spirits

THE HEARTLAND TRILOGY
#1: *Under the Empyrean Sky*
#2: *Blightborn*
#3: *The Harvest*

ATLANTA BURNS SERIES
Atlanta Burns

NONFICTION
The Kick-Ass Writer: 1001 Ways to Write Great Fiction,
  Get Published, and Earn Your Audience

CHUCK WENDIG

BLACKBIRDS

SAGA PRESS

LONDON SYDNEY **NEW YORK** TORONTO NEW DELHI

SAGA PRESS
AN IMPRINT OF SIMON & SCHUSTER, INC.

1230 AVENUE OF THE AMERICAS, NEW YORK, NEW YORK 10020

TO THE DEAD,
WHO CAN TEACH
YOU A WHOLE
LOT ABOUT LIFE

PART ONE

ONE

THE DEATH OF DEL AMICO

Car lights strobe through busted motel blinds.

When the headlights come in, Miriam regards herself in the dirty mirror.

I look like something blown in off a dusty highway, she thinks. Dirty, torn jeans. Tight white tee. Bleach-blonde hair, the roots coming up, those dark, earthen roots.

She puts her hands on her hips and cocks them this way, then that. With the back of her hand, she wipes away a smear of lipstick from where Del kissed her.

"The lights need to be on," she says to nobody, foretelling the future.

She clicks the lamp by the bed. Piss-yellow light illumines the ratty room.

A roach sits paralyzed in the middle of the floor.

"Shoo," she says. "Fuck off. You're free to go."

The roach does as it's told. It boogies under the pull-down bed, relieved.

Back to the mirror, then.

"They always said you were an old soul," she mutters. Tonight, she's really feeling it.

In the bathroom, the shower hisses. It's almost time now. She sits down on the side of the bed and rubs her eyes, yawns.

She hears the squeaking of the shower knobs. The pipes in

the walls groan and stutter like a train is passing. Miriam balls up her monkey toes and flexes them tight. The toe-knuckles pop.

In the bathroom, Del is humming. Some Podunk fuckwit country tune. She hates country. That music is the dull, throbbing pulse-beat of the Heartland. *Wait. This is North Carolina, right? Is North Carolina the Heartland? Whatever.* The Heartland. The Confederacy. The Wide-Open Nowhere. Did it matter?

The bathroom door opens, and Del Amico steps out, wreathed in ghosts of steam.

He might have been attractive once. Still is, maybe, in this light. He's middle-aged, lean as a drinking straw. Ropy arms, hard calves. Cheap, generic boxer-briefs pulled tight on bony hips. *He's got a good jaw, a nice chin,* she thinks, *and the stubble doesn't hurt.* He smiles big and broad at her and licks his teeth— bright pearly whites, the tongue snaking over them with a squeak.

She smells mint.

"Mouthwash," he says, smacking his lips and breathing hot, fresh breath in her direction. He rubs a scummy towel up over his head. "Found some under the sink."

"Super," she says. "Hey, I have a new idea for a crayon color: cockroach brown."

Del peers out from the hood formed from his towel.

"What? Crayon? The hell you going on about?"

"Crayola makes all kinds of crazy colors. You know. Burnt umber. Burnt *sienna*. Blanched almond. Baby-shit yellow. And so on, and so forth. I'm just saying, cockroaches have their own color. It's *distinct*. Crayola should get on that. The kids'll love it."

Del laughs, but he's obviously a little confused. He continues toweling off, and then stops. He squints at her, like he's trying to see the dolphin in one of those Magic Eye paintings.

He looks her up and down.

"I thought you said you were gonna be out here . . . getting comfortable," he says.

She shrugs. "Ooh. No. Truth be told, I'm never really that comfortable. Sorry."

"But . . ." His voice trails off. He wants to say it. His mouth forms the words before he speaks them, but finally: "You're not naked."

"Very observant," she says, giving him a thumbs-up and a wink. "I got bad news, Del. I am not actually a truck stop prostitute, and therefore we shall not be fucking on this good eve. Or morning. I guess it's morning? Either way, no fucking. No ticky, no laundry."

That jaw of his tightens. "But you offered. You owe me."

"Considering you haven't actually paid me yet, and *further* considering that prostitution is not exactly legal in this state—though, far be it for me to legislate morality; frankly, I think what people do is their business—I don't think I owe you dick, Del."

"Goddamn," he says. "You love to hear yourself talk, don't you?"

"I do." She does.

"You're a liar. A liar with a foul little mouth."

"My mother always said I had a mouth like a sailor. Not in an *arr, matey* way, but in a *fuck this* and *shit that* way. And yes, I am a big fat liar. My dirty, torn-up jeans on fire."

It's like he doesn't know what to do. She sees it; she's really steaming his bun. His nostrils are flaring like he's a bull about to charge.

"A lady should be respectful" is all he manages through gritted teeth. He pitches the towel in the corner.

Miriam snorts. "That's me. My fair fuckin' lady."

Del takes a deep breath, moves over to the dresser, then slides a grungy, ain't-worth-nothing Timex over his bony wrist. It isn't long before he sees what she's laid out for him next to the watch.

"What the—?"

He holds up photos, picks them up as a bunch, flips through them. A woman and two young girls at a Sears portfolio special. The same kids on the playground. The woman at someone's wedding.

"I found those in your car," Miriam explains. "Your family, right? I thought it kind of interesting, what with you bringing a prostitute—er, *supposed* prostitute—back to a motel room. Doesn't seem like the kind of thing a good husband or daddy would do, but what do I know? Then again, maybe that's why you hide them all the way in the glove compartment. It's like a mirror—if you can't see them, they can't see you."

He pivots, heel to toe, the wallet photos in a quaking grip.

"Who are you to judge?" he seethes.

She waves him off. "Oh, hush, I'm not judging. I'm just waiting. Since we're waiting, I should *probably* also tell you that I've been following you for a couple weeks now." His gaze narrows again, and he's looking at her like maybe he recognizes her, or is trying to. She keeps talking. "I know you like hookers. Pros and hos. All kinds, too! You're the kind of fellow who'll eat every candy out of the chocolate box. Variety is the spice of life; good for you. I *also* happen to know that, outside of some relatively boring sexual proclivities, you like to hit women. Four prostitutes. Two with black eyes, one with a cut chin, the fourth with a busted lower lip—"

Del moves fast.

Bam. A tight coiled fist hits her right in the eye and knocks her back on the bed. Capillaries burst. Fireworks on a black background. Gasping, she scrambles backward, thinking he's going to advance and try to beat her or choke her, but by the time she's in a crouch and ready to kick, bite, or collapse his throat with a forearm, she sees he hasn't moved one inch.

He's just standing there. Shaking. Angry, sad, confused; she can't tell.

She waits it out. He doesn't move toward her. He isn't even looking at her now—Del's staring off at a nowhere point a thousand miles from here.

Gingerly, Miriam reaches over to the nightstand and turns the alarm clock so she can read it. It's an old-ass clock, the kind with the numbers that turn like Vanna White's flipping them. Each with a *click*.

"It's twelve forty," she says. "That means you have three minutes."

"Three minutes?" He narrows his gaze, trying to suss out her game.

"That's right, Del, three minutes. Now's the time to ask yourself: Any thoughts you want to share? Grandma's corn bread recipe? Location of a buried pirate treasure? Any poetic last words? You know, *Either the wallpaper goes, or I do?*" She waves him off. "I know, an Oscar Wilde reference. I reached too far for that one. My bad."

He doesn't move, but he tightens up. Every muscle pulled taut to bone.

"You think you're going to kill me?" he asks. "*That* what you think?"

She clucks her tongue. "No, sir, I do not think that. I'm not the killer type. I'm more *passive*-aggressive than aggressive. I'm a wait-and-see kind of girl. More vulture than falcon."

They stare at each other. She feels scared and sick and a little excited.

Click.

The 0 flips to 1.

"You want to hit me again," she says.

"I just might."

"You think, *I'll hit her again, and then I'll fuck her like she deserves*—that's, of course, provided you can get Little Dale Junior to race. I saw the dick pills in your glove compartment. Next to the OxyContin."

"You shut the hell up."

She holds up a finger. "Let me ask you one question, though. You hit your wife and daughters?"

He hesitates. She's not sure what that means. Does it mean he feels guilty about it? Or that he'd never consider touching a hair on their pretty little heads and would die if they found out?

"At this point," she says, "it's not like it matters. I'm mostly just curious. You bang hookers and punch them in their faces, so we've already established that you're not gonna win Father of the Year. I'm just trying to feel out the *depth* of your character—"

He lets out a frustrated whoop and swings at her—a clumsy, wide throw, telegraphed loud and clear like his body was using a bullhorn. Miriam leans back. The fist catches the air in front of her nose, *whiff*.

She stabs a heel out and catches him in the balls.

He staggers backward, buttbone thunking against the wall, moaning, grabbing.

"You only get one freebie with me," she hisses. "Swing and a miss, asshole."

Click.

The time is now 12:42.

"One minute," she says, easing off the bed.

He still doesn't get it. They never do.

"Shut up," he whimpers. "You fuckin' whore."

"This is how it's going to go. Any second now, we're going to hear a car honking out in the parking lot—"

A car honks outside. Once, then twice, then a third time when the driver lays on the horn just to get the message across.

Del looks from Miriam to the window, then back again. She's seen the look before. It's the look of a caged animal. He doesn't know where to go, where to run, but the truth is, he can't run anywhere. He's trapped. What he can't understand is *how* or *why*.

"What comes next, you ask?" She snaps her fingers. "Some-where, outside, someone starts yelling. Maybe it's the car-honking guy. Maybe it's the dude the car-honking guy was honking *at*. Who cares? Because . . ."

She lets her words trail off, only to be replaced by someone yelling out in the parking lot. The words were indecipherable, just a muted, Neanderthal rant.

Del's eyes go wide.

Miriam forms her thumb and forefinger into a gun, and points it at the alarm clock. She lets the hammer—her thumb—fall.

"Boom," she says, and—

Click.

The time is now 12:43.

"You have epilepsy, Del?"

The question registers, and she knows now that he does. It explains what's about to happen. A moment of calm strikes him, a kind of *serene confusion*, and then—

His body tightens.

"And here it is," Miriam says. "The kicker, the game ball, the season-ender."

The seizure hits him like a crashing wave.

Del Amico's body goes rigid, and he drops backward, his head narrowly missing the corner of the motel dresser. He makes a strangled sound. He sits upright on his knees, but then his back arches and his shoulder blades press hard against the matted Berber.

Miriam rubs her eye.

"I know what you're thinking," she says as Del's eyes start to bulge like champagne corks ready to pop. "*Jeez, why doesn't this broad stick a wallet under my tongue? Couldn't she do me a solid?* Or maybe you're thinking, *Hey, I've had seizures before, and none of them killed me. A guy can't actually swallow his own tongue, right? That's just a myth?* Or maybe, *just maybe,*

9

you think I'm some kind of batshit highway witch with magical powers."

He gurgles. His cheeks go red. Then purple.

Miriam shrugs, wincing, watching it unfold with grim fascination. Not that this is the first time she's seen it.

"Not so, my friendly neighborhood whore-puncher. This is your destiny, to choke on your own mouth meats, to expire here in this God-fucked motel in the middle of Hell's half acre. I'd do something if I could, but I can't. Were I to put the wallet under your tongue, I'd probably only push the tongue in deeper. See, my mother used to say, 'Miriam, it is what it is.' And this, Del Amico, is that."

Froth bubbles out over Del's ashen lips. The blood vessels in his eyes burst.

Just like she remembers it.

His rigid body goes limp. All the fight goes out of him. His wiry frame slackens, his head tilts at a bad angle, his cheek hits the floor.

Then, insult to injury, the cockroach runs out from under the bed. It uses Del's twisted upper lip as a step ladder, and squeezes its fat little body up into his nostril before disappearing.

Miriam takes a deep breath and shudders.

She tries to speak, tries to say she's sorry, but—

She can't stop it. She runs to the bathroom and pukes in the toilet.

Miriam kneels like that for a while, her head leaning up against the base of the sink. The porcelain feels cool, calming. She smells mint. The clean scent of cheap mouthwash.

It often hits her like this. Like some part of her is dying along with them, some part that she has to gag on and purge and flush away.

And, as always, she knows what will really make her feel better.

She crawls out of the bathroom, over Del's cooling body, and fetches her messenger bag from the far side of the bed. Fishing around, she finds what she's looking for and pulls out a crumpled pack of Marlboro Lights. She taps one out, plugs it between her lips, and lights it.

Miriam exhales smoke, a jet from each nostril. Like steam from a dragon's nose.

The nausea recedes, a septic tide washing the poison back to sea.

"Much better," she says to whoever is listening. Del's ghost, maybe. Or the cockroach.

Then she goes back into the bag to find Item Number Two: a black notebook with a red pen tucked in the spiral. The notebook is almost at its end. Just ten more pages left. Ten blank pages, a great gulf of awful potential: an unwritten future that's already been written.

"Oh, wait," she says. "I'm getting sloppy over here. Can't forget this—"

Miriam goes and grabs Del's pants and digs in for his wallet. Inside, she finds just shy of fifty bucks and a MasterCard. Enough to get her on the road, put a meal in her belly, move her on to the next town.

"Thanks for the donation, Del."

Miriam props up some pillows against the bed's headboard and leans back. She flips open the notebook, and she writes:

Dear Diary:
I did it again.

TWO

OF SCAVENGERS AND PREDATORS

I-40. Quarter past one in the morning.

It's just finished raining. The highway glistens.

The air smells of wet asphalt, which is an odor Miriam associates with fat nightcrawlers stretched across moist macadam.

Car tires *shoosh* and *hiss* by. Everything is a smear of headlights in one direction and brake lights in the other.

Miriam's been out here now for twenty minutes, and she wonders why this isn't easier. Here she is, tight white T-shirt—a tight, white, *wet* T-shirt with no bra in sight—and her thumb out for a ride. Prime, Grade-A Road Trash, she thinks. And yet, nobody stops.

A Lexus speeds past.

"You're a dick," she says.

A white SUV rumbles by.

"You're a *super*dick."

A rust-fucked pickup approaches, and she thinks, this is it. Whoever's driving this junk-bucket is sure to think he can score with this thin slip of road pussy. The truck slows; the driver wants a looky-loo. But then it speeds up again. The truck's horn honks. An empty Chick-Fil-A cup pirouettes through open air and narrowly misses her head. Hillbilly guffaws Doppler past.

Miriam turns her hitchhiker's thumb into a middle finger, and she yells out, "Eat a dick and die, fuckpie!"

She expects them to keep going.

But: red flash. Brake lights. The truck stops hard, then reverses onto the shoulder.

"Shit," Miriam says. Just what she needs. She half expects the identical twin of the dearly departed Del Amico to step out of the truck, scratching his gut through his wife-beater. What she gets instead is a pair of frat boys.

They're grinning.

One's got that fireman's build and a pair of clear, mean eyes beneath a mop of blond. The other's shorter—squat, really. Fat, freckled cheeks. Tarheels cap overlooking a pair of puckered butthole eyes. Clean suburban white-boy clothes.

Miriam nods. "Nice truck. The Tetanus Express."

"It's my dad's," Blondie says, coming right up on her as cars continue to pass. Squats—that's how she thinks of the other one—trundles up behind her.

"It's a real nice ride," she says.

"You *need* a ride?" Squats asks from behind her. His tone isn't friendly.

"Nah," she says. "I'm just out here flippin' the bird to pass the time."

"You're a Yankee," Blondie says. Ironic, because he doesn't have much of the Southern pluck to his voice. Those icy eyes roam all over her. "A cute Yankee."

Miriam massages her temples. She thinks for a moment about indulging these two frat-tards in some clever roadside banter, but the truth is, she's damp, she's tired, and the blacked eye is really starting to pound.

"Listen. I know how this goes. You two boys think you're going to get some. Maybe tag me at both ends, maybe just push me around, maybe see if I have any money. I get it. Like any good scavenger, I know predators when I see them. You know what, though? I *just* don't have the time. I'm fucking tired, for real. So.

Get back in your lockjaw jalopy, and head back to the highway from whence you came."

Blondie steps up on her. He doesn't touch her, but he's nose-to-nose.

"I like the way you use your mouth," he leers.

"Last warning," she says. "You see the black eye, and you think I'm good to go, but sometimes a girl lets herself get hit for all kinds of complicated reasons. I won't let that happen again tonight. You picking up what I'm putting down?"

Apparently not, because Squats puts his sausage fingers on her hips.

Miriam reacts.

Her head snaps back, pops Squats's nose—

Squats is in his fifties now, fatter than ever, his nose one big gin blossom, and he's yelling at some woman in a yellow dress, and sweat is beading on his brow, and flecks of spit are flying out of his mouth, and suddenly, he plants his fat hand on the kitchen counter as the heart attack tightens the left half of his body and turns his every nerve ending into a roadmap of pain.

—and he howls, and Miriam thinks to turn up the volume by reaching back and gripping his crotch in a crushing claw. Blondie's taken aback, but she knows she doesn't have long. She spits in his eye, which buys her another second, so she uses her free hand to punch him once, then twice in the throat—

The cancer is eating him up, juicing his bowels into a tumor-squeezed mess, but he's old, at least in his late seventies, and he lies there surrounded by the boops and beeps and blips of hospital equipment, and he's got his family there. A young boy grips his hand. An old woman bends down to kiss his forehead. A woman in her forties with her blonde hair pulled tight and a peaceful look on her face pats him on the chest once, then twice, and that's it—the old man cries out, shits blood, and dies.

Squats tries to slap at her, a clumsy grizzly-bear move, but

14

she steps out of the way and his meaty palm swishes through air. Miriam's elbow catches him hard in his already-busted, already-bleeding nose, and Squats goes down.

Blondie, face red, still choking, rushes at her with all the finesse of a tumbling boulder. She pulls her upper torso back to dodge him, but lets her knee hang out there and catch him right in the breadbasket. Blondie grunts, a hard *oof* of air, and slips on some gravel. He goes down.

"You think I come out here and I don't know how to protect myself?" she screams at them. She picks up a handful of gravel and pitches it at Blondie, who moans and protects his head. Miriam hawks up another loogie and spits it in his hair. For good measure, she grabs the Tarheel hat off Squats and pitches it onto the highway. "Assholes."

Then: harsh white. Headlights. Big shadow grumbling.

The hiss of hydraulic brakes.

A bobtail—the truck part of an eighteen-wheeler, this one without its trailer—pulls up onto the shoulder, gravel popping underneath its massive tires.

Miriam shields her eyes, sees the driver's silhouette. *Jesus,* she thinks, *it's a goddamn Frankenstein. Where are the torches and pitchforks when you need them?*

The Frankenstein is holding a crowbar.

"Everything okay here?" Frankenstein asks. The voice booms, even over the rumble of the idling truck.

"We're just having a little friendly tussle," Miriam yells over the truck's engine.

She can't see his face, but she sees that Frankenstein pivots his cinder-block head, getting a good luck at Squats and Blondie. He shrugs. "You need a ride?"

"Me or the two moaning assholes?"

"You."

"What the hell," she mumbles, then heads over to the cab to get in.

THE INTERVIEW

Miriam takes a drink from her water bottle. *Nope, still not vodka,* she thinks.

Above her head, sparrows rustle their wings in the eaves of the warehouse—dark shapes, stirring.

She lights another Marlboro. Bats the ashtray back and forth the way a cat might play with a mouse. Blows smoke rings. Drums her fingers so her nails—some chewed to the cuticle, some left long—click on the top of the card table.

Finally, the door opens.

The kid comes in, a notebook and pages tucked under his arm, a laptop bag hanging at his side, a digital recorder dangling from a cord around his neck. His hair is a mess.

He pulls up a chair.

"Sorry," he says.

Miriam shrugs. "Whatever. Paul, right?"

"Paul. Yeah." He offers to shake her hand. She stares at the hand like it has a dick and balls attached to it. He doesn't get it at first, but then it dawns on him. "Oh. Ah. Right."

"Do you *really* want to know?" she asks.

Paul pulls his hand back and gently shakes his head no. He sits down without saying another word. He gets out the notebook, a couple copies of his 'zine (headlines like ransom notes, printed on pages of fluorescent fuchsia, eye-punching lemon, nuclear lime), and delicately places the digital recorder in the center of the table.

"Thanks for the interview," he says. The kid sounds nervous.

"Sure thing." She sucks on the cigarette. After an exhale of smoke in his direction, she adds, "I don't mind talking about it. It's not a secret. It's just that nobody listens."

"I'm listening."

"I know. You bring me what I asked?"

He pulls a crumpled brown bag, sets it down in front of her with a *thunk*.

She snaps her fingers. "It isn't gonna unwrap itself, is it?"

Paul hurries to pull the bottle of scotch—Johnnie Walker Red Label—from the bag.

"For me?" she asks, waving him off. "You shouldn't have."

She unscrews the cap and takes a swig.

"Our 'zine—it's called *Rebel Base*—gets, like, a hundred readers or something. And soon we're going to be on the Internet."

"Welcome to the future, right?" She fingers the moist rim of the scotch bottle. "I don't really care, by the way. I'm just happy to talk. I like to talk."

"Okay."

They sit there, staring at each other.

"You're not a very good interviewer," she says.

"I'm sorry. You're just not who I expected."

"And who did you expect?"

He pauses. Looks her over. At first, Miriam wonders if maybe he's hot for her, wants to jump her bones, maybe. But that isn't it. On his face is the same look one might have while marveling at a two-headed lamb or a picture of the Virgin Mary burned into a slice of toast.

"My uncle Joe said you're the real deal," he explains.

"Your uncle Joe. I would ask how he's doing, but . . ."

"It happened like you said."

Miriam isn't surprised.

"I haven't been wrong yet. For the record, I liked Joe. I met him in a bar. I was drunk. He bumped me. I saw the stroke that'd kill him. Fuck it, I thought, and I told him. Every detail—that's where the devil lives, you know, right there in the goddamn details. I said, Joe, you're going to be out fishing. It's going to be a year from now—well, technically, three hundred seventy-seven days, and it took me some noodling around on a napkin to get the number and the date. I said, you'll be out there in your hip waders. You're gonna catch a big one. Not the biggest, not the best, but a big one. I didn't know what kind of fish, because, fuck, I'm not a fishologist—"

"I think it's an ichthyologist."

"I'm also not an English major, nor do I care to become one. He said it would probably be a trout. A rainbow. Or a largemouth bass. He asked me what kind of bait he had on the line, and I said it looked like a shiny penny, one flatted by a train so it makes a smooshed oval. He called it a spinner, said that's what he used to catch trout. Again, I'm not an ick, uhhh, ithky, a *fish*ologist."

She taps the cigarette into the ashtray, crushing it.

"I said, Joe, you'll be standing there with this fish in your hand, and you'll be smiling and whistling even though nobody's around, holding it up for God and all the other fish to see, and that's when it'll hit you. A blood clot will loosen and fire through your arteries like a bullet down a rifled barrel. *Boom!* Right into the brain. You'll lose cognitive function, I said. You'll drop into the water. Nobody'll be there for you. You'll die, and the fish swims on."

Paul is quiet. He worries at his lip with the too-white teeth of a teenager.

"That's how they found him," Paul says. "Pole in hand."

Miriam chuckles. "Pole in hand."

Paul blinks.

"Get it? Pole? In hand? You know, like, his dick?" She waves him off, and pulls out another Marlboro. "Well, screw you, then. Joe would've liked it. Joe appreciated the finer points of a double entendre."

"Did you sleep with him?" Paul asks.

Miriam feigns shock. She fans herself like a wounded Southern debutante.

"Why, Paul, what do you think of me? I am the very model of chastity." He isn't buying it. She lights the cigarette and waves him off. "Dude, I discarded the key to my virginity belt long ago—just up and tossed it into a river, I did. That being said—no, Paul, I did not bang your uncle. We just drank together. Closed out the bar. And then he went on his way and I went mine. I wasn't sure he really believed me until you found me."

"He told me about it a month or so before he died," Paul says, running his fingers through his unkempt hair. Paul stares off at a distant point, remembering. "He totally believed it. I said, just don't go fishing that day. And he shrugged and just said, but he really wanted to go fishing, and if that's how he was going to die, then so be it. He got a thrill out of it, I think."

Paul reaches over and turns on the digital recorder. He watches her carefully. Is he looking for her approval? Does he think she'll reach over and bite him?

"So," he asks. "How does it work?"

Miriam takes a deep breath. "This thing that I have?"

"Yes. Yeah. That."

"Well, Paul, this thing? It's got rules."

THREE

LOUIS

Long highway. Everything else is black, pulled away into shadow. All that exists is what the headlights reveal—the glowing middle line, the center divider, a pine tree or exit sign as it emerges from darkness and passes back to darkness.

The big trucker is as his shadow suggested: canned-ham hands, shoulders like hunks of granite, a chest like a bunch of barrels strung up together. But he's clean-shaven, with a soft face and kind eyes, hair the color of beach sand.

Probably a rapist, Miriam thinks.

The cab of the truck is clean, too. Almost *too* clean, not a speck of dust or road grime. A control freak, clean freak, rapist serial killer wear-the-skins-of-women freak, Miriam thinks. The radio and CB sit mounted on a chrome plate. The seats are brown leather. (Probably *human* leather.) A pair of dice—hollow aluminum, with the dots punched out—hang from the rearview, lazily spinning.

"All of life is a roll of the dice," she says.

Frankenstein looks at Miriam as if he's confused by her.

"Where you headed?" he asks, studying her.

"Nowhere," she answers. "Anywhere."

"You don't care?"

"Not so much. Just get me away from that motel and those two douchebags."

"What if I'm going to another motel?"

"Long as it's not *that* motel, we're square."

Frankenstein looks pensive. His big hands pull tight around the wheel. His brow furrows. She wonders if maybe he's thinking about the things he's going to do to her. Or maybe what use he might get out of her bleached skull. A candy dish would be nice, she imagines. Or a lamp. She was in Mexico, what, two years ago? During the Day of the Dead celebrations? All those colorful *ofrendas*—the bananas, the *pan de muerto* bread, the marigolds, the mangos, the red and yellow ribbons. But what really stays with her are the sugar skulls: hardened meringue *memento mori* dotted with colored confections, each wide-eyed and grinning, blissful in its delicious demise. Maybe this guy will be cool enough to do something like *that* with her skull. Lacquer it with sugar. Tasty.

"I'm Louis," Frankenstein says, interrupting her fantasies.

"Dude," she says, "I don't want to be friends. I just want to get away."

That'll shut him up, she thinks. And it does. But he only grows more preoccupied. Frankenstein—*Louis*—gnaws on a lip. He taps on the wheel. Is he mad? Sad? Ready to rape her early? She can't tell.

"Fine," she blurts. "You want to talk, great. Sure. *Yes.* Let's talk."

He's surprised. He says nothing.

Miriam decides she's going to have to do all the heavy lifting.

"You want to know about the shiner?" she says.

"The what?"

"The bruise. The black eye. You saw it as soon as I stepped into this truck; don't lie." She clears her throat. "Which is a very nice truck, by the way. So shiny." She thinks, *You probably polish it with the hair you scalp from pretty girls like me.* Miriam takes a moment to commend herself. Normally, she'd say that sort of thing out loud, which would probably get her kicked out onto the rain-slick highway.

"No," he says. "I mean, yes, I saw it. But you don't need to tell me—"

Miriam opens her bag and starts rooting through it. "You look flummoxed."

"Flummoxed."

"Yes. Flummoxed. That's a good word, isn't it? It sounds like a made-up word, like maybe a word a three-year-old would use in place of another word. You know, like, *Mommy, my flummoxed hurts, I think I ated too much pasghetti.*"

"I . . . never thought of it like that."

She screws a cigarette between her lips and starts flicking the lighter.

"You mind if I smoke?"

"I do. You can't smoke in here."

She frowns. She could really use a smoke. Scowling, she puts the lighter away but leaves the cigarette dangling from her lips.

"Whatever. Your truck. Anyway. The black eye, that's what you want to talk about."

"Did one of those boys give it to you? We could call the police."

She snorts. "Does it look like either of those frat-fucks gave me a black eye? Please. I can handle myself. No, this shiner was dutifully applied by my boyfriend."

"Your boyfriend hits you?"

"Not anymore. I'm done with scum like him. That's why I don't want to go back to the motel, see? Because that prick is back there."

"You left him."

"I left the shit out of him. Get this. He's lying there on the bed, all smug and satisfied after popping me in the eye and then popping his cookies—at least he didn't pop his cookies *in* my eye, am I right?—and the dumb fucker falls asleep. Ooh. Bad move. He starts snoring like a drunken bear with sleep apnea, and I think, *It's over.* I'm tired of getting pushed around. Tired of the cigarette burns, tired of the belt and the golf cleats and all that shit."

Louis stares dead ahead, like he's not sure what to make of the story. She continues.

"So, I grab a pair of handcuffs—sorry for the sordid details, but the jerkoff likes to get kinky and has a real power-trip fetish. I take the handcuffs, and gently, so as not to wake him, I handcuff his one wrist to the bedpost." Miriam pulls out the cigarette, twirls it betwixt thumb and forefinger like a cancer baton. "I take the key, and I go chuck it into the toilet, then I pee on the key for good measure. But that's not all—as they say on TV, *Wait, there's more.*"

Miriam, it must be said, loves to lie. She's very good at it.

"I took one of those little plastic bears, the ones filled with honey? Again, I know, kinky details, but the guy liked food-play. Whipped cream on my tits, a lollipop in my mouth, a hunk of broccoli up his ass, whatever. So I take the honey bear, and I drizzle the sticky golden goo all over his—"

She makes a swirly motion over her crotch region with her index finger. For added emphasis, she whistles.

"Christ," Louis says.

"Not done yet. When I blew out of there, I left the door wide open. Windows, too. I figure whatever kind of animal wants to come in and snack on his Honey Nut Cheerios, so be it. Flies, bees, a stray dog."

"Christ," Louis says again, his jaw set firm.

"Made some Pooh bear very happy, I hope." She clears her throat, then sticks the cigarette back between her lips. "Or some homeless guy."

For the first minute, Louis doesn't say anything. The trucker just sits, stewing. His shoulders tense. He looks pissed. Does he know that she just lied? Is this when he slams on the brakes, puts her through the windshield because she's not wearing her seat belt, then rapes her broken body on the soaked macadam?

Bam. He pounds his hand against the steering wheel.

Miriam doesn't have anything smart-ass to say. A slow realization creeps up on her: *I can't take this guy. He'll crush me like a bug.*

"Goddamn assholes," he says.

She narrows her eyes. "What? Who?"

"Men."

"You're gay?" It's the way he says it.

He pivots his head, levels his gaze at her. "Gay? What? No."

"I just thought—"

"Men don't know how good they have it. Men are basically . . . children. Pigs."

"Pig children," Miriam offers, a quiet addendum.

"We never see what's in front of us. The women that are kind enough to be in our lives, we just treat them like garbage. It's nonsense. Plain nonsense. And men who hit women? Who take advantage of them? Who don't just fail to appreciate what they have but they outright . . . abuse what's been given to them? My wife—when she left me . . . I didn't fully *appreciate* . . ."

He hits the steering wheel again.

That's when Miriam decides she likes this man.

It's the first time she's felt even the tiniest bit inclined toward anyone in . . . years. Something about him: sweet, sad, damaged. She knows who he reminds her of *(Ben, he reminds you of Ben)*, but she doesn't want to go there, and she shoves that thought back into the darkest corners of her brain.

And then, she can't help it. She has to know. She has to *see.* It's a compulsion. An addiction. She offers her hand.

"My name's Miriam."

But he's still fuming. He doesn't take the proffered hand.

Shit, she thinks. C'mon. Grab it. Shake it. *I need to see.*

"Miriam's a pretty name," he says.

Hesitantly, she withdraws her hand. "Nice to meet you, Lou."

"Louis, not Lou."

She shrugs. "Your truck, your name."

"I'm sorry," he offers. "I don't mean to get pissy. It's just . . ." He waves it off. "Been a long couple weeks. Just coming down off a backslide from Cincinnati and have to head down to Charlotte to pick up another load."

He takes a deep breath through his nose, like he's trying to ratchet up his courage.

"Thing is, I've got a few days down there before I grab the next haul. I don't get too many days off, I usually go straight through, but . . . I was thinking. Maybe you'll be down in that area. It's only an hour south of here. And maybe, if you *are* in that area, and you have a spare night, well. We could do dinner. A movie."

She puts out her hand. "It's a deal."

He doesn't grab it, and Miriam wonders how bold she'll have to be. Reach up and tweak his ear? *She only needs skin to skin to see. . . .*

But then he smiles and takes her hand in his own, and—

The lantern room is encased in glass. One windowpane is broken out, and the wind howls madly through the gap. Thunder rumbles in the distance. Gray light filters in through the dirty windows and illuminates Louis's face, a face encrusted in dried blood.

Somewhere, the sound of the ocean.

Louis is bound to a wooden chair next to the lighthouse lantern. A dizzying array of optics sits above his head. Brown extension cords affix his wrists to the chair arms, and another pair holds his feet to the chair legs. His head is held fast by black electrical tape wrapped around his forehead, fastening his skull to base of the lighthouse's pedestal clockworks.

A tall, thin man approaches. He is entirely hairless. No eyebrows. No eyelashes, even.

In one of his smooth, spidery hands he holds a long fillet knife.

The man admires the blade for a moment, though it is pocked with rust and smells not-too-faintly of fish guts.

"Get away from me," Louis stammers. "Who are you? Who are you people? I don't have what you want!"

"That no longer matters," the man says. He has an accent. Nebulous. European.

The man moves preternaturally fast. He stabs Louis in the left eye with the knife. It does not go to the brain and only ruins the eye: a choice the hairless man has made. Louis screams. The attacker withdraws the knife. It makes a sucking sound as he extracts it.

His thin lips form a mirthless smile.

He pauses. He admires.

Louis's good eye darts to somewhere over the man's shoulder.

"Miriam?" Louis asks, but it's too late. The man stabs him again, this time through the right eye, and this time, all the way to the hilt.

All the way to the brain.

FOUR

THE MILLION-DOLLAR QUESTION

She can still hear the sound as the knife pulls out of the one eye and the sound as it plunges into the other. And him speaking her name . . . *Miriam?* It bounces around her skull like a ricocheting bullet.

Her hand feels like it's touching a hot stove. She gasps and jerks, pulling it away.

Her head slams into the passenger-side window. Not enough to crack it but enough where she sees stars. The unlit cigarette drops from her lips and tumbles into her lap.

"Do you know me?" she asks, blinking away the white spots. Louis, of course, looks confused.

"I don't know if anybody knows anybody," he says.

"No!" she barks, sharp, *too* sharp, and shakes her head. "I *mean*, have we met? We don't know each other?"

Louis still has his hand hanging out there from where she grabbed it, but now he slowly pulls back, like any fast movement might cause him to lose it.

"No. We don't know each other."

She rubs her eyes. "Do you know *anyone* named Miriam?"

"I don't think so. No."

He's watching her now like she's a rattlesnake. He's got one hand on the wheel and the other hanging free—just in case the rattlesnake decides to bite, she thinks. He probably thinks she's on drugs. If only.

Shit. She knows how this adds up. This is a bad equation. Her guts roil.

"Stop the truck," she says.

"What? The truck? No. Let me get to a—"

"Stop the goddamn truck!" This time, it's a hoarse scream. She doesn't mean it to be, but that's how it comes out. And the reminder of how little control she really has only furthers the feeling that she is weightless, dizzy, spiraling into a yawning black hole.

Louis is kind enough not to punch the brake. He eases it in, slow. The hydraulics whine. He brings the truck over to the shoulder and lets it idle.

"Okay. Calm down," he says, putting his hands out.

Miriam grits her teeth. "That's the worst thing you can ever say to somebody who's not calm. It's just gas on a fire, Louis."

"I'm sorry. I'm not . . . trained in this."

This? He means dealing with crazy people. Which she is, probably.

"I'm not trained in being this way, either." *Though,* she thinks, *I'm getting better with it. Week by week, month by month, year by bloody year.* One day, it'll be water off a duck's back.

"What's wrong?" he asks.

"That's the million-dollar question."

"You can tell me."

"I can't, I really can't. You wouldn't . . ." She takes a deep breath. "I have to go."

"We're in the middle of nowhere."

"It's America. Nowhere is nowhere. Everywhere is somewhere."

"I can't let you do that."

She fishes the cigarette from her lap and, with trembling hands, tucks it behind her ear. "You're a very nice man, Louis. But you *will* let me get out of this truck, because you know now that I am off my bloody rocker. I see the look on your face. Already you're thinking, *She's not worth the trouble.* And I'm not. I'm a curse. I'm an infected boil on your neck. Best thing I can do for you is get away from you. Best thing *you* can do is lance the boil."

Grabbing her messenger bag, she pops the door.

"Wait!" he says.

She ignores him and hops out onto the cracked and crumbling highway shoulder. Her feet plant in a murky puddle, soaking through.

Louis slides over to the passenger side and pops the glove box.

"Wait, here," he says, going through the compartment. He pulls out a white envelope, and as he cracks it, she sees what waits within:

Money. A thick wad of it, all Andrew Jacksons.

With a callused thumb and forefinger he peels out five bills, then thrusts them at her.

"Take it."

"Go fuck yourself."

He looks hurt. Good. She needs to hurt him. She hates doing it. But it's like medicine. Everybody needs their medicine. Tastes bad. Does wonders.

"I have plenty."

It's the last thing she wants to know. It makes him a mark. She can't help but picture him as roadkill now, and her picking at his exposed guts with a vulture's beak.

"I'm not a charity case," she says, even though she knows she is.

His hurt has already scabbed over and become something else. He's angry now. He grabs her hand, hard enough to force her but not so it hurts, and presses the money into her palm.

"It's a hundred dollars."

"Louis—"

"Listen. *Listen.* Walk the way we were driving. It'll be a half hour or so. You'll find a motel down that way, a motor lodge; it's like a . . . a series of bungalows. There's a gas station and a bar.

You keep walking, you'll find it. But get off the road. You don't know what kind of weirdoes are out here at one o'clock in the morning."

"I know what kind of weirdoes are out here," she says, because she's one of them. Miriam takes the money. She looks into Louis's eyes: He's trying to be firm, but even now the anger is melting, the scab drying up and flaking away.

"You going to be okay?" he asks.

"I'm always okay," she says. "You best forget you ever met me."

Miriam pulls away from him and walks off. Head down. *Don't look back, dummy.*

She needs a drink.

THE INTERVIEW

"The first rule," Miriam says, "is that I only see what I see when skin touches skin. If I touch your elbow and you're wearing a shirt, then nothing. If I wear gloves—and I used to, because I didn't want to bear witness to all this craziness—then it prevents the vision from happening."

"That must be horrible," Paul says. "I mean—sorry. I just mean, over and over again, you can never get close to somebody, I mean—"

"Relax, Paul. I can take it. I'm a big girl. But this speaks to rule number two. Or maybe number three. I should really write them down. The rule is, it's one and done. I get the vision once. It doesn't keep happening over and over again—though, I'll tell you, some of the really bad ones will keep a girl up at night." She pauses and tries not to think of any. In her mind's eye, so much blood, so much suffering, so many last moments play out. Theater of the macabre, the curtain forever open. Dancing skeletons. Chattering skulls.

"So, what is it that you see?" Paul asks. "You're like, what, an angel floating above the scene? Or are you the person who's dying?"

"An angel. That's funny. Me with my wings." She rubs some sleep boogers from the corner of her eye. "This speaks to the next rule. I'm the impartial observer. My viewpoint hovers above the whole thing, or maybe off to the side. I'm privy to certain details but not others. I know how the person tap-step-shuffles off this mortal coil, for one. Intimately. Death isn't always obvious, you know—a guy clutches his head and falls over, could be a lot of things. But I know what it is. I know if it's a brain tumor or a blood clot or a bumblebee that's burrowed its way into his cerebral cortex.

"I also know when. Year, day, hour, minute, second. It's a red pushpin stuck in the great timeline of the universe, and I can see it. The pushpin I *can't* see, oddly, is where. The location remains a mystery. Outside visual cues, of course. I see a chick's head explode in the parking lot of a McDonald's with street signs at the corner of Asshole Boulevard and Shitbird Lane and she's wearing a DON'T MESS WITH TEXAS T-shirt, then I can use my Sherlock Holmesian deductive reasoning to figure out that pesky riddle. Or I just use Google. I fucking love Google."

"So, how long?"

"How long what?"

"How long—er, how much do you see? One minute? Five minutes?"

"Oh. That. Well. I used to think it was a minute, right? Sixty seconds on the clock, go. Turns out, not so much. I seem to get whatever time I'm supposed to get, if that makes any sense. A car accident might happen over the course of thirty seconds. A heart attack or whatever could unfold over a five-minute period. I see what it lets me see. The weird part is, even if I see five minutes in my mind's eye, it doesn't take more than a second or two in real life. I'll space out, and then I'm back. It's certainly jarring."

Paul frowns, and Miriam can tell that, despite the thing with his uncle, he doesn't quite believe her. Not that she blames him. She finds times, even still, that she herself doesn't buy it. The easier answer is that she's just bugfuck nuts. A real moonbat. A shithouse spider.

"You're witness to the last minutes of human lives," he says.

"Well put," Miriam says. "Lots of human lives. You know how many people you bump into on the subway during summer? Everybody in short sleeves? It's all elbows, Paul. Death and elbows."

"So, why don't you stop it?"

"Stop what? Death?"

"Yeah."

Miriam chuckles, the sound of I-Know-Something-You-Don't. The sound of irony, that mirthless cad, expressed. She tips the bottle to her lips but does not yet drink.

"Why don't I stop it from happening," she ruminates over the lip of the bottle. "Well, Paul, that right there is the last—and cruelest—rule."

She sucks back a cheek-bulging mouthful of Johnnie Walker and explains.

FIVE

BUG LIGHT

Miriam's been walking for a half hour, and the thoughts that run through her mind have serious legs. Terrible thoughts jog swift laps.

The man, the trucker, the Frankenstein. Louis. He is going to die in thirty days, at 7:25 p.m.

And it is going to be a horrible scene. Miriam sees a lot of death play out on the stage inside her skull. Blood and broken glass and dead eyes form the backdrop to her mind. But it's rare that she sees murder. Suicide, yes. Health problems, all the time. Car accidents and other personal disasters, over and over again.

But murder. That is a rare bird.

In a month's time, Louis is going to say her name right before he dies. Worse, he *looks* at someone before the knife punches through his eye and into his brain, and *then* says her name. He sees her there. He's speaking to her.

Miriam goes over it and over it in her head, and not once does it make sense.

She cries out some hybrid of "fuck" and "shit"—she's not really sure—and punctuates it by picking up a hunk of broken asphalt from the shoulder and chucking it against the dead center of an exit sign. It *clangs*. Wobbles.

And just past it, she sees the place: Swifty's Tavern.

Neon beer signs glow bright against the storm-tossed, late-night sky. The bar is a bug light, and she is the fly (fat from feeding off death). She makes a beeline for the place.

Her mouth can taste it already.

Inside, the bar is like the unholy child of a lumberjack and a biker wriggling free from some wretched womb. Dark wood. Animal heads. Chrome rims. Concrete floor.

"An oasis," Miriam says out loud.

The place isn't busy. A few truckers sit at a table, playing cards around a foamy pitcher. Bikers mill around a lone pool table toward the back. Flies orbit a mess of old cheese fries that have dried into a shellacked mound to the left of the door. Iron Butterfly growls from the jukebox. "In-a-Gadda-Da-Blah-Blah, Baby."

She sees the bar, its edges bordered with heavy-gauge chain. It will be her home, she decides, until they evict her.

She tells the bartender, who looks like a pile of uncooked Pillsbury dough stuffed into a dirty black T-shirt, that she needs a drink.

"Fifteen minutes until close," he mumbles, and then adds, "Little girl."

"Cut the 'little girl' shit, Paleface. If I only have fifteen minutes, then I want whiskey. Your cheapest and shittiest. Think lighter fluid mixed with coyote piss. And you can put a shot glass down, but if you're amenable to it, then I'd damn sure like to pour my own."

He stares at her for untold seconds, then finally shrugs. "Sure. Whatever."

Paleface plunks down what might have once been a plastic jug for antifreeze, and from the look of the murky whiskey within, antifreeze might be the healthier choice. He waves away a haze of gnats. They're probably getting high off the vapors.

He uncaps it. He leans back coughing, and rubs his eyes. The smell—or, really, the *sensation*—hits Miriam a few seconds later.

"It feels like someone is pissing in my eyes," she says. "And up my nose."

"Buddy of mine across the Tennessee border makes it. He uses old oil drums instead of oak barrels. He calls it bourbon, but I dunno."

"And it's cheap?"

"Nobody'll ever drink it. Whole jug'll go to you for five bucks, you want it."

It smells like it'd burn barnacles off a boat hull; she can't imagine what it will do to her insides. She needs that. She needs to purge. She slaps down a five-spot, and then taps the bar.

"Then all I need is the glass."

Paleface *thunks* a shot glass next to the fiver, then grabs the money with a greasy hand.

Miriam takes the antifreeze jug and tops off the glass. Liquid spills on the bar, and she's surprised it doesn't eat through the lacquer.

She stares into the muddy whiskey. Flecks of something float at the top. But something else floats to the top, too: Louis. His face. Two ruined eyes. A mouth moaning her name.

Suck it up, she tells herself. None of this is new. This is how it's been for eight years. She sees death everywhere. Everybody dies, just like everybody poops. This guy's no different than anybody else (*except,* a little voice says, *the part where he gets stabbed in the eyes with a rusty fish-gutter and he says your name before getting his brain skewered*), so why should she care? She doesn't care (she does), and to prove it, she drinks the shot. One gulp.

It feels like firecrackers soaked in Drano going off in her throat and belly. She can *feel it* start to explode her liver. It is the worst thing she has ever put in her mouth.

Perfect. She pours another.

Paleface watches, amazed.

She bangs back the second shot, and a creeping numbness

starts to settle in. It fuzzes the edges. It takes those terrible thoughts running laps in her head and loops a piano wire around their necks. It drags them to the edge of a filthy kiddie-pool. It holds their heads underwater. They kick and thrash. They start to drown.

One last thought wriggles free from the pack.

She thinks of a Mylar balloon floating up over a highway.

She shuts her eyes and pours another shot. Miriam doesn't hear the bar door open. Doesn't even notice when someone sits next to her.

"You gonna drink that shot, or is this just foreplay?"

Miriam looks up. He's got a boyish face. Oily black hair in a tangle, like a teepee made from raven wings. Clear eyes. A boomerang smile with a sharp edge.

"I woo all my drinks," she responds.

"You drink that one, I'll buy you another." He looks at the jug. "Or something that doesn't look like mop water."

"Just let a girl die in peace."

"C'mon," he says. "You're too pretty to leave for dead. Even with that black eye."

She can't help it. Her heart skips a beat. She feels a tingling between her legs. He's got a pretty voice. Lyrical, almost, like he could sing the wings off an angel. But not feminine, either. A cocky, balls-to-the-wall confidence lives there. No Southern accent, to boot. He looks like bad news. That turns her on. She *likes* bad news. It starts to make her feel normal, whatever passes for normal where Miriam is concerned.

Though—his face looks familiar. She just can't place it.

He orders a beer from Paleface. Tips it back. But he watches her. Studies her.

"What do you tell a girl with two black eyes?" she asks him.

"Nothing you haven't told her twice already," he answers, whip-quick.

"Way to blow the punch line," she says. "I thought I had one up on you."

"Nope. Not me." That smile again. Sharp. Too sharp. So hot. Shit. "Besides, I only count one black eye on you."

"Then maybe I haven't learned my lesson yet."

"My name's Ashley. Ashley Gaynes."

"Ashley's a girl's name."

"That's what my dad would say before he'd beat my back with a belt." He says it, but the smile never leaves his face. In fact, it gets bigger, broader.

Miriam's mouth forms an O. She winces and laughs. "Holy shit, dude. You know the punch line to my joke and then you come back with a knee-slapper about child abuse? You know what? Fine. When the apocalypse finally comes, I promise to let you live. My name's Miriam."

"Miriam's an old lady's name."

"Well, I do feel old."

"I can make you feel young again."

She rolls her eyes. "Oh, hell. You were doing *so well*."

"Tell you what, how about this one?" he says, idly peeling the label from his sweat-slick beer. "I'm going to go to the Little Wranglers' room, paint the urinal a prettier shade of yellow. Then I'm going to preen in the mirror, because I want to look good for you. I'll wash my hands, of course. I'm dirty, but not *that* kind of dirty. When I'm done, I'll dry off, and then come back out here."

"Thanks for the play-by-play. You gonna diddle your balls while you're in there?"

He ignores her. "If you're still out here, then it's on. I'm going to hit on you like kids on a piñata. You'll laugh. I'll laugh. You'll touch my hand. I'll touch your hip. And you'll come home with me."

Ashley smirks, crumples up the wet label, and shoots it right into her shot glass.

"Ass," she says.

He gets up and strolls to the back.

She watches his ass as he walks. Bony. Enough to grab hold of, though.

She watches as he passes a trio of bikers hovering around the pool table. An old guy peers out from behind a curtain of feathered gray hair. Fella next to him is short and stocky, his whole body stacked like a pack of hot dogs. The last guy, looking like an extra from Thunderdome, is a living, biological mountain. Six-six, his big bones layered with a topography of muscle and fat. His tree-trunk arms are home to a mess of ink: an old lady's face, a tree on fire, a bunch of skulls, a motorcycle on fire. He's a Fat Dude.

Fat Dude is just about to shoot. Stick back. Giant melon head peering over it.

Ashley pushes past him. His bony hip bumps the pool stick.

The stick scrapes the table green and nudges the cue ball into the corner pocket.

A scratch.

Fat Dude turns on Ashley. If they were outside, he would block out the sun. The ground would tremble. Magma might belch up from the fractured earth.

Ashley smiles. Fat Dude seethes. A fly—probably fattened from an earlier meal of floor-stuck cheese fries—is caught in the airspace between these two, then hurries right the fuck out of there.

"You fuckin' prick," Fat Dude says. "You fucked my shot."

Ashley just smiles that smile, and that's when Miriam knows they're in trouble.

SIX

CLOSING TIME

"So reshoot," Ashley says, eyes twinkling.

"Can't do *that*," Fat Dude says, as if Ashley just suggested he fuck his own mother. "Rules are rules, asshole."

The old biker with the curtain of hair—who Miriam can't help but think of as Gray Pubes—steps up behind Ashley. The other one, Hot Dog, comes in from the side, like one of the velociraptors from *Jurassic Park*.

Paleface disappears behind the bar and doesn't emerge.

Miriam takes that as another bad sign.

"I'm sure your two friends here are happy to let you take the shot over," Ashley says.

Gray Pubes shakes his head. Hot Dog mumbles something.

"My friends don't fuck with the rules," Fat Dude says.

Ashley just shrugs and says, "Okay. Fuck you."

Fat Dude moves faster than Miriam would have thought possible. Gray Pubes twirls Ashley around like a top, and Fat Dude pulls the pool cue, horizontally, up under Ashley's chin. It's drawn tight against his windpipe.

He hoists Ashley into the air like the Beanstalk Giant with Little Jack.

"I'ma squeeze the dogshit outta you," Fat Dude thunders.

Ashley's jaw works around a mouthful of gurgles and burbles as the back of his head is pressed into Fat Dude's copious muscle-tits. His legs start to kick. His lips go blue, and Miriam can't help but think back to Del Amico.

Miriam knows she shouldn't get involved. Best thing would be to slink out of the bar with the antifreeze bourbon under her arm, never give a look back. Of course, she's never been the Queen of Good Decisions.

She meanders over. She takes her time, and when she finally gets there, Ashley's lips have gone full purple, like two earthworms wrestling or making love.

Miriam tugs on the hem of Fat Dude's leather jacket.

"Excuse me," she says, mustering girlish politeness. "Giant man? May we speak?"

He turns his tremendous skull toward her. She can practically hear the grinding of stone as the mountain pivots to regard the buzzing gnat at his side.

"What's up?" he asks, like not much else is going on.

Ashley's legs start to go limp.

"That guy you're choking to death?"

"Uh-huh."

"He's my brother. He's . . . got problems. One, he's got bad manners. Two, his name is *Ashley*, and with a name like that, he might as well have a couple vaginas in his pocket, am I right? Three, he's *at least* half-retarded. Though I'm willing to put money on two-thirds retarded, if you're up for a friendly wager. Mom used to feed him lawn fertilizer when he was a kid, I think as some kind of retroactive abortion attempt."

Ashley's eyes roll back in his head.

"Now," she continues, "if you'd be so kind as to stop choking him and let me know what it is that you fine gentlemen are drinking, I think I have just enough cash to buy you another round before they close up shop for the night."

"Oh, yeah?" Fat Dude asks.

Miriam offers up two fingers: a scout's honor, though it also looks like a proctologist's silent threat.

Miriam can see the tectonic plates beneath the man's rubbery skin start to shift. The cue pulls away from Ashley's neck, and Ashley drops to his knees hard, gasping, wheezing, rubbing his throat.

"Thanks so much," Miriam says.

Fat Dude grunts in reply. "You should leash your brother. Get him a tard helmet."

"I will consider that."

"We're drinking beer. Coors Light. But I think we'd like some shots. Tequila."

"Tequila it is."

"The good stuff, too. Not that cheap-ass cactus juice."

Miriam gives him a thumbs-up, then offers her hand to Ashley. The gasps have stopped for the most part. He coughs once more. But he doesn't take her hand.

He looks up at her and smiles. She sees it coming, but like with a car wreck, she's powerless to stop it.

Ashley punches Fat Dude in the groin.

It doesn't *do* anything, of course, because Fat Dude's got balls made of basalt. Fat Dude doesn't even flinch. He does look a bit surprised, though.

"Not cool," Fat Dude says.

Then he swings a roundhouse fist at Ashley's face, which remains at crotch level.

Ashley, though, he's ready for it. He pulls his head back, and Fat Dude's boulder-fist whiffs through open air to connect with the corner of a two-seater bar table. Miriam sees the table break the first two fingers on Fat Dude's hand; they spring out like clothespins. She hears the break. Like someone splitting a branch over his knee.

Fat Dude, to his credit, doesn't cry out. He just slowly brings his busted hand to his face, examining it the way a gorilla might regard a stapler, or an iPod.

Chaos erupts.

Gray Pubes wraps his hands around Ashley's neck, but Miriam's fast: She gives a nearby high-back chair a good kick, so the tippy-top of it drives right into the guy's gut. He doubles over. Ashley, meanwhile, shoulders into Hot Dog's stubby knees, and the guy goes down.

Then: *crack*. A pool cue over Ashley's head. Fat Dude's left holding the broken half in his good hand. He laughs. This is fun for him.

Before she means to be, Miriam's in the middle of it. A fist is thrown; she's not sure by whom. She feels the air current pass by her chin—a narrow miss. Ashley's up, eyes crossed, and then he's back down again as Fat Dude throws him, his shoulder against the two-seater, the table flipping up like a seesaw.

Miriam sees a glint: Gray Pubes, clutching his nuts with one hand, draws a knife.

Hot Dog's hands shove her forward.

Fat Dude's raising the busted pool cue above Ashley's skull.

It's all happening so fast and yet so slow. She's dull at her edges. Half-drunk, frankly.

Time to end it. Time for Momma's Little Lifesaver.

Miriam reaches in her pocket as Gray Pubes advances on her. She sidesteps Hot Dog. Fat Dude bellows something, and his fingers—even the broken, crooked ones—curl tight around his weapon. Miriam's hand finds what she's looking for. She has it out. And she's using it.

It's pepper spray. Fine grain. Shoots in a stream, not in a fog. Good for dogs, bears, and Fat Dudes.

She whips it around wildly. The stream hits Fat Dude's eyes, and he howls, swatting at the stream like somehow that'll help.

A blade swishes through air and she blasts Gray Pubes, too. Hot Dog makes a play, grabbing her wrist with his hand—

A baby deer on wobbly legs runs out into the middle of the road and stops there, standing in the darkness, framed by the bright circle of a motorcycle headlight. Hot Dog's too busy kissing some old tattooed chick with a volcanic archipelago of cold sores around her mouth to see, and by the time he extracts his tongue from her snaggletoothed maw, it's too late. He turns the bike, just missing the deer's little white flicking tail. Tire catches gravel. The bike skids, then flips. Hot Dog isn't wearing a helmet. Face meets road. Gravel and asphalt form a belt sander. It takes half his face off like it wasn't more than ground beef. Eye tumbles from shattered socket. Rag-doll body folds end over end, his spine bowing, then snapping. The chick flies overhead like some confused superhero, her arms pinwheeling. She cries out. The baby deer runs into the brush.

—and Miriam sidesteps, thrusts the pepper spray into his mouth, and fills his throat with the stuff. It only takes two seconds before he falls backward, throwing up onto the bar's cold concrete floor, face red, eyes like blisters, snot and sweat in a steady stream.

Miriam pulls Ashley up.

"We have to run," she says.

Fat Dude claws at his eyes with a broken hand.

Ashley grabs the other half of the broken pool cue and smashes it over Fat Dude's head. Miriam shoves him.

"I said, *run!*"

Ashley bolts, laughing.

On the way out, Miriam hurls a twenty-dollar origami boulder behind the bar, where Paleface is hiding. Her shoulders hit the door, knocking it open. The outside air hits her, along with the smell of wet asphalt and spilled beer. It's almost dizzying. She damn near trips on a hunk of broken parking lot. The piss-yellow streetlights are otherworldly. The distant sound of cars on the highway fills her head. She feels lost. Where to go? Where to run?

Ashley's hand finds the small of her back.

"This way," he says.

She follows. He fumbles in his pocket for a set of keys, and before Miriam knows it, he's popping the driver's-side door of a white late-1980s Ford Mustang.

"Get in!" he yells.

Like the cockroach from Del Amico's motel room, she does as told.

The car's interior is dark, cluttered, dingy. Vinyl is torn in places. Coffee cups and plastic soda bottles form a sticky trash pile at her feet. A pair of playing card deodorizers dangle from the mirror, but they've long lost their ability to conceal the cigarettes-and-feet funk.

Ashley twists the key in the ignition, but the engine sputters. It turns over again and again—*guh-guh-guh-guh*, a stuttering asthmatic—but never starts.

"What the fuck?" she asks. "C'mon!"

"I know," he barks back at her. His foot taps the gas pedal. *Guh-guh-guh-grrrrr-guh.*

The bar doors—a hundred feet away, maybe less—explode open.

Fat Dude tumbles out. Even in the ruined-liver light of the parking lot, Miriam can see the white ring of spit spackling his rage-howl mouth, the mucus swinging from his nostrils and eye corners like he's some frothing bull.

She can *also* see the shotgun in his hand. She has no idea where it came from—behind the bar?—but it doesn't matter, because it exists, and he has it, and he's pissed.

"Go, go, go!" Miriam screams. "Gun!"

The car heeds her panic and rumbles to life. The engine pops and shudders, but it's up-and-at-'em time. Ashley throws it into reverse and guns it backward—unfortunately, toward the angry mountain with the pump-action shotgun.

The gun goes off.

The back windshield explodes against the seats. A rattle and patter of glass bits.

The Mustang, like the wild horse for which it is named, bucks when Ashley slams it into drive. The car kicks back a cloud of stone and exhaust. It gallops forward like someone's trying to stick a riding crop up its ass. Another booming roar from the shotgun, and Miriam hears pellets punch little holes in the back end of the car, but it's too late for Fat Dude.

The car busts out of the parking lot, tires squealing. Ashley laughs.

SEVEN

LITTLE DEATH

Night.

A small house sits on a curvy back road. Wisteria—beautiful in its own way but listed as a weed species by the great state of North Carolina—chokes one half of the house, binding it in thick vines like strangling fingers and purple flowers like clusters of pale grapes.

Somewhere, a dog barks. Crickets chirrup.

The sky is black and host to a million visible stars.

A white Mustang sits in the driveway, a big hole in the back window and a starburst of little holes perforating the trunk.

Inside the house, a deeper darkness. Everything is still. Shapes and the shadows of shapes merge seamlessly to maintain calm immobility.

Then: sound.

Outside the front door, keys jiggle in the lock. Then someone drops them. Someone giggles, and someone says, "Shit." The keys are back in the lock now. More jingling. More fumbling.

The door flies open, nearly rocked off its hinges. The shadows of two shapes circle each other, reaching, then withdrawing, then reaching again. They have a mad gravity, crashing together. The two bodies slam into each other, a supernova; they pivot, pirouette, hips into a side table, mail knocked on the floor, a piece of framed art sent there soon after. Glass shatters.

A palm slams against the wall, searches blindly for a light switch.

Click.

"Fuck," Miriam says, "that's bright."

"Shut up," Ashley says, and pins Miriam against the arm of a pale microfiber sofa, his hands on her hips, holding her fast.

He presses his face against hers. Lips meet lips, teeth on teeth, tongue on—

Ashley sits in a wheelchair, and he's an old man whose hairless scalp is a checkerboard of liver spots and other marks. His frail hands rest, steepled in his lap atop a blanket the color of Pepto-Bismol, and

—tongue, and she bites his lower lip and he bites back. She raises her knee and wraps her leg around his bony denim-clad hip and pulls him tight, and then flips him around so he's the one against the couch's arm.

She takes off her shirt in one fell swoop. His hands grip her sides tight, hard, painfully—

an oxygen tank sits on the floor next to him, the tube snaking up under the pink blanket and back out, up to his nose. He's small like a crumpled cup, like a slowly composting sack of bones ill-contained by a powder blue bathrobe, but his eyes, his eyes are still young, flashing like wicked mirrors. Those eyes look left, look right, suspicious, or looking to see who is suspicious of him, and

—and the balled-up shirt disappears over her shoulder. Again they kiss.

Clothes peel away, leaving a trail of fabric from the living room into the bedroom.

Before too long, it's *all* skin on skin, and as they topple onto the bed, she gasps—

he spies two orderlies chatting and chuckling in the corner, telling some bullshit story to break the monotony of their jobs, to help them forget about how many times they have to shower and

scrub and shampoo to wash away that pissy-pants old-people
smell. But nobody's watching. The ancient and antediluvian
inhabitants of the old folks' home orbit the room in various
stages of languor; a woman with orange-dyed hair fiddles with
a pair of crochet hooks without any yarn between them. A
skinny octogenarian drools. A potbellied man lifts his shirt and
scratches under his waistband, empty eyes half-following an old
SpongeBob *cartoon on the TV*

—and the bed isn't long for this world; they tumble to the
floor. She bites his ear. He pinches her nipple. She digs nails
into his back. His hands are on her throat, and she feels the
blood ballooning in her head, a dull roaring pulse that grows
with each beat, and she closes her eyes and shoves her thumb in
his mouth . . .

and all the while Ashley sits, his body still, his eyes moving.
He pulls the blanket up to his chest, and as he does so, it reveals
his legs. A plastic flip-flop dangles from his right foot, but he
has no left foot. The left leg dead-ends in a stump past the faded
plaid pajama bottoms. It has no prosthesis. Ashley stares down
at it, wistful, sad, scowling.

Her foot touches his, and it sends an electric, awful thrill
through her body. She feels equal parts ecstatic and disgusted,
like she's one of those people who gets hot under the collar at
car accidents, but she doesn't care. She's lost to it. Dizziness
enrobes her. His hands tighten around her throat. He laughs.
She moans. Her leg kicks out. Toes cramp.

Her foot lifts up the bed skirt, and she sees a glimpse of
something—a metal suitcase, a combination lock, a black lacquered handle—but then her vision is filled with Ashley, her
ears lost to the sound of the pulsing blood-beat.

Miriam pulls Ashley's hands off her throat, and she flips him
over onto his back. His head cracks into the leg of a nearby table,
but neither of them care. She chokes him now. He cranes his

head and bites the flesh just south of her clavicle. Miriam feels alive, more alive than she's felt in a long time, nauseated and giddy and wet like a storm-thrown wave, and she wraps her hips around his and she feels him inside of her—

and the lids of his eyes close, and when they open, the clarity is gone. What remains is just a muddy haze. He pulls the oxygen tube from his nose and lets it flop over the side of his wheelchair. His eyelids flutter. His chest heaves once, then twice. A rattling wheeze squeaks from his throat, like a tire's air pushed through a pinhole in the dark rubber. The wheeze turns wet; the fluid in his lungs builds, and he starts to struggle for air, a fish on the dock, his lips working but finding nothing. He's drowning in his own body, and finally one of the orderlies—a reedy black dude with a silver nose ring—sees and rushes over, shaking the old man gently. He picks up the tube and looks at it like he doesn't under-stand what he's seeing, and the orderly asks, "Mister Gaynes? Ashley?" He gets it now. He sees what's happening. "Oh, hell. You in there, old man?" Ashley's in there for one last second. But then he's gone. The orderly says something else, but it's all fading to black, because dead is dead is dead, a wheezing whimper.

Miriam cries out, not a whimper but a *bang*, riding the intense mixture of emotions inside her to a throttling orgasm.

It surprises her.

THE DREAM

A red snow shovel hits dead in the center of her back. It slams her to the floor. Her chin hits hard tile; her teeth bite through her tongue. She tastes a mouthful of blood. The shovel comes down again, this time against the back of her head. Her nose breaks. Blood squirts.

Everything is ringing, distorted, a high-pitched whine.

She looks up through teary eyes.

Louis sits on a toilet in a stall. His pants are up. The rickety walls can barely accommodate his broad shoulders, big body. Both of his eyes are gone, replaced with Xs formed out of electrical tape. He clucks his tongue.

"You're a real man-eater," he says and whistles. "Del Amico. Me. That old bastard out of Richmond. Harry Osler up in Pennsylvania. Bren Edwards. Tim Streznewski. See a penny, pick it up. Am I right? Oh, and let's not forget that little boy out there on the highway. So many dead boys. The names go on and on, all the way back to . . . what? Eight years ago. Ben Hodge."

Miriam spits out blood. "Women, too. And I don't kill them. I don't kill anybody."

Louis laughs.

"You keep telling yourself that, little lady. Whatever helps you sleep at night. Remember, just because you're not pulling the trigger doesn't mean you aren't a killer."

"It's fate," Miriam says, red drool swinging from her lower lip. "It's not me. It's how fate is. What fate wants—"

"Fate gets," Louis says. "I know. You say that a lot."

"My mother used to say—"

"It is what it is. I know that old chestnut, too."

"Fuck you. You're not real."

"Not yet. But just shy of a month, I will be. I'll be another skeleton in your closet, another ghost in your head. Dangling and swinging and moaning and groaning."

"I can't save you."

"Apparently not."

"Go to hell."

He winks. "Meet you there. Watch out for that—"

The shovel comes down between her shoulder blades. She feels something break deep inside of her. Her thighs grow wet. The pain is intense.

"—shovel."

EIGHT

DIE JOBS

The morning after.

Five men (counting the frat-tards). One death. Lots of violence. A banner night for Miriam Black.

Hands on the sink in Ashley's bathroom, she stares at her reflection in the mirror. She smokes a cigarette, blows the plume against the reflection, watches smoke meet smoke.

All told, it's the orgasm that really bothers her.

It isn't the *sex*. Sex happens—hell, sex happens often enough that it's a hobby for her like scrapbooking or collecting baseball cards is for other people. Who cares? Her body is no temple. It might have been once, but it lost its sanctified status long ago (*just over eight years ago*, that wicked little voice reminds), with too much blood spilled at the altar.

The orgasm, though. That's new.

She hasn't had one in . . . She takes another drag of the Marlboro, tries to figure it out. She can't. It's like doing hard math half-drunk. It's been *that* long.

And then last night? Boom. Bang. Fireworks. Fountains shooting off. Twenty-one-gun salute, rocket blasting to the moon, a Pavarotti concert, the universe exploding and then imploding and then exploding again.

A blinking red light. An alarm going off.

And what was it that did it?

She presses her head against the mirror. It's cold against her skin.

"It's official," she says into the mirror. "You're totally broken. Unfixable." She has an image of a cracked porcelain doll being dragged through puddles of blood, mud, and shit and then punted into midair, its arms cartwheeling, until it smacks head-long into the grill of an oncoming eighteen-wheeler. The doll looks like her.

(*A red balloon rises to the sky.*)

Time to do what Miriam does best.

"Time to dye my hair!" she chirps.

This is her true gift: the ability to shove it all out of her mind. Just crowd it out with hard elbows and headbutts. Zen and the art of repression.

She opens her bag, takes out two boxes. She bought them a few days before at a grimy CVS in Raleigh-Durham, and by "bought," she means, "with a five-finger discount."

It's hair color. Cheap-ass punk color for cheap-ass punk girls. An adult female with any self-respect would never buy a brand like this, would never dye her hair these colors—Blackbird Black and Vampire Red. But, while Miriam legally qualifies as an adult, she certainly doesn't count as one with even a dram of self-respect, does she? H-e-double-hockey-sticks no.

She pokes her head out of the bathroom door. Ashley lies back on the bed, heavy lids half-closed. The TV is playing (*SpongeBob SquarePants*) some kind of daytime talk show.

"Long day at the office, honey?" she asks.

He blinks. "What time is it?"

"Nine-thirty. Ten. Shrug."

"Did you just *say* shrug instead of actually shrugging?"

Miriam ignores the question and instead holds up the two boxes for display, one in each hand. "Check it out. Blackbird Black. Vampire Red. Pick one."

"Pick one what?"

She makes an exasperated sound. "A candidate for the presidency of the moon and all its provinces."

He stares, confused.

"A *hair color*, retard. I'm dying my hair. Blackbird Black"—she shakes that box—"or Vampire Red?" She shakes the other box.

He squints, face slackened to indicate minimum investment or comprehension. Miriam growls and stomps over to him, dropping her bag. She thrusts the two boxes up under his chin and makes them do a little dance, like the "Let's All Go to the Lobby" parade of treats.

"Black, red, black, red," she says.

"Yeah, I don't actually care. It's too early for this shit."

"Heresy. It's never too early for hair dye."

"I dunno," he croaks. "I'm not really a morning person."

"Let's go through this," she says. "Vampires are cool. Right? Modern vampires, at least, they're all black leather and sexy moves and pomp and circumstance. Plus, they're pale. I'm pale. Except, vampires are slicker than goose shit on a glass window. Suave. Sultry. I'm neither of those things. Plus, I don't really feel like being one of the slag-whore bitches in Dracula's brothel, and all that goth and emo shit gives me a rash."

She holds up the other box. "Blackbirds, on the other hands, are cool birds. Symbols of death in most mythology. They say that blackbirds are *psychopomps*. Like sparrows, they're birds that supposedly help shuttle souls from the world of the living to the world of the dead." A little voice tries to say something, but she shushes it. "Of course, on the other hand, the genus—or is it species, I always get them mixed up—of the common blackbird is *Turdus*, which, of course, has the word *turd* in it. Not ideal."

Ashley watches and listens. "How do you know all this?"

"Wikipedia."

He nods gamely.

"Still nothing?"

He shakes his head.

"Dude, seriously. You have a chance here to sway my fate. If you subscribe to the thought that a butterfly's wings flapping in Toledo can cause a hurricane in Tokyo, you'd know right now that you have *tremendous power* in your hands, the power to shape destiny, to direct the course of the entire breadth and scope of human history, *right* here, *right* now."

He blinks. "Fine. Vampire Red."

She makes a *pshhh* sound.

"Fuck that noise." She hurls the Vampire Red box at his head. "I was always going to choose Blackbird Black, dummy. You can't sway fate. Tsk, tsk, tsk. And that, dear boy, is the lesson we learned here today."

And with that, she darts back into the bathroom and slams the door.

NINE

THE NOTEBOOK

Ashley hears the faucet start.

"Perfect," he says. He hops down, grabs Miriam's messenger bag sitting by his feet where she dropped it, and hoists it up onto the bed.

He casts one more paranoid glance at the door. She should be in there a while. A home dye job isn't quick work. All that washing, all that combing through, all that waiting.

Satisfied, he starts going through the bag.

Item after item ends up in his hand, then on the bed. Lip balm. Hair ties. Small MP3 player so scratched and dinged, it looks like it has been run through a wood chipper. Pair of tawdry romance novels (one with Smooth Blond Fabio on the cover, another with Dark Goateed Fabio). Clark's Teaberry gum (he doesn't know what the fuck "teaberry" is). A squeaky toy for dogs; it looks like a squirrel clutching an acorn in his mouth. Before he has time to think on that, out come the weapons. A can of pepper spray. A butterfly knife. *Another* can of pepper spray. A hand grenade—

"Jesus Christ," he says. Swallowing hard, he gently sets the grenade down on the pillow behind him. He steadies it, takes a deep breath, and then goes back into the bag.

Finally, he finds what he's looking for.

The diary.

"And Bingo was his name-o."

It's a black notebook, its plastic cover nicked. The book is swollen, like a tumor filled with words instead of blood. He gives it a quick flip-through: tattered pages, some dog-eared, all colors and styles of pen (red, black, blue, Sharpie, ballpoint, Uni-ball, one in fucking *crayon*, by the looks of it), each page dated, each page starting with *Dear Diary* and ending with *Love, Miriam*.

"So, what about you?" Miriam asks, and Ashley damn near voids his bowels. He looks up, heart racing, expecting her to be standing there, but she's not. She's still on the other side of the bathroom door—she's yelling through, talking to him while she rocks the dye job.

He takes a deep breath. "What about me, what?"

"Where you from? What do you do for a living? Who are you?"

He flips to the front of the diary.

"Uh," he says, trying to focus on the words. "I'm from Pennsylvania. I'm an, uh, a traveling salesman."

"Yeah, right," she calls back. "And I'm a circus monkey."

"I've never had sex with a circus monkey before."

He flips a few more pages. His eyes drift over the words. His mouth starts to go dry. His heart races. It makes sense, but . . . He turns another ten pages and reads more. He mouths the words he reads without speaking them aloud—

Like trying to derail a train with a penny or kicking a wave back into the ocean, I can't stop shit, I can't change shit.

Flip.

What fate wants, fate gets.

Flip.

I am a spectator at the end of people's lives.

Flip.

Bren Edwards shattered his pelvis and died in a culvert. He had two hundred bucks in his wallet—I'm going to eat well tonight.

Flip.

It is what it is.

Flip.

Almost done with you, Dear Diary, then you know what happens.

Flip.

Just need a rich guy to bite it. That'll be the day.

Flip.

Dear Diary, I did it again.

His eyes catch something else in the messenger bag flopped on its side. He reaches in, pulls out a small year-long planner.

"I'm from Pennsylvania, too," Miriam calls out from the bathroom.

"That's great," he mumbles. He flips through the datebook. Most days are empty, but others? Others have names. Times. Little icons, too—stars, Xs, dollar signs.

And causes of death.

June 6, Rick Thrilby / 4:30 p.m. / heart attack

August 19, Irving Brigham / 2:16 a.m. / succumbs to lung cancer

October 31, Jack Byrd / 8:22 p.m. / eats a bullet, suicide

And on, and on.

"Find anything interesting?" Miriam asks.

Ashley, startled, drops the book and looks up. She narrows her eyes and darts her gaze between him, the diary sitting next to him, the grenade on the pillow, and her fallen bag.

"Listen," he starts, but she interrupts him.

With a fist. A straight clip to the mouth splits his lower lip. *Pop.* His teeth rattle. He's surprised, though he probably shouldn't be. She's been on the road for years now. Somewhere along the way, she learned how to throw a punch; and by the looks of that black eye, she knows how to take one, too.

"You're a cop," she says. "No. Not a cop."

"Not a cop," he mumbles around the palm pressed to his bleeding lip. He pulls his hand away, sees a streak of red.

"A stalker. A psycho."

"I've been following you since Virginia."

"Like I said. *Stalker. Psycho.* You know what? Eff this." She pushes past him, fetching her books, her armory, her other debris and detritus, and cradles it all before upending it into the open mouth of her messenger bag. Ashley grabs her wrist, but she'll have none of it. She wrenches free. He reaches again, but she backhands him off the bed.

By the time he realizes what's happened, the front door is already open, and she's gone.

TEN

THE SUN CAN GO FUCK ITSELF

Birds tweet. Bees buzz. The sun shines, and the air is heady with honeysuckle perfume. Miriam squints against the bright light, wishes she had a pair of sunglasses. A sour feeling sucks at her gut; her bowels feel like ice water. She hates the sun. Hates the blue sky. The birds and the bees can go blow each other in a dirty bathroom. Her pale skin feels like it's about to split open like the skin of a microwaved hot dog. She's a night owl. The day is not her domain, which makes her reconsider—*maybe I should've gone Vampire Red, after all.*

Her boots stomp down the deserted back road. She's been walking for fifteen minutes now, maybe more. It feels like a lifetime.

She feels vulnerable. Like she got played. Miriam hasn't felt this way in a long time. She's the one with all the secrets. With the edge. Her nerves are electric. Anxiety nibbles. She doesn't know why. What's to worry about? What's he going to do?

She keeps walking.

The road twists and turns. Up a hill. Under a copse of trees. Around the bend sits a post-and-rail fence, a hand-painted mailbox, a half-collapsed barn and farmhouse. Perfectly pastoral. Miriam feels like smashing handfuls of gravel into her eyes and rubbing vigorously. She's not even sure why she's so angry.

She hears a car coming up behind her. It slows.

A white Mustang. It's Lying Sneaky Asshole.

It pulls up alongside of her, the passenger window down. Ashley leans over, one hand easy on the wheel. He peers out at her. The smile is gone. He's all serious-faced.

"Get in," he says.

"Suck my dick."

"Nowhere to go."

"I got my getaway sticks. They take me all kinds of places."

"I know who you are. I know what you do."

"You don't know rat rubes from rum punch. Whatever you think you know damn sure isn't the half of it. Keep driving. Get away from me."

She keeps walking. He continues to ease the car alongside her.

"I'm not going to sit here and drive along like an asshole," he says. "I'm done arguing. Just get in the car. Don't be a twat."

Miriam reaches in her bag, and with a quick pivot of her wrist, the butterfly knife is out; metal gleams, and the blade flies free of the split handle.

"Hey—" he says.

She lags behind a second and kneels. He tries to see what she's doing, but by the time he gets his head out the window, it's too late. One thrust and the knife punctures the back tire of the Mustang. Air hisses from the rubber, a whispering fart.

"What the—?" he yells out from the car. "Where are you—oh, Jesus Christ."

By the time he's taking the Lord's name in vain, she's already at the opposite back tire, slicing a new mouth in the rubber. It, too, leaks a steady hiss.

The rubber flaps on asphalt with each turn of the tire: *thup thup thup thup*.

She passes by his driver's-side window while he's still looking out the passenger side, and calls in, "See? Told you my getaway sticks will do the trick. Don't go driving on that thing. You'll dick up the rims."

Then she gives him the finger and jogs away, leaving the hobbled Mustang behind.

ELEVEN

THE SUNSHINE CAFÉ CAN GO FUCK ITSELF EQUALLY

Miriam enjoys a lumberjack's meal.

All around her are the sounds of breakfast: spoons clanking in mugs as they stir, the hiss of griddles, the scrape of fork tines against plates. She's keeping her head down, focused on the monstrosity before her. Two eggs, over easy. Two buttermilk pancakes that seemed the size of manhole covers before Miriam got to them. Four link sausages. Wheat toast. And on a separate plate, a grilled cinnamon bun. Everything but the bun sits soaked in a congealing ooze of maple syrup. *Real* maple syrup, like from a fucking tree, not that flavored diarrhea from the grocery store.

You curse like a sailor, her mother always said. *And you eat like a lumberjack.*

Still. Despite the gut-expanding, tongue-pleasing meal, she doesn't want to look up, lest her eyes explode from all the cheeriness.

The Sunshine Café. *Ugh.*

Bright yellow walls. Sunlight filtered through gauzy curtains. Powder-blue stools at the counter. Farmers, migrants, truckers, and country yuppies all milling around together. Each one of them probably goes to church, puts change in the collection plate, and tries to be a good American citizen, smiling all the while. Miriam shakes her head. She reminds herself to one day get drunk and urinate on a Norman Rockwell painting.

Miriam wads up a hunk of toast, ruptures an egg yolk, lets the runny ooze swirl together with the syrup swamp she's created.

And then someone sits down across from her.

"You owe me for the tow truck," Ashley says.

Miriam shuts her eyes. Breathes deep through her nose.

"I'm just going to pretend you're a pink elephant. You'll kindly take this opportunity to get up and slink out of this place like a rat before I open my eyes, because if I open my eyes and still see you there, O Figment of My Diseased Imagination, I'm going to stab you in the neck with my fork."

Ashley snaps his fingers. "Or, alternate scenario: I call the police."

Her eyes snap open. She watches him. He grins, the middle of his bottom lip bisected by a dark, scabby line. So smug. So satisfied.

"You won't. You're road scum just like me. They won't believe you."

"Maybe," he says. "But they'll believe pictures. That's right—I got photos. And the coincidences will seem more than a little strange, won't they? Since Richmond, you've been, what, at the scene of *three* different deaths?"

Her jaw tightens. "I didn't kill those men."

"All of them conveniently missing the cash from their wallets. And I'm sure if someone were to do a little bit of digging, they'd find the credit cards missing, too. Credit cards that sometimes get used, then thrown in trash cans or ditches. Digging even deeper, they'd find a trail of the dead, wouldn't they? With your footprints walking them backward through time. They'd find your diary. They'd find your weird little datebook."

Miriam's guts go cold. She feels trapped. Cornered. A butterfly pinned to a corkboard. For a second, she genuinely considers sticking her fork in Ashley Gaynes's neck and bolting.

"I didn't kill them," she says.

Ashley watches her. "I know. I read enough of the diary."

"But you don't believe it."

"I maybe do," he says. "My mother was into all kinds of mystical blah-blah. Crystal gazing, psychic phone line, all that. I figured it for garbage, but sometimes, I wasn't so sure. I always wanted to believe.

"Plus, these three I've seen, they each died in different ways, didn't they? The bike courier in Richmond—the black kid? Traffic accident. Hard to call that murder, though you *are* a crafty little cunt, aren't you?"

"Nice. You go down on your mother with that mouth?"

Ashley visibly tenses. His grin doesn't fade, but he damn sure isn't happy.

"Don't talk about my mother," he says. He continues: "The most recent appears to have choked on his own tongue after a particularly severe epileptic fit. Again, could've been murder, but the guy had a history of epilepsy, right? The one from Raleigh, the old man, what was his name? Benson. Craig Benson. I'm actually not sure how he died. Company bigwig, had lots of security and cops and the like; I couldn't get close. But you did. Was he just old?"

Miriam pushes aside her plate. She's no longer hungry.

"His dick killed him," she says.

"His dick."

"His erection, more specifically."

"You banged CEO Grandpa?"

"Jesus, no. I did flash him a tit, though. He was so pumped full of dick pills—and not prescribed stuff but shit from, like, some village in China—that it killed him. My chest isn't exactly impressive, but I guess it's enough to kill an old man."

"So, him you *did* kill."

"Bull."

"Gun or tit, you were the one firing the weapon."

She waves him off. "Whatever."

The waitress comes by—skinny up top but a big round bottom that Miriam can't help but think of as "birthing hips"—and asks Ashley what he wants. He orders coffee.

"So, you've been following me for two months now?"

He tells her just about, yeah.

"How? How'd you find me?"

The waitress comes, pours him a coffee, tops off Miriam's, too. "The bike courier. I saw you picking the corpse's pockets. I had the same idea."

"You just *happened* to be there?"

"Nah. I'd been working the courier for a week. He was dirty. Delivering packages for all kinds of shady types. I was running a scheme, trying to convince him that he and I could take one of those packages and offer it to a higher bidder, but really, I was just going to take the package and run." He sips noisily at his coffee. "Obviously, you came and fucked that up."

"You're a con man, then."

"I prefer con *artist*."

"*I'm a dancer, not a stripper.* Keep saying it; see if it magically becomes true." She feels a headache from the Bourbon of Doom stretching its legs in the back of her skull, like it needs to get up and roam around. She needs a smoke. Or a drink. Or a bullet to the temple. "Let's cut to the chase. You see what you see, and you follow me for *two months*. Why?"

"Initially, it was professional curiosity. I figure, hey, check it out—another con artist, just like me. Maybe I can learn a thing or two, and maybe I'll pull something over on her, or maybe she'll pull something over on me. Either way would've been interesting."

"I'm not a con artist."

"Maybe you are, maybe you aren't. Maybe this whole thing is a ruse, and maybe you're conning me right now. The diary, the datebook, the hair dye. Maybe you knew about the game I was trying to run on the courier, and maybe you thought I was the bigger fish." He shakes his head, waggles a finger. "But I don't think so. Because things don't add up. The courier had a package. You didn't take it. You only emptied his wallet. In fact, that seems to be all you do. You empty their wallets, maybe take a few other items—like the kid's scarf, or the old man's watch."

"It's all stuff I need. It was cold, so I wanted a scarf. And I didn't take Benson's watch. Cop must've taken that. I have my own watch—" She holds up her wrist with the old-school calculator watch attached. "Of course, batteries are dead now, but that's not the point. From Benson, I took a pen because I needed a pen. I need to eat and sleep, so I take money for food and hotel rooms."

"And that's it? You don't angle for more?"

She upends three packets of sugar into her coffee. "I don't get greedy."

"You don't get greedy," he repeats, laughing. "That's cute. I like that. A little ointment for the soul never hurt anybody."

She shrugs.

"Let's say all of this is true," he says.

"It *is* true; that's why we're *saying* it."

"You can see how people are going to die."

"You read the diary. That what the diary said, you nosy fucker?"

He chuckles. "Okay. You have this weird gift. So, do me."

"I *did* you last night."

"Cute again. No, I mean, with the whole voodoo-death-touch-vision thing."

She rolls her eyes. "That's what I mean. Yeah, I did you with my vagina, but I also did the voodoo-death-touch-vision trick. It doesn't take much. Skin on skin." He starts to speak, but she cuts him off. "No way, dude. I am not telling how you're going to die. I will not give you that satisfaction. Besides, you don't want to know. It ain't gonna be pretty."

He flinches. His eyes pinch at the edges. She got to him. He thinks it's close, that it's coming. Way she sees it, people fall into one of two categories: those who think their death is imminent, and those who figure they have long, healthy lives ahead of them. Nobody ever thinks it's somewhere in between.

Ashley nods, then clucks his tongue.

"I see what you did there. You're trying to mess with me. That's cool. You know what? I don't wanna know. But here comes the waitress. Do her."

"You're serious?"

"Serious as a pulmonary embolism."

The waitress, she of the big hips and swaying caboose, comes up to the table's edge and lays down a check. In her other hand, though, she's got a coffee pot.

"I'll take that whenever y'all are ready," she says, sweet as a mouthful of honey. "Meantime, you need a top-off, sweetie?"

Miriam says nothing, just slides her coffee mug closer to the waitress in acknowledgment. She gives the woman a faint smile of concession, and as the woman pours the brew, Miriam brushes the back of her hand with her—

The Honda hatchback barrels down a winding country road. It's summer, two years hence. The forests and meadows blink with fireflies. The waitress is at the wheel, and she's let her hair grow out—no longer the big bouffant; now she's got a small ponytail in the back, and while it's two years later, it makes her look younger. She looks happy. And tired. Like she's just come back from a bar. Or a party. Or a good lay. Kenny Rogers's "The Gambler" plays on the radio, and she sings along: "I met up with the gambler; we were both too tired to sleep." The car zips around curves. The buzz of the Honda's engine.

The waitress's eyelids droop. She blinks away sleep, rubs her eyes, yawns.

Her head dips slightly. She takes a turn too fast. Car's back wheel bumps off the road, hits gravel, can't get purchase, and the waitress is awake now. Her hands work the wheel as she gasps, and the car hops back on the road; a deep sucking relieved breath. She cranks the radio. Puts her head out the window like a dog would, just to keep herself awake.

It doesn't help. Five minutes later, her eyelids flutter. Chin dips.

Tire bounces into a pothole. Her eyes bolt open.

The car is coming up on a T-intersection with a big oak tree at the end of it. The Honda's racing up too fast. White knuckles grip the wheel. Her foot pounds the brakes. Wheels squeal like they're driving over a ghost. The car's back end sways like the waitress's own wide bottom when she walks, and the car fishtails toward the tree, and then . . .

The Honda stops, just inches from that big bad oak tree. The car stalls. The only sound is the cooling engine making this little tink-tink-tink noise.

The waitress first looks like she's going to cry, but then instead, she laughs. She's alive, she's crazy, the air is warm, nobody saw what happened, and she's rubbing tears of embarrassment and joy out of her eyes, and this means she doesn't see the truck coming. Two headlights stab the darkness. A pickup truck the color of primer.

She looks up. Sees what's coming.

She races to undo her seat belt. Clumsy fingers. Slow going.

She honks her horn. Truck keeps coming.

Her mouth opens to yell, to scream, but by the time her brain sends the signal to her mouth to make some goddamn noise, the truck slams into her at eighty miles an hour. The door crumples up into her midsection, shattering her chest. Her head whips back under a rain of glass. The sound of the car honking, of screaming metal, of

—fingertips. Miriam, still hearing the sound of the accident, gently pulls her hand away and clears her throat. "That's fine. Thanks."

"Sure thing, hon."

Miriam takes a deep breath.

"So," Ashley asks, eager. "How does it happen?"

"I need to go to the bathroom."

She stands up and pushes her way through the little café. Her hand brushes a farmer's elbow—

The old farmer's riding along in his white T-shirt with the pit stains and a green-and-yellow John Deere hat even though he's riding an orange Kubota ("Buy American," they say, but end up on a Korean tractor) and the old man's got an inner ear condition and it makes him woozy, so he tumbles off the tractor seat and into the tilled earth below, crying out only moments before the big tiller—going around for its second pass—tills right over his body, curved claws tilling his skin and muscle and bone, all that blood pushed down into the overturned earth

—and she yanks away, but then some redheaded teen brushes up against her—

The kid's not a kid but a thirty-year-old man and he tastes the gun oil on his tongue as the pistol's sights scrape the roof of his mouth and then comes a hot, hollow flash and the bullet plows through his brain pan

—and she brings her hands tight to her chest, the way Mighty T. Rex might walk, and she barrels into the bathroom, leaving someone behind her asking, "Just what the heck is wrong with that girl?"

It's a question she can't help but echo.

THE INTERVIEW

"Fate's an immovable object," Miriam says, tracing her finger up the neck of the bottle. A warm haze saturates the edges; the scotch is doing its glorious, God-given duty. "The course is charted. Fate's already got everything mapped out. This conversation we're having? It's already on the books. It's already been written. We feel like we have control over it, but we don't. Free will is bunk, bupkes, bull-puckey. You think that you go buy a coffee, you kiss your girlfriend, you drive a school bus full of nuns into a fireworks factory, that's your choice. *You did that.* You made that decision and acted upon it, right? *Bzzt.* Wrong-o. All of our lives are just a series of events carefully orchestrated to culminate in whatever death fate has planned for us. Every moment. Every act. Every loving whisper and hateful gesture—all just another tiny cog in the clockwork ready to ring the alarm for our ultimate hour."

Paul says nothing. He just stares, wide-eyed. He tries to say something, then doesn't.

"What?" she asks.

"That's . . . dark."

"No kidding."

He shifts uncomfortably. "So, you've tried to change things."

"Yup. For the first couple years, I tried a lot. Let's just say it never worked out."

"And then one day, you just stopped trying?"

"No. One day I met a little boy with a red balloon."

TWELVE

THE PROPOSAL

The bathroom is unisex, and the place only has one. Someone's rattling the doorknob. She mumbles for them to piss off, but she doesn't have the heart to say it loud enough for anybody to hear; a rare moment.

It's like a closet in here. Tight. Bright. Blue. Everything is blue. Robin's egg blue. Sky blue. Picasso's blue period. The blue of *someone choking on a meatball and dying* blue.

She hears the distant *clang* of a red snow shovel. She feels its heavy weight on her back.

In the mirror, she sees a glimpse of ghosts from future and past: Del Amico, his throat almost comically swollen with his own tongue; Ben Hodge, the back of his head blown out like a juiced pomegranate; the old man, Craig Benson, stroking his bent erection with hands curled into arthritic claws; Louis, an electrical-tape X over each eye, mouthing her name again and again. A shiny balloon floats up, and for a moment, it seems to blot out the light above her head, even though she knows it's not real. . . .

The door rattles again. The ghosts are gone. Miriam pushes her way out of the bathroom, past some blonde country yuppie in pink.

The waitress approaches, carrying an almost-impossible armload of plates.

"Your friend said you were done eating?" she asks Miriam, gesturing to the plates with her chin.

"Uh. Yeah. Yes, thanks." She pauses. The words come out of

her mouth before she even thinks to speak them: "Do you have a Honda? A Honda hatchback?"

"No," she says, and Miriam's heart leaps like a bullfrog with a dart stuck in his ass. A tiny glimmer of hope grows wings and starts banging against her insides, a bee against a window. "But you know what? I have been thinking about getting one. Old Tremayne Jackson down on Orchard Lane, he has one sitting out in his driveway. Was his daughter's, I guess, but she got a scholarship—first one in the family to go to college—so now the car's just sitting there, collecting pollen and leaves and whatnot on the hood. He said he'd sell it to me, but I hadn't decided yet. Heck—maybe I'll go for it! I'd forgotten about it until now."

Miriam's insides tighten. She screams within her own head. The thoughts rage at her, throw things, kick down mental doors, and hurl bricks through windows: *See what you did? See how it all happens? You say something, and bad shit happens. Before, she wasn't sure about buying that goddamn car, but now you open your lippy bitch mouth, and now she's got the idea planted in her head like a bad seed growing an ugly tree, and one night, she's going to get crunched into that tree by some drunk dumb fuck in a pickup truck—way to go. You have to keep trying, don't you?*

And even then, a littler voice chimes in: *Tell her no. Tell her that Honda hatchbacks are known to spontaneously burst into flames when you turn on the radio. Or better still, go down to Orchard Lane and stuff a rag in the gas tank and blow that sucker to Timbuktu. Or maybe take fate into your own hands right now—grab a butter knife off the counter and saw this stupid woman's head clean off. If you kill her first, it doesn't count, right?*

But Miriam just smiles, shrugs, and pushes past.

The waitress watches her go, equal parts confused and pleased.

Miriam sits, and Ashley's polishing off his coffee.

"So, how's Flo bite it?"

"Car accident. Truck slams into her." He cocks an eyebrow. "What, do you want me to prove it? Hold on, we just have to get to my time-traveling DeLorean parked out back by the Dumpster. We'll go back to the future and you can see I'm telling the truth."

"All right, all right, let's say I believe you."

"Lucky me."

"I have a proposal for you."

"No, I will not marry you. The baby's not yours. It's a mixed-race baby, and last I checked, you don't look Eskimo."

"I want to work together."

"Work." She says the word like she's looking at a dog turd. "Really? Us? Work together?"

"Like a volleyball team. You set 'em up, I spike it. Let's be frank, Miss Black—you need my help bad."

"I need neither shit nor Shinola from you." Under her breath, she adds: "Not that I know what Shinola is."

"The old bastard. Benson. With the dick-pill problem. He had a safe, right?"

"So?"

"So, people keep things in safes. Important things. Money. Guns. Jewels. Gold doubloons, whatever. I can crack a safe."

"Who can actually do that? Is that what they're teaching at community college these days? You're telling me you can actually crack a safe."

"You bet."

"I don't need what's in a safe. I told you, I don't get greedy." She reaches into her bag, finds some money, tosses it atop the bill. "There. I'm paid up. This is where we part ways. Thanks for the fun time last night. All that . . . violent monkey sex? With the choking and shit? It was a lovely time. But I'm done here. You have a great life."

She stands.

He puts his hand on her wrist. He tightens his grip. It doesn't hurt. Not yet.

"You're only going where I tell you to go," he says, giving her a flash of that winning smile. He loves this; she can tell. "I will call the cops. I will sell you up the river. Furthermore, I've got one more little surprise for you."

Miriam ponders breaking his nose. It'll draw attention, though.

"I did a little look-see into your past. It's not like a girl like you has a big trail, but it did lead me to your mother. She's alive and well. Maybe you knew that, maybe you didn't. But I can see the way your lip is twitching that this is getting to you. It's okay. I have a mother, too, and I know how it can be. Love and disappointment, those perpetual dance partners, right? You bail on me, and I'll go to her. I'll tell her everything. Maybe she'll believe me, maybe she won't. But I think she'll know the scoop. I think she'll be sad to know that you're out there, banging rednecks and losers, stealing from the dead, and just being an all-around tramp. You want that?"

Her teeth grit together so hard, she thinks they might snap into little pieces.

"Are we in business together?" he asks.

"You going to tell me what's in that metal suitcase under the bed?"

"Nope." He smirks.

"I hate you" is her response.

"You love me because we're the same." He stands up and reaches in to get a kiss. She turns her cheek, and that's where it lands.

Ashley lets go of her wrist and heads to pay the bill.

Everything feels like a wave crashing down on her. She closes her eyes and thinks maybe this is how it has to go. This is fate, after all. Destiny. The undertow will pull her down one of these days. It'll drag her out to sea. Forever lost within the swaying seaweed and fish bones.

The diary will be done, and that will be that.

It is what it is.

PART TWO

THIRTEEN

HARRIET AND FRANKIE

Maker's Bell, Pennsylvania.

A black Oldsmobile Cutlass Ciera with Florida plates slides down the streets and alleys, the roads a drunken spider's web of cracks meeting at pothole junctures. The whole town calls to mind a lunarscape: gray, cratered, dust-blown. The car rumbles past house after house whose windows are half-lidded eyes, whose porches and doors are forever yawning. Many look empty. Others appear occupied, but only by the dying—or the living dead.

The car pulls up to a driveway of uneven limestone gravel. A wooden mailbox sits out front, the mallard duck it was shaped as now barely recognizable. The paint has flaked off. The wing— the mailbox's flag—swings limp and loose, squeaking in the wind. The duck sits crooked, like one day soon it will tumble off its roost, dead.

Three black numbers—iron, rimmed with rust—identify the house as 513.

The doors to the car open.

"This the place?" Frankie asks of his partner, Harriet.

"It is," she says, her voice flat.

They get out of the car.

The two figures are opposites of each other in many ways. Frankie is a tall drink of water with a Droopy Dog face and a Sam the Eagle nose. Harriet barely cracks five foot two and echoes Charlie Brown—pudgy, round face with small and deeply set eyes.

Frankie Gallo is Sicilian somewhere down the line. His skin is like greasy, cakey cinnamon. Harriet Adams is whiter than an untanned ass, bleached like ocean-soaked bone.

Frankie's hands are large, the knuckles bulbous; Harriet's hands are little mitts, wormy fingers connected to flat, fat palms. His eyebrows are two caterpillars lying dead; hers are auburn slashes penciled in above her pinprick stare.

And yet, despite these differences, the two share an aura of menace. They belong together. He in his dark suit, she in her wine-colored turtleneck.

"Jesus, fuck, I'm tired," Frankie says.

Harriet says nothing. She stands, staring, like a mannequin.

"What time is it?" he asks.

"It's eight thirty," she answers without looking at her watch.

"It's early. We didn't eat breakfast. Want to go get some food first?"

Again, she says nothing. Frankie just nods. He knows the drill. Business before pleasure. And with her, it's always business. He likes that about her, though he'd never say so.

The house in front of them has gone to shit. A blue Victorian with shuttered windows. Ivy has been pulling it apart with slow fingers for the last twenty or thirty years.

A chill wind kicks up, sweeping leaves off the porch and jangling tangled wind chimes. Two gray cats, startled by the noise, dart down the steps and around the back of the house. Frankie makes his own noise in response.

"Ungh. She a cat lady?" he asks.

"I have no idea. Does it matter?"

"It matters." His eyes scan the house's face, and he spots what he doesn't want to find: an orange tabby peering out of a second-floor window, a tortoiseshell cat with a monkey-colored face hanging out on the porch roof by bent gutters, and a trio of white kittens peering out from under an out-of-control rose-glow shrub.

He sighs, rubs his temples. "Yep. She's a cat lady."

"Then let's just hope she's alive in there," Harriet says, and she starts walking to the front porch. Frankie stops her, grabbing her shoulder; he's one of maybe two people in the world who is allowed to do that without ending up dead.

"Wait. What does *that* mean?"

"I never told you about the Cat Lady of Brookard Street?"

His eyes widen. "No."

Harriet's mouth tightens. "When I was a little girl, we had a cat lady in town. We called her Mad Maggie, though I don't know that Maggie was her name. She had a great many cats, dozens upon dozens, and she kept getting more. She'd take in strays. She'd go to the shelters and take the ones marked for death. Rumor suggests she even stole cats from other people to add to her collection."

"Oh, fuck. I hate cats. I don't want to hear the rest of this story."

"The woman was very, very old. My mother said that when she was a child, Mad Maggie was an old lady even then. She had her routines: come out, get the mail, get the paper, water the mostly dead flowers that grew up out of a spare tire planter by her mailbox, repeat. Most hours of the day, she'd stare out the window. Then one day, we didn't see her anymore."

"Christ. Is this going where I think it's going?"

"Soon, a smell emerged. It wafted from the house when the wind blew. Sickly sweet, like spoiled meat."

"Great. She died. Probably from catching cat AIDS or something. Let's go inside."

"That's not the end of the story. Yes, she died, and no, I don't know from what. But the story is her body sat there for days. She had no family. Nobody came to check on her. And more important, nobody took care of the cats. They started at her extremities—fingers, nose, eyes—and then moved inward. The muscles. The organs. Everything."

"I am gonna puke."

"The cats bred, too. Even after people found the body, nobody dealt with the cats. They multiplied until they became a colony. A hundred feral cats, maybe more. The walls and floors were spackled with feces and ammonia, a home to parasites and disease. Someone did the merciful thing and burned the place down a year or so after." Harriet stares off in the distance. "I still remember the sound of fire crackling and cats wailing as they burned."

Harriet walks off, up to the porch. Frankie trails.

"You're one broken cookie," he says.

"Knock on the door."

"You said parasites. What kind of parasites?"

"*Toxoplasma gondii*—causes toxoplasmosis. Cat feces have it. Gets on people's hands. Or in raw meat. Often survives the cooking process. It messes with dopamine levels. It changes the brain chemistry of the host. Some speculate that the parasite is the very reason for 'cat lady syndrome,' as it rewires the brain so that the person loves cats, going so far as to hoard them. There may also be a link between it and schizophrenia. Now knock on the door."

"You're fucking with me. I can never tell when you're fucking with me."

She pushes past him and knocks on the door.

"I'm not touching anything in there," he says. "I don't want to ingest particles of cat shit and have cat worms reprogram my brain."

Harriet knocks again, more forcefully.

They hear something within: a bump, a shuffle. Then, footsteps. The locks rattle one after the other: one, then three, then six. The inside door opens, and an older woman's head peeks out, her nose pressing against the mesh of the screen door. A tube snakes up her nose. An oxygen tank on wheels sits at her feet.

"Go away," she rasps. "I don't want your damn magazine. I *told* you that. I don't want to hear any nonsense about 144,000 seats in Heaven—that doesn't make any damn sense! Billions of people have come and gone on God's green earth, but he only likes 144,000 of them? What kind of crazy god is that? Answer me!"

"We're not Jehovah's Witnesses," Harriet says.

"Like hell. What are you, then?"

"FBI," Frankie says, and flips his ID and badge like they do in the movies. The woman squints at it. Harriet shows hers, too, with a less ostentatious gesture.

"FBI? Whatever for?"

"It's about your son," Harriet says. "We'd like to talk to you about Ashley."

Harriet can see the channels in which the old woman moves; the woman is a hoarder, albeit an organized one, and her rooms are formed of canyons carved through the piles of debris. *National Geographic* stacks form mountains, each peak capped with a potted violet. The tops of furniture peek out over a laundry basket and an ironing board and mounds of paperback books—it's like wreckage floating atop a sea of more wreckage.

The smells of mold and dust mingle in her nose. It doesn't bother her. It does bother Frankie, from what Harriet can tell—he slides past twin magazine towers to find a chaise longue, on which he sits, his gangly limbs giving him the look of a daddy longlegs failing to find comfort amid the ordered chaos.

His eyes dart to and from a distant staircase, where golden eyes peer out from between the railing bars. Another mangy cat sits ill-concealed behind one of the magazine stacks.

The woman, Eleanor Gaynes, sits in a chair, her hand curled around the top handle of her oxygen tank. "This is about Ashley, you say."

Harriet doesn't sit. She stands but doesn't pace. She remains stock-still.

"That's right. Have you seen him?"

"No."

"No contact with him?"

"I told you, no. Haven't heard hide nor hair from him. Not a peep. He's gone. Flown the roost years back when I got emphysema, and I guess he's never coming back. We done?"

The old bitch is lying. It's only partly true that people have certain universal hooks that indicate when they're lying, but everybody has *individual* tells. It takes a certain instinct to know when someone is slinging a lie. Harriet has that instinct. It's no one thing that tells her. It's in the woman's inflection, how she blurts out the information, as if *she doth protest too much*. It's in the way her hand curls tighter around the top of the oxygen tank, pulling it closer. Harriet has an animal's sense. She can practically smell the deception.

"Mrs. Gaynes. Your son. I'd hate to think you're impeding our investigation. We are trying to help him, you know. We're trying to protect him from some very bad people."

The old woman's lip quivers. Her brows darken.

"You leave him alone," she hisses. "He's a good boy. He sends me money."

"Money. How much money?"

"Enough for my treatments."

"Do you know anything about a suitcase? A metal suitcase?"

Fidgeting with the oxygen tube, Mrs. Gaynes shakes her head.

Harriet finally moves. She doesn't move swiftly; she simply approaches and enters the woman's personal space. Her knees nearly touch the oxygen tank. Harriet folds her hands in front of her.

"I see you're on oxygen," she says.

"I told you, emphysema. Got it from smoking. Most of my lung capacity is gone. Got about twenty percent left, the doctors say. You can't get it back, they say. Damn doctors."

"You need the oxygen to breathe."

Mrs. Gaynes picks at the fraying edges of the blanket across her lap. "That's the idea." The words come out sarcastic and bitter.

"Interesting fact about oxygen," Harriet says, "as I'm sure you're aware from the many warnings on the tank and nozzle—"

Harriet pulls out a Zippo lighter with a pawprint painted onto the metal.

"—is that it's flammable."

Frankie moans. "I'm going to go make some tea or something." Harriet's okay with this. She doesn't need Frankie for this kind of thing. This is her thing, not his. They both have their niches. Still, sometimes she wonders: Is he losing the taste for this work? Does he really have the stomach for it?

As Frankie exits the room, Mrs. Gaynes remains transfixed by the lighter.

"You're not FBI," the old woman hisses, watching her reflection in the chrome.

"I should clarify," Harriet says. "Oxygen is not exactly flammable. Technically, it's considered an accelerant. That's how fire burns—it feeds on oxygen. It helps flame to spread quickly and efficiently. The problem with the air around us is that the oxygen is diluted. But what you're breathing is the real deal. Incredibly pure. Perfectly concentrated."

"Please," the old woman says.

Harriet's face shows no emotion, but inside, her heart is a leaping gazelle. This is her favorite part of the job. It is a small pulsing center of warmth inside her mind.

"Were I to light a lighter," Harriet continues, "the presence of the tank and the precious oxygen whispering from the tube would help the flame sweep over your frail, withered body. Have you ever seen someone set aflame?"

"My son—"

"Forget him. Think of yourself. I was . . . on-scene at a car fire. A woman and her husband sat trapped in the car, held fast by crumpled metal and melting seat belts. It was not a quick death. All that screaming. All that thrashing about. Such movement only helps to churn in more oxygen and give the fire more meat for its ragged teeth."

Mrs. Gaynes sobs silently as Harriet pops the tubes from the old woman's nose. From the end of the tubes come a faint susurration: *fssssssss*, the sound of something once life-giving, now potentially deadly. Harriet brings the lighter close, pops it, massages it with her thumb.

"Now. Your son. Where is he?"

"I can't—"

"You will. *Your son.* Or you burn. This whole place burns."

She sobs, cries out, "He's innocent!"

"Innocence is a fable." Harriet lights the flame but holds it away, then slowly draws it closer—like a mother playfully bringing a spoonful of food to a stubborn child. "Tell me where your son is, or you can die amidst the wails of your filthy cats."

"North Carolina," comes Frankie's voice from behind them. Harriet frowns and backs away, flipping the lighter closed and extinguishing the flame.

Mrs. Gaynes loses the tension in her muscles and just flops forward, moaning, crying.

"How do you know?" Harriet asks.

In one hand, Frankie's got a can of generic ginger ale, which he takes a delicate sip from, as if to make sure his lips don't touch any secret cat-shit germs. In his other hand he holds a postcard, which he waves around.

"The stupid dickhead sent her a postcard from North Carolina, and the equally stupid old broad hung it on the fridge like it was his third grade art project. Postmarked a week ago." He frowns and reads the postcard again. "He's been sending her money, like she said."

Harriet takes the postcard. Looks it over. On the front, *Greetings from North Carolina!* The name of the state plays host to mountains, the ocean, some city hall. On the back, Ashley writes, *Mom. In a town called Providence. Not far from Asheville. Met somebody who will join the team, help me meet my sales quota. Soon moving on to bigger and better. Get well. Will send money again soon. Love you. Ash.*

"Well," Harriet says, disappointed. "That concludes our business here."

She knows she should be pleased. They have the answer they need with a minimum of effort. No bodies to clean up. And fire is a chaotic, uncontrollable element.

And, yet, sometimes you just want to burn an old lady.

"Ashley," the old woman mutters.

Harriet tries to find a way to pull her mood out of its tailspin. She thinks of sticking it to the old woman, of telling her the truth about what her son does for a living, but the old woman probably already has a sense of it, and besides, Harriet just feels tired.

Instead, she simply says, "Kill her, Frankie. I'll be in the car."

Outside, Harriet taps the postcard against the palm of her hand.

From behind her, two pops. Frankie's gun.

That, she reminds herself, is Frankie's gift. Every tool in the toolbox has its function, and this is Frankie's. He cleans up messes. Maybe he complains. Maybe he's squeamish. But, for now, he does what he's told and she's thankful for that. Harriet knows that dispatching the old woman wouldn't be something she could do—not because she doesn't have the stomach for it,

BLACKBIRDS

but just the opposite. She has too much heart for it. She'd make it last. She'd enjoy herself.

Frankie emerges from the house looking like nothing happened.

"Thank you," she says.

He cocks an eyebrow. She doesn't usually thank him.

"We have to bring Ingersoll in on this." She throws him her phone. "Call him."

"But he likes you best."

"Call him."

"Shit."

He picks up the cell.

FOURTEEN

TERMINAL

Miriam stands in the thick of it.

It's night. She's no longer sure what time. She smells the stink of exhaust as another bus comes and goes, purging its people like a bulimic, then gorging on more. Across the way, sitting on a blue bench is Ashley, who makes an impatient roll of his index finger to say, *Move, move, move.*

Once more, she thinks of running. Maybe just get on a bus and go; not like she hasn't done it before. Her feet stay glued. She's not sure why.

(You like him. You like this. You deserve this.)

The Charlotte downtown bus terminal looks not unlike a giant airplane hangar—open air, big arched canopy, skylights allowing a faint glow from the moon above. It makes her feel very small.

She wades into the crowd, hands out.

Same plan as the last hour, and the hour before that, and the hour before that—her hands graze the hands of others, or she touches an exposed shoulder as someone passes. She takes a step, and—

Three years from now, the woman grips the edges of the hospital bed, soaked with sweat, pushing, pushing, trying to push a bowling ball out a gap the size of a small fist, and the child crowns, a meager mop of wet black hair already on the baby's empurpled head, and the face is out now, and it's covered in something that looks like red ambrosia salad, but then the vitals start going crazy, and a doctor who looks more than a little like Sulu from Star Trek *says something about an "obstetrical hemorrhage." A gush of blood, the woman screams, the baby slides out, a raft on red, and flatline.*

Miriam blinks away the image. She steadies herself. Not like she hasn't done this before. She's amazed at how many hospitals she's inadvertently seen the inside of. She lets her bare shoulder brush the shoulder of a man in a tank top as he reaches in to hug his wife—

The man is alone, thirty-three years from now, in a hospital. He's bald. The cancer's all through him, like rats in the walls. He sits in a chair in the corner and he reaches over to the bedside table and finds a bottle of pills there, and he counts out one, then two, then pauses. He regards these two pills and finally just upends the bottle into his hand and gets maybe two dozen of them, all of which he swallows. He sits there for a while, not feeling anything, just staring at the floor tile, the ceiling, his face looking woefully alone, and he starts to cry; a numbness creeps in around the edges. His head droops. Jaw slackens. Drool oozes. And then

Fine, whatever, Miriam thinks. Guy gets old, gets sick, kills himself. She won't be sad. He makes it to old age; good for him. Most do. That's what she realizes. Most people make it into their sixties and die of some "old person" disease—cancer, stroke, heart attack, cancer, heart attack, on and on, forever and ever. Throw in a little diabetes. A dash of pneumonia.

Most people don't die young, at least not here in America. Tragedy is unavoidable, but in this country, it doesn't usually come in the way one dies but rather in the way one lives. Failed marriages, fucked-up children, abuse of self, abuse of wife, abuse of dog, loneliness, depression, loathing, yawn, whatever.

Congratulations, she thinks, *most of you douchebags and assholes are going to live your shitty lives well into your golden years.*

Of course, this makes her job more difficult.

Ashley wants her to find a mark. A mark who will die soon, someone they can take for all he's worth. More important, he wants a place to squat. As it turns out, the house up in the middle of nowhere wasn't his; he just ganked the keys from some guy taking an airplane trip overseas. Took the house, settled in residence, hid all the framed photos. Instant bachelor pad.

He figures, if they can find someone who's going to die, who has money, and who has some crash space for them while they're in town, perfect. He looked at her datebook. It didn't have anything in it coming up soon enough for his impatient tastes. Ashley is hungry for more than just food.

So, he said, go somewhere with a lot of people.

Miriam offered, "A dance club." You get lots of people, most of them younger, a lot of them with risky behaviors. Coke-snorters, baseheads, unprotected sex monkeys, drunk drivers, the whole gamut. Ashley said no. Bus station. *Let's hit a bus station.*

Except, Miriam explained, that's not the best place, because at least half the people aren't coming; they're *going.* Which means, were she to *find* someone who was going to bite it soon, she and Ashley wouldn't be on scene for the event, not unless they wanted to hop a bus to Des Moines. And nobody wants to go to Des Moines.

No, Ashley said. Ashley thought he knew the score. Thought he was so damn smart. She'd been doing this for eight years now, but *he's* going to tell *her* a thing or two? Straighten her out, help her to "up her game"?

Fine. Bus station, she conceded. Whatever.

And here they are.

Across the way, he looks impatient. Foot tapping. Head lolling back. Mouth open, catching flies, like this is torture for him. What an asshole, she thinks. Torture. For *him*.

Hilarious.

By now, she's tired and pissed. She steps off the curb to cross in front of a bus and—

He's on his cycle, a road bike with tires so thin they look like they were squirted out of a pipette, and he's got all his tight Lycra cyclist gear on like he's being sponsored by Goodyear or Kellogg's or some shit, and the tire hits a stone and he skids, flips, and then there's a screeching of brakes and a bumper crashing into him, shattering his hip, and his body (like a marionette whose strings were cut) slides up onto the hood and his helmeted head cracks the windshield and then everything's blurry and black and brain bleeding and

—she turns, finding a man waving to another man, saying good-bye, be they friends or lovers. She doesn't expect it. She was just walking along, lost in her own thoughts, and his hand must have grazed her own. It doesn't help. Yes, he dies. No, it's not tomorrow. One year from now—well, really, one year, two months, and thirteen days. Still. He looks like he has money. It's close enough that she'll consider marking it in her datebook later. *(If you're around later . . .)*

Shaking it off, she darts in front of an incoming bus (wondering for a moment, *Will it hit me? Is this my time?*) and steps up to Ashley, who gives her the stink eye.

"Anything?" he asks.

"This is like fishing without bait."

"So, that's a no."

"Yes. No."

He shrugs. "Well, get back out there. Do your . . . psychic thing."

"This is really your idea of a partnership? You sit on your ass while I go and do the work?"

"My gifts don't come into play until you've hooked a fish, sweetheart."

"Your *gifts*? Seriously? Spare me. So far, your only gift to this world is that winning smile of yours. Everything else is taking up precious air and space."

"The smile's just the window dressing. But it *is* a key weapon in my arsenal of charm."

"Arsenal of charm," she repeats. "I'm hungry."

"I don't care."

"You damn well should care."

He yawns. "Listen. We don't have a place to stay. We need a place to stay. When we have shelter, then we'll think about food. Besides, you wouldn't want me to, oh, I *don't know*, cast you adrift, call the police, call your mother, that sort of thing?"

"I get it. You're holding the cards. Good for you. But quick biology lesson—this girl's gotta eat. I'm human. We humans thrive on food, not to mention liquor and cigarettes. I've got money. Let's hit a Waffle House? Then a motel? It's on me."

He seems to ponder. Then nods. "Fine. Yeah. Let's do it."

THE INTERVIEW

"The boy with the balloon," Miriam says, her face tightening.

"Yes," Paul says. Waiting.

She hates this story. Hates thinking about it. Hates retelling it worst of all.

"It was about two years after."

"After you—"

"After I earned this unique ability."

Paul lifts his brow. "That's an interesting word. Earned?"

"Yeah. Never mind that," she says, waving him off. "I was hungry, and I was tooling around this yuppie suburb of DC, and so I went to a Wendy's to get one of their . . . whatever their milkshake-without-the-milk product is called. A McSlurry."

"A Frosty."

"Whatever. I paid. I got my chemical-byproduct-industrial-foam-sugared-lubricant in a cup, and I went to throw away my trash like a good citizen. And there he is."

"He?"

"Austin. Little towhead with a head full of freckles. He has this red Mylar balloon with a picture of a blue birthday cake with yellow candles. He was nine years old. I know because he told me. He came up to me and said, 'Hi, my name is Austin; it's my birthday, and I'm nine years old.'"

Miriam worries at a fingernail. She knows that if she keeps

up with it, she'll soon bite it down to the cuticle, so to stop herself, she taps out another cigarette and lights it.

"I told him, I dunno. Good for you, kid. I'm not exactly the sentimental type, but I liked Austin. He had that bold, dumb-kid outlook—everybody's your friend, and the best thing that can happen to you is to have a birthday. At that age, a birthday is like this . . . big bucket of potential—a piñata exploding with candy, a toy box upended onto the floor. You get older, and you start to see how each birthday is really just a turnstile, and it takes you down, down, deeper, deeper. Suddenly, the birthdays are no longer about potential and become entirely the inevitable."

"And then you touched him," Paul says.

"You make it sound like I molested him in a van. For the record, *he* touched *me*. The kid grabbed my hand and went to shake it, like we were business partners now or something. Probably something his daddy taught him. How to shake hands properly like a big boy. He shook my hand, and that's when I saw."

Miriam describes it:

Austin would run out into traffic. Little sneakers pounding ground.

He'd be reaching up. Looking up. Little fingers reaching, waggling, as he bolted forth.

Chasing a Mylar balloon.

A white SUV would come out of nowhere.

It would knock his shoes off and send the boy's body tumbling like a doll across the asphalt.

It would happen twenty-two minutes after Miriam met him.

Paul sits there, quiet. He tries to say something, but then doesn't.

"Exactly," Miriam says. "Dead kid. Up until that point, I'd seen how lots of people were going to die. And yeah, I'd seen how a few kids were going to bite it, but they were always going to die . . . for lack of a better word, normally. Forty, fifty years later. They'd have their lives. Sad, but we all have to suck the pipe and take the Great Dirtnap. But this kid. Dead at age nine. Dead on his birthday."

She takes a long drag off the cigarette.

"And it was going to happen on my watch. I was there. I figured, here's my chance. I can stop this. I can be—what's the word? Proactive. Up until that point, all my efforts were passive. Guy's gonna die in two years in a drunk-driving accident, I tell him, 'Hey, dumb-fuck, don't drink and drive, at least not on June third,' and he can do what he wants with that information. But here? Now? A kid's gonna run out into traffic? How hard is it to stop a kid from running out into traffic? I figure, I'll show him something shiny. I'll just . . . Indian leg-wrestle the kid to the ground. I'll stick him in a goddamn trash can. Something. Anything.

"I got this great big swell of hope in me, you know? Like a bubble. I suddenly felt like . . . here it was. This was my purpose. This horrible thing that happened to me, this horrible so-called 'talent,' maybe it has a reason after all. Even if I stop one stupid little idiot kid from sucking a bumper at age nine, then it's all worth it, forever anon."

Miriam closes her eyes. She feels the anger rising in her, still.

"And then I met the cunt."

Paul blanches.

"What?" she asks. "You don't like that word?"

"It's just . . . a harsh word."

"Harsh word for harsh times, Paul. Don't be a girl about it. In England, they say it all the time. It's just part of the language."

"We're not in England."

"No shit?" Miriam snaps her fingers. "I guess I'd better stop driving on the left side of the road, then. Explains all the honking. And the fatal car crashes."

Paul's mouth forms a grim line. "So, you met some . . . woman."

"Austin's bitchy cunt whore mother. Twat bitch ax wound prostitute witch. She's got her designer handbag, her Botox-paralyzed smile, her hair pulled back so tight, she can't fucking blink without tearing her eyelids off, her little cell phone Bluetooth robot antenna shoved up into her ear or her ass or whatever. I went up to her and I said, 'Lady, I need your help. Your kid. He's going to die soon unless you help me save him.'"

"How'd she react?" Paul asks.

"I'm going to go with 'not well' for two hundred dollars, Alex."

"I think it'd actually be, 'What is "not well"?' Because it's *Jeopardy!*"

Miriam takes a last drag of the Marlboro and chain-lights another off the cherry. "You really know how to take the energy out of a story, Paul."

"Sorry."

"Twat-cunt looked at me like I just took a piss on her complete set of *Sex and the City* DVDs, so I went ahead and repeated myself. The woman mumbled something at me about being crazy, and I reached over to grab her arm—I got ahold of her shirt, not her skin—and she didn't like that very much.

"Fast-forward twenty minutes, and I'm yelling at the cop, she's yelling at me, the cop is just trying to make sense of everything—"

"Wait. Cop?" Paul asks.

"Yes, Paul, the cop. I said we were fast-forwarding twenty minutes, c'mon. Catch up. She marched outside and called the police, said some crazy lady was threatening her son."

"And you didn't run?"

Miriam flicks ash at Paul; he blinks it away.

"No, remember? I was trying to save the kid's life? I figured a cop on the scene could only help, not hurt. Maybe he'd drag us all downtown, which would solve the problem right out of the gate. I wasn't just going to . . . leave the scene, let it all happen."

Her hand tightens into a fist, and she pops her knuckles.

"But I should've. I should've run away. Because while we were all standing there yelling at one another outside a fucking Wendy's, Austin saw a penny on the ground. Even now, I can hear his voice play out, but at the time, I wasn't giving it any thought, you know? I was *so* caught up in giving his stupid god-damn mother a piece of my goddamn mind that I didn't really *register* what was happening.

"Austin says, 'See a penny, pick it up!' and he reaches down to pick up this . . . this penny. And when he does, the balloon slips from his grip. Now, I don't know how long he'd been carrying around the balloon, but the helium had started to go south, so it didn't float away. Instead it just . . . hung there, in midair, until a wind came and nudged it along."

Paul swallows a knot.

"The balloon picks up speed. He chases after it. I see him run for it. And I try to yell, but the mother is yelling at me, not watching her son. And the cop is watching the mother, because she looks like she's about to rake my eyes out. I scream and start to run but the cop pulls me back.

"It's still there. In my head. The balloon drifting past. The SUV. His body. His shoes. It's unreal. Like something you'd see on the Internet. Like a joke."

Silence.

Miriam blinks away the start of some tears. She won't let them come.

"That's messed up," Paul says finally.

She grits her teeth. "No, what's messed up is what comes later. After you pull yourself out of that moment, after you find a way to escape the loop of images your brain keeps playing, you start to make some connections. You realize all of life is written in a book, and we all get one book, and when that book is over, so are we. Worse, some of us get shorter books than others. Austin's book was a pamphlet. Once it's over, it's over. Throw it away. Say good-bye, Gracie."

"That's morbid."

Miriam stands, kicks over her chair, then picks it up and wings it hard—it clatters against the warehouse floor, spinning away.

"Paul, don't you get it? I tried to save this stupid little kid's life, and in trying to save it, I'm the one who doomed it. *I killed him.* If I didn't have that vision, if I didn't *act* on that vision, his dog-fucker of a mother would've probably dragged him into a shoe store or back home and she'd *never* have been distracted by the crazy girl, and her kid would never have made it to the highway. It's like some sick snake-biting-its-own-tail bullshit. Fate had a plan, and I was part of that plan all along even though I thought I was being slick and wriggling free from destiny's grip. By trying to stop it, *I* made it happen."

The chair is far away now, so Miriam sits down on the floor. She smokes quietly, huddled over, breathing heavy and deep.

"That's why I don't try to save people," Miriam finally says.

"Oh."

Miriam stubs her cigarette out on the hard concrete floor.

"Now," she says. "What you really want to know is, how did I get this way?"

FIFTEEN

OUROBOROS

Waffle House, a staple of the American South, is essentially a greasy yellow coffin. It's small. It's boxy. Half the people inside are little more than animated corpses, stuffing their mouths full of hash browns and sausages and the requisite waffles, their bodies bloating and swelling, their hearts dying. Miriam thinks it's awesome. She eats here because it's just one more nail in the ol' pine box; she can *hear* her arteries clogging, crunchy and crispy like the skin on fried chicken.

The irony, she thinks, is that you can't smoke in here anymore. Now only the Waffle House waitress is the *approved death merchant*.

Miriam stands outside now. It's spitting rain. Cars drive past. She sees a defunct Circuit City through a haze of smoke, and a little Korean place across the highway sitting next to a Jo-Ann Fabric and Crafts. In the distance are the yellow lights and dark silhouette of the Charlotte skyline, a neatly arranged picket fence of skyscrapers, hardly the tumbling monstrosity that is New York or Philly.

She feels perched on an edge. Precariously balanced. She doesn't want to think about the future—she so rarely does anymore, usually just letting life carry her along like she's a discarded Styrofoam cup floating on a lazy, crazy river. But it keeps nagging at her. Worrying with little teeth.

She's heard that in lab studies, rats and monkeys who are given the illusion of choice end up relatively healthy. Even if they only have two choices, a lever that doles out an electric shock and a lever that doles out a different electric shock, they at least *feel* like they have some say in their outcome, and end up being much happier and more productive. Rats and monkeys who just get the shock arbitrarily, no choice at all, end up anxious, agitated, chewing out fur, and biting holes in their little hands and little feet before dying of cancer or heart death.

Miriam feels like she has no control. She wonders how long it will be before she's chewing her own fingers down to the bone.

Of course, it might also be Louis.

He haunts her. He's not even dead, and she sees his ghost. A chance meeting once, and now she sees glimpses of him in places: standing in a crowd, driving a nearby minivan, in the reflection of the smeary Waffle House window—

"Miriam?"

She wheels.

The ghost is talking to her.

"Hey," the ghost of Louis says. Except—normally, the ghost has those Xs of electrical tape over bloody eye sockets. This one, not so much. Real eyes. Warm eyes. Watching.

"You're not a ghost," she says aloud.

He pauses. Pats himself down as if to make sure he's still physically present. "Nope. And neither are you, from the looks of it."

"That's debatable." She feels shaken.

In her head, Louis is dead. It's easier that way. This is harder.

"What are you doing here?" she asks.

He laughs. "Eating."

"I guess that makes sense." She feels embarrassed. A blush rises to her cheeks; that never happens. She tries to think of a witty retort. She can't. She feels unmoored, woefully unprotected. Stripped bare.

"You want to join me?"

She wants to run.

Instead, she says, "I just finished."

"Sure," he says.

And then they stand, sharing silence and the whisper of rain.

"Listen," he finally says. "I think I maybe messed things up back in the truck. I think maybe I gave off the wrong impression, like I was some kind of weirdo. And heck, maybe I am. It's just—I don't meet a lot of nice people. I didn't mean to get strange or act out, and I didn't mean to put you on the spot about going out sometime."

Miriam tries not to laugh, but she laughs. He looks hurt, and she waves him off. "I'm not laughing at you, dude, I'm laughing at me. At the situation. Irony is alive and well. You're the farthest thing from weird. You're a *thousand million miles* from weird. Trust me. I'm the odd duck. Not you. You're just a guy. A very nice guy. I'm the crazy bitch who had a spaz attack."

"No, I get it—long night, long highway, stressful situations; it's all good." Louis pulls a crumpled receipt from his jeans pocket and fishes out a pen. He presses the receipt up against the Waffle House window and writes something, then gives it to her. "That's my number. My cell; I don't have a landline anymore. I can't pick up another load for a few days—the economy basically fell off the horse and it hurts the little guys like me—but that means I'm still around."

"You're still around," she says. *Knife in eye. Slurping sound. Miriam?* "Well. I dunno."

"Who's this?" Ashley asks, coming out of the Waffle House, rangy arms crossed, a defensive posture. "Friend of yours?"

"No," she says. "Yes. I dunno. He gave me a ride."

Louis towers over Ashley. He's a pillar, a monolith. Ashley is just a windblown blade of grass in his shadow. Doesn't stop him from sticking his chin out and puffing up his chest. The two men stare bullets at each other.

"This your old boyfriend?" Louis asks.

"What? The black-eye boyfriend?" Miriam can't help but laugh. "No. Gods, no."

"Good meeting you, big guy," Ashley says. "We gotta split. See you later."

"Okay," Louis says. "I get it. I'm going to go inside, get a waffle."

Ashley smiles. "Smart way to play it, buddy."

Louis just grunts, and it's like the air has been sucked out of him. He's a big guy, like Ashley said, but suddenly he looks very small. Louis tosses Miriam a sad look over his shoulder, then heads inside. Ashley makes a jerk-off motion with his hand.

"Toodle-oo, fucker," he says, laughing.

SIXTEEN

GRAVITY

Still night. Still pissing rain.

Ashley presses her up against the brick wall. He parked the car. He said he wanted to show her something. They got out, and now here they are. The city's noises play around them—mild for a city, but still loud: the honking, the yelling, the laughing, the music drifting from somewhere far away.

Miriam feels the brick against her back. Ashley's up against her.

"Fuck off of me," she says, pushing him back. But he moves right back into place, like one of those clowns you punch down just so he can stand back up, grinning.

"You knew him," he whispers, chuckling. "The trucker."

"He gave me a ride. He's just a guy."

She smells his breath. Mint. She's surprised to see him lolling a Life Saver around on his tongue. Miriam hopes her breath smells like an ashtray.

Ashley's nose touches her own; then his cheek is against her cheek. His skin is smooth. No stubble. Feminine, almost. Hot breath reaches her ear.

"Just a guy? I don't buy it. You like him."

"I don't like him."

"No, you don't like *me*. But you do like him."

He bites her earlobe. Not hard enough to draw blood. But hard enough.

She pushes him away. He laughs. His hands hold her hips.

"I don't give a shit about that guy. I don't give a shit about anybody."

Ashley searches her face. She feels his eyes on her. The way his gaze roams, it's like a pair of hands. She gets a rush. Her heart flutters like a bird with a broken wing.

"Something else is going on here," he says. His thumb undoes the top button of her jeans. His fingers play idly around the waistband. His eyes widen. Revelation. "He's your mark."

"Fuck you. Get your hands out of my pants."

She says it and doesn't mean it.

He asks her the big question.

"When does he die?"

His hand slides down deeper. His fingers tease at her. She's getting wet like a hot summer day, sodden like a swamp, and she hates it.

"Go to hell."

His fingers move up inside her. She gasps.

"Let me help you."

"I don't need your help." She wants to moan. She stifles it.

"He's a trucker. Truckers have lots of money. I'll help you get it."

"I said, I don't need—" He does this thing with thumb and forefinger. She shuts up. She feels weak. Controlled. Like she's a robot and he's got the remote control.

"You definitely need something."

His fingers thrust harder.

He laughs.

Motel room. Floral print bedspread. Gold-rimmed mirror with the old showbiz-style lights marking its perimeter. A painting of a magnolia tree on the wall. The room is clean but smells of mold ill concealed by disinfectant.

Miriam sits at the edge of the bed, smoking. She eyes the metal suitcase, wondering what's in it.

Naked, she massages the carpet with her toes. Another motel. Another fuck. Another cigarette. Circles and circles, the spinning snake, the endless carousel. She wants a drink to drown in.

Ashley comes out of the bedroom, brushing his teeth with one hand, hiking on a pair of boxers with the other.

"Rapist," she says.

"Can't rape the willing," he snaps back with a wink.

"I know. Besides, I could've broken your jaw. I just want you to feel icky, is all."

Around the toothbrush, he gleefully mumbles, "I don't."

"I know that, too."

Back in the bathroom, he swishes, spits, and swishes again.

"No means no," she calls after him.

"Not usually," he calls back before exiting the bathroom. He wipes toothpaste froth from his chin with the back of his hand. "So let's hear the deets."

"The deets."

"Of the trucker's death."

"Louis. His name is Louis."

"Uh-huh. Whatever. His first name is *Mark*. His last name is *Victim*. He's got money, I know that much. Truckers always have money. They get big paydays but don't have the time or the place to spend it—unless they're married. He married?"

"Wife left him, he says."

She feels queasy. Traitorous. A dirty quisling.

"Then he's got money. Probably doesn't keep it in a bank, either, because one day you're in Toledo, the next you're in Portland, the third day you're in Assfuck, New Mexico—if you can't find a bank, and you want money, you gotta pay all those fees. Plus, half these trucker assholes are cranked up on amphetamines they buy at rest stops. Dealers and pimps don't take debit cards. Trust me."

"He's not a dope fiend."

Ashley shrugs. "Yeah, you know him *so well*. So, back to the original question: How does he bite it? Car wreck? That'll suck, because he probably keeps the cash in his truck. Won't help us if it all burns up."

"He dies in a lighthouse. In—" She does some quick math. "Two weeks. Fourteen days."

"How?"

"I'm not telling."

"That's awfully fourth-grade of you."

"It's private. It's his death."

"You get to know it."

She takes a drag off her smoke. "And I wish I didn't."

"Fine. Whatever. A lighthouse is at least a scenic way to go, so how nice for him. We're in North Carolina, and up the coast are what I imagine to be a shit-ton of lighthouses." He starts pacing. "Okay, here's the plan. Get close to him. Call him tomorrow. Go out with him. We got two weeks, so we need to know where he's going to be when he sucks the pipe."

"That's your genius plan? *That's* why I need you?"

He shrugs. "I didn't hear you come up with it."

"And tell me, why don't we just take his money while he's still alive?"

"*Because* people who are alive don't like you taking their stuff. People who are dead make fewer calls to 911."

She watches him carefully. "And none of this bothers you? You're not jealous?"

"I don't mind being green with envy if I'm also green with a wad of hundred-dollar bills," he says. "Now let's hit the sack. I'm beat."

SEVENTEEN

BLOOD AND BALLOONS

Miriam jolts awake. A shadow passes over her eyes.

She sits up. Her eyes adjust to the darkness. Ashley lies next to her, unmoving.

Her eyes catch sight of the shadow again—it eases into the corner, then ducks into the bathroom, a whispery, crinkly sound accompanying the drifting shape.

She reaches down over the edge of the bed, her hand darting into her messenger bag and coming up with the butterfly knife, a knife she bought at a flea market in Delaware for six bucks. Soundlessly, she flips open the blade.

Her feet touch carpet. Gentle steps stalking the shape.

Her free hand slides along the wall around the doorframe of the bathroom. Fingers find the light switch.

Click. Harsh, garish light.

Her heart stops.

A red Mylar balloon floats in the upper corner of the bathroom. It bobs and shifts. On the balloon is a picture of a cake, and above the cake, written in the cartoony flames of the cake's candles, is a message: HAPPY BIRTHDAY, MIRIAM.

"It's not my birthday," she says, apparently talking to the balloon.

The balloon shifts—another whispery crinkle—and drifts to the center of the room. Miriam looks at herself in the mirror. Both eyes are bruised. A rime of crusted blood rings her nostrils.

"This is a dream," she says.

The balloon turns slowly—on the back is another message.

A skull and crossbones are where the cake should be. From the skull's open mouth, emerging through crooked, jaunty teeth, a comic strip word bubble: HAPPY DEATHDAY, MIRIAM.

"Cute," she says, and she thrusts up with the knife.

The balloon pops.

And it sprays blood everywhere. Black blood. Thick with clots. Miriam wipes it off her face, spitting. It runs down the mirror, globs of rusty treacle. Bits of pale tissue are trapped in the flow like maggots in tree sap. She's seen this before, seen this kind of blood. (*On the floor, on the bathroom floor.*)

She doesn't know why, but she runs her hand across the mirror, wiping a clear spot away so she can see her reflection.

What she sees surprises her.

It's still her, the reflection. But she's young. Chestnut hair pulled back and tied with a pink scrunchie. No makeup. Eyes wider, fresher, that glimmer of innocence.

Then, movement behind her, in the reflection, obscured by coagulating clumps of gore.

"Nine more pages," says a voice. Louis's voice.

Miriam wheels, but it's too late. He's got a red snow shovel.

He cracks her across the head, laughing. All goes dark. As she's drawn deep into the well of unconsciousness, she hears the squalling cries of a child, and then that fades, too.

She wakes to the antiseptic stink of a hospital. It crawls up her nose. It nests there.

Her hands clutch the sheets. She struggles to get out of bed, to swing her feet over the edges, but the sheets have tangled her, and the bed is edged with a metal rail that she cannot, not for the life of her, seem to overcome. It's as if they form an invisible perimeter. It's hard for her to get air. Her lungs won't draw full breaths. She feels trapped, like in a box, in a coffin. *Sucking breath, tight throat, gasp.*

Hands reach out suddenly—hard hands, heavy hands—and they grab her ankles and, no matter how hard she struggles, buckle her feet into cold rubber stirrups. The palms feel greasy, wet. A face emerges from the edge of the bed, rising up from between her legs.

It's Louis. He tugs aside a mint-green surgical mask with blood-stained fingers.

"There's been a lot of blood," he says.

Miriam struggles. The sheets have coiled around her hands. "This is a dream."

"Could be." Louis reaches up and scratches the edges of the electrical tape *X* over his right eye. "Sorry. The tape itches."

"Get my legs out of those stirrups."

"If it's just a dream," he says, "why not just wake up?"

She tries. She really tries. She cries out, *willing* herself to wake.

Nothing. The world remains. Louis cocks his head. "Still think it's a dream?"

"Fuck you."

"Such a dirty mouth. It's why you'll be an unfit mother."

"Fuck *your* mother."

"You're like that girl in that movie, the one where she gets possessed by the devil? You know the one. All that vomit. All that angry rage slagging our blessed Lord and Savior."

Miriam pulls again at the stirrups. Sweat beads on her brow. She grunts in frustration, anger, fear. *Why can't I wake up? Wake up, you stupid girl, wake up.*

"We're going to have to stitch you up," Louis says. He leers toward the exposed space between her legs and licks his lips. "Tie it shut, *nice and tight*."

"You're not Louis. You're just a phantom in my head. You're my own brain, toying with me."

"It's *Doctor* Louis, I'll have you know. Respect the credentials."

He pulls out a needle. It's huge, like a knitting needle. Like a baby's finger. He sticks out his tongue to concentrate and, even blind, is able to thread a dirty, fraying cord through the eye of the fat needle. "You don't even know my last name, do you?"

"You don't have a last name," she huffs, trying to free her hands. "You're a figment. A fragment. I don't care about you. I don't care about ghosts and goblins."

"You feel guilty. That's okay. I'd feel guilty, too. We can talk about that, but before we do, I really need to stitch up your naughty place. That's medical lingo, by the way: naughty place. But I know you're fond of certain words, so let me rephrase that: I need to sew shut this stinking, worm-choked cunt of yours so that you can *never* have another baby, because the last thing the world needs is for you to breed true once more and crack your whore's pelvis giving birth to whatever little godless maggot decides to wriggle free from your scabbed womb."

Miriam is horrified—horrified at the words coming out of his (*her?*) mouth. She wants to say something, but her voice is just a squeak, a hoarse squeal. She tries to say no, tries to reach out and stop him—

But his head dips down and the fat needle pierces her labia, and she feels a gush of blood and she tries to scream but no scream will come—

Long highway—tapering to nothing in one direction, and tapering to nothing in another. Gray, blasted, pale, cracked. Desert on both sides: red earth, pale scrub. Blue sky above, but far off, a rolling thunderhead like an anvil tumbles end over end over end.

Miriam stands on the shoulder of the highway. She catches her breath, as if she just emerged from the icy waters of a winter lake.

She feels her thighs, her crotch. No pain. No blood.

"Jesus," she gasps.

"Not quite," a voice from behind her.

Louis, again, with those dead-*X* eyes.

He smiles.

"Don't come near me," she warns. "You come near me, I will break your tree-trunk neck, I swear to all that is holy."

He chuckles, shaking his head. "C'mon, Miriam. You've already established that this is a dream. You already know that I'm you. So, are you saying you want to break your own neck? That's very counter-productive. Suicidal, really. You should seek professional help."

Louis starts to pace, and as he moves, Miriam sees two crows in the middle of the highway. Dark beaks peck at a smashed armadillo, pulling up strings and tendons of red. The dead animal almost looks like a cracked Easter egg. The birds peck at each other.

"Maybe I'm not you," Louis says, slowly ping-ponging from dusty shoulder to dusty shoulder. "Maybe I'm God. Maybe I'm the Devil. Could be that I'm the living manifestation of fate, of destiny, of that thing you curse every morning you wake and every night before you lay your head to sleep. Who can say? All I know is, it's time to *meet ze monsta*."

Miriam begins to pace along with him. They are like two preda-tory cats, stalking each other on two sides of the same cage.

"Get me out of this dream," she says.

He ignores the request. "Maybe I really am Louis, though. Maybe I'm his sleeping mind, psychically calling out to you—because, after all, you're so sensitive. Poor little psychic girl. Maybe I know what's coming, and I'm begging for you to make it stop. *Please, make it stop, Miriam.* Boo-hoo."

"I can't make it stop."

"Maybe. Maybe not. You still have choices. I'm going to die in two weeks, but instead of trying to stop it—or, at least, trying to make my life a little better during that time—you're going to haunt me like a ghost and steal from my dead, eyeless body."

"Girl needs to eat." Miriam sneers.

He stops pacing. "Is that how you justify what you do?"

"You don't know what I do or why I do it," she says, even though she suspects the opposite must be true. "I'll be with Louis—and trust me, you're not him—and maybe I *will* make his life better for those two weeks."

"Blow jobs are nice," Louis says. "Try one of those."

"Fuck you. I can make him happy during that time. But don't ask me to save him—"

"Save *me*."

"—because it ain't happening. It can't happen. It won't let me."

"It."

"Fate. You. God. Whatever."

He shrugs. Then he looks somewhere over her shoulder.

"Hey," he says. "What's that?"

She falls for it. She looks.

It's a Mylar balloon. Drifting over the road top, caught in a heat haze, dripping blood onto the asphalt, where it sizzles as if on a hot griddle.

Miriam turns to say something to Louis, or not-Louis, or whatever he is, but—

He's gone.

He's been replaced by a white SUV, and it strikes her dead in the chest, and she feels something break inside of her.

The crows caw. A baby cries.

When Ashley wakes, he finds Miriam in the corner, soaked in sweat. She's sitting there, back against the two walls joining, and she's furiously scribbling in the notebook.

"What are you doing?" he croaks.

"Writing."

"I see that, Hemingway. Writing what?"

She looks up then. Mania glints in her eyes, and a mad smile plays.

"Wrote two pages, that's what. Only seven pages left."

Then she goes back to scribbling.

EIGHTEEN

THE NOT-QUITE-REVENGE OF FAT DUDE

The trailer park reminds Harriet of a graveyard. Single-wides and double-wides. Gray and white boxes. All lined up, one after the next. They're like headstones, she thinks. Or rows of tombs, each marked with dead and dying flowers.

Frankie kicks a stone. It ricochets off a rusty watering can, pelts a dirty garden gnome in his mushroom hat. "This place is disgusting."

Harriet steps up and knocks on the door of a double-wide at the end of the row.

A human mountain—his flesh a tattooed landslide in mid-collapse, answers the door.

Fat Dude. More specifically, naked Fat Dude. Two fingers splinted.

His frame fills the trailer door. A fire-breathing serpent, inked and linked with another serpent, encircles his belly button crater. The second serpent runs down to Fat Dude's mammoth thigh and coils inward so that—

Frankie blanches.

"Oh, c'mon," he mumbles, shielding his eyes.

"What?" Fat Dude asks, pissed.

Frankie wrinkles his nose. "Man. You got your *dick* inked?"

"You lookin' at my dick?"

"Well, it's right fuckin' there!" Frankie yells, pointing. "It's like a cucumber. A *sea* cucumber. I think it's looking at me, to be honest with you."

Fat Dude growls, "It'll spit in your mouth if you don't quit flappin' your lips."

"You sonofabitch—"

"We need to ask you a question," Harriet interrupts, holding back Frankie.

"I don't answer questions from dykes and dagos," Fat Dude says, proud of himself.

"Fuck you, fat-sauce!" Frankie says, stepping up.

Fat Dude reaches out with his left hand—the one with unsplinted fingers—as if to grab Frankie's lower jaw and rip it off his head. His hand never gets that far.

Harriet lets out a small sigh and darts in with a fast hand, pinching one of Fat Dude's testicles between her small fingers. She squeezes like she's trying to unscrew a sparrow's head. The mountainous man yelps like a kicked puppy and swings a meaty paw at Harriet's head. She leans backward, and Fat Dude's hand cracks into the moldering doorjamb of his own trailer. His index and middle finger bend backward in a way that's wholly not natural and crack like sticks breaking under a heavy foot. He howls.

Harriet finds this terribly satisfying. Two more broken fingers. Symmetry pleases her.

She lets go of Fat Dude's empurpled nut and shoulders him backward.

It's now possible to see the rest of the trailer—the mound of dirty dishes collecting flies, the couch with fabric so rough it could grate cheese, the bathroom door that's actually just a strip of accordion plastic pulled taut and latched with a rusty hook. A real palace.

Against the back wall sits a cot bowed deep, Harriet presumes, from Fat Dude's tremendous bulk. At present, a skinny girl, maybe eighteen, maybe younger, sits watching the whole thing unfold with heavy, heroin-lidded eyes. She holds up a blanket as if to feign modesty, but one tiny tit pokes out the top with a cigar-butt nipple standing at attention, a fact to which the girl seems oblivious.

"Hold his head," Harriet commands.

Frankie grabs the biker's pale pumpkin head and slams it down against a carpet crusted with food stains and other biological blemishes.

"Now lift his head."

Once the head's back up, Harriet thrusts a photo under Fat Dude's nose. His watering eyes try to focus on it.

"This man's name is Ashley Gaynes," Harriet explains. It's a photo of Ashley at a party, laughing, a cup of something that might be beer in his hand. He and everyone else stand bathed in the glow of red Christmas lights. "A bartender across town said you might know him."

"Yeah, yeah," Fat Dude squeaks. "I know him. You shoulda just showed me the picture to begin with. I woulda rolled on that little asshole like it weren't nothing. He's the one who broke my . . ." He can't seem to bring himself to finish the sentence. He lifts the splinted hand off the carpet and waves it like a penguin's busted flipper.

"Gonna be tough to jerk off now," Frankie says, grinning ear to ear.

"He have a metal suitcase with him?" Harriet asks.

"No. No suitcase. Just some blonde bitch."

"Blonde?"

"Blonde like white blonde, like beach sands—a dye job. And he drives a Mustang. Early 90s. White. Back window busted out."

Harriet nods to Frankie, who lets go of Fat Dude's face. It booms into the floor like the boulder tumbling after Indiana Jones.

"That's all for now," Harriet says. "Thank you for your time."

"Fuck you people," he whimpers.

Clucking her tongue, Harriet whips the tip of her boot into Fat Dude's mouth, shattering teeth. He rolls over, coughing, blood bubbling up over his lower lip. One tooth slides out on an oozing river of red. It plops to the carpet.

"Let's go," Harriet says to Frankie, who follows after, chuckling.

NINETEEN

DATE WITH DEATH

Fuck him, she thinks.

He's dead soon, anyway. His ticket's punched. His clock is set. Fate has taken a thumb of black ash and smeared it on his forehead. Nobody's marked his door with lamb's blood. God's got his number. Too bad. Sayonara, big guy.

The dude's got big cash. That one envelope alone had enough green in it to feed her, clothe her, give her a place to stay for weeks on end.

Not your fault. You didn't hunt him down and kill him. You're not a predator. You're a scavenger. A vulture, not a lion. You just found the body. Might as well pick its bones.

Yeah. Fuck him.

Then she sees him.

Miriam's standing in the parking lot of the motel, smoking a cigarette, and he shows up in his truck—the brakes hiss, he gets out, and she sees how he's cleaned himself up real nice. It isn't high fashion: blue plaid shirt, straight-leg jeans with nary a fraying hem or cut in the denim, big black cowboy boots (scuff-free).

And here she waits, plain white T-shirt, hair dyed the color of an oily crow, a pair of jeans with the left knee out and a series of crooked slashes up the right thigh. No boots, just a set of once-white Chuck Taylors, now so stained, they're the color of storm clouds.

She feels outclassed. Her mouth goes dry. This isn't like her.

"Shut this shit down," she mumbles to herself as he approaches. "Close it off. Be tough. Don't be a douche. Don't be a coward. Suck it up. We all die."

He gets closer, and she feels small—she is reminded again of his tremendous size, the broad shoulders, the ham-hock hands, the Herman Munster boots. And yet, his face is soft. His eyes cast downward. He's vulnerable. *An easy takedown,* she thinks, but isn't convinced.

"Hey," he says. It's got an aww-shucks vibe to it. He's nervous. That helps her. It's a cruel thing, but she finds herself forever empowered by the weaknesses of others. "You find the place all right?"

"I did," she replies. She drove here in Ashley's Mustang—borrowing his car took some convincing, like she was asking Daddy if she could cavort around town in his Benz.

"It's good to see you."

"You look . . . clean."

The comment puts him off-balance. She feels mean and awkward.

"I did shower," he says.

"I like that in a man."

"I didn't think you'd call."

She pitches the cigarette. It hits a puddle and sizzles. "Oh, yeah?"

"I figured, you were with the—"

"The other guy? Oh, gods, no. That's my brother, Ashley."

Louis looks relieved. Like the wind just caught in his sails. "Your brother?"

"Yep. That's actually why I'm here. Visiting him. I'm thinking of getting a job in the area, an apartment." The lies keep flowing. Once she turns the spigot, the faucet won't stop pouring; her knobs and handles are long broken. "Of course, *he's* between jobs, though—Mom and Dad always said he was pretty worthless. Me, I've got a real competitive spirit. I figure I can come down here, find him work, show him who's boss, humiliate him into getting his slacker ass in gear."

"Hope it works. Charlotte's a nice city."

"Nice," she repeats. "Yeah, it's certainly very nice." *Nice*. She says the word in her head, and it sounds mocking, whiny. The city is nice in an antiseptic way, in a clean-lines-and-polished-metal way. She'd much rather have New York, Philly, Richmond: the dirt, the grime, the odd angles, the chemical air, the smell of garbage intermingling with the odor of strange foods.

"You ready to go?" he asks.

The pit of her stomach goes sour. She's not ready to go. She's really not.

"Of course," she says, and she steps toward him to take his hand. "The chariot awaits."

The movie sucked. Dinner was mediocre.

Miriam feels like she's lost her way. The two of them sat next to each other during the movie, and across from each other at the Italian joint, but it felt like they were a thousand miles apart. He'd move in—a question, a look, a reach across the table—and she'd recede—a dismissal, a look away, her hand withdrawn to her lap. Two magnets turned the wrong way, repelling instead of attracting.

This isn't working, she thought again and again.

Now they sit, back in the truck, rumbling through stop-and-go traffic on the inaptly named Independence Boulevard. Miriam doesn't feel independent. She feels trapped. Shackled.

"My wife is dead," Louis suddenly says as they're sitting at a red light.

Miriam blinks. It's so unexpected, a boat anchor thrown overboard, a jarring splash.

He keeps talking: "I lied to you earlier. I said she left me.

That's true only in the . . . dumbest way. She's dead. That's how she left me."

Miriam looks down on the floormat, expects to see her jaw sitting down there, unhinged, the tongue flopping about like a dying fish.

"I don't know what to say" is all she can say.

Louis sucks in a deep breath that he doesn't seem to exhale.

"I killed her," he says.

Miriam's not easy to surprise. She's seen many things, and over time, those things act like steel wool; they abrade any presuppositions she has about the world. She's seen an old black lady taking a shit on the side of the highway. She once watched a woman beat a man to death with his own fake leg because she thought he was cheating on her. She's seen blood and vomit and car wrecks and X-rays where dudes have weird stuff shoved up their asses (like light bulbs and 8-track cassettes and rolled-up comic books) and at least *two* instances where guys were stomped to death by the horses they were trying to fuck. By now, the human animal is hardly a mystery; his depravity, his madness, his sadness, all these things are all well catalogued in her mind, and she's not even thirty years old yet.

But Louis. She didn't expect this.

Him? A *killer*?

"I was drunk," he explains. "We had a good night. It was warm. We ate dinner out on the patio of our favorite restaurant, this . . . this little café that overlooked a river. We talked about where we were going, what we were doing. We talked about having kids. About how it was time—maybe not time to *try* for children, but maybe time to stop trying *not* to. If that makes sense. We were laughing, and we both had margaritas, and—"

He stops then. Dams up the stream; closes the floodgates. His eyes are steel dots—gun barrels pointed at the horizon, or at nothing at all.

Miriam has an image in her head of Louis wrapping his giant hands around his wife's neck and choking her the way you squeeze a pimple—maybe a tequila worm made him do it, maybe the worm crawled up out of his windpipe and bored deep inside the meat of his big brain.

"We got in the car, and I was dizzy and all torn up from those drinks, but I didn't think anything of it, because I felt like we were unstoppable, that the road was wide open. I lost control of the car five minutes into the trip back home. It wasn't raining or anything, and I'd driven that road a hundred times before, but there was this one curve, and—I took it too fast, reacted to it too slow, and the road followed along the river, and . . ."

He finally exhales that breath.

"Car went in the water," he says. "Windows, doors wouldn't open. I don't remember getting out. But I ended up on the banks, and I watched the water move around the four tires sticking up out of the river. My wife—Shelley—she was still there. Still in the car. They found her, still buckled in. Lungs full of muddy river water."

Miriam's not sure if she should speak.

Louis runs his fingers through his hair. "After that, I sold everything we had, including the house. I quit my job at the factory and took one of those truck driver classes to get my CDL, and then I hit the road. Haven't been back home since. I'm just out here now."

"You really know how to say the sweetest things to a girl," Miriam says. It's a smart-ass comment, hurtful, but she can't help it. It just comes out of her.

He shrugs. "I figured things weren't going so well tonight, so what did I have to lose?"

She laughs, and then he laughs. It's an unanticipated sound.

"You're damaged goods," she says.

He nods. "I suppose I am. I also suppose that's not particularly attractive."

Miriam feels a hot rush rise to her cheeks.

He doesn't know how wrong he is.

She's on him in the motel room, white on rice, chrome on a bumper, a hungry velociraptor on a chained-up goat. Miriam can't refuse the scent of a damaged soul. The stink of death is in her nose, and she knows it's deeply fucked, but as her mother would say, *It is what it is*, and what *she* is is hot to trot, ready to roll. She wants to be ridden hard and put away wet.

Louis, he's like a goddamn building—she has to climb him like King Kong. Hand on his shoulder, she brings her hungry mouth to his ear, she slides her hand around his barrel chest, she tangles her own leg around his. It must look cartoonish, she thinks, but fuck it. They're not making a porno. This isn't for public consumption.

He moans. He's not sure. He's not comfortable. "I don't know—"

No, uh-uh, he's not allowed to finish that sentiment. Her mouth on his mouth, her tongue is a snake in the grass, a worm in the apple. With her one free hand, the one not clinging to his shoulder like a mountain climber, she starts trying to undo the buttons of his shirt, but they're stubborn as shit, so she just rips them. They hit the wall, a clattering rain.

He protests, but the words are swallowed by her mouth.

So, there she is. Hungry. Lustful. Driven into a froth.

And she sees a shadow behind them.

She's on Louis, but behind them is *another* Louis.

And he's standing there, and he peels up the black electrical tape over his left eye, and a river of maggots starts to tumble out of the puckered, ruined hole.

"Shhhh," Ghost Louis says.

Miriam doesn't mean to, but she bites Real Louis's tongue.

"Ow," he says.

She winces. "Sorry."

She wants to scream to the ghost, *You're a figment, shoo, go sleep with the cockroaches. This is a celebration of life over here. It's not twisted. It's not fucked up. Totally normal.*

Ghost Louis pulls up his other homespun eye patch. A coughing burble of black blood runs out next to the still-streaming spout of maggots. He smiles.

"You're going to let me die and steal my money," Louis says, and Miriam drops to the ground and steps backward, her heart hammering against her breastbone like an iron fist. She doesn't know *which one of them said it.*

"What?" Louis, *Real Louis,* asks.

"Maggot, vulture, parasite, hyena," croons Ghost Louis in a chirpy singsong.

Miriam cries out in frustration.

Real Louis looks confused. He looks behind him, and for a moment, she half expects him to see his own ghostly reflection. But now Ghost Louis is gone, and she's certain that her mind has completely gone, too.

"What is it?" he asks. "Did I do something?"

She wants to say, *Yes, you manifested as a ghost or demon from my own subconscious and taunted me while I was trying to get some action.*

"No," she says, instead, waving him off. "No, it's just me. I can't, uhh. I can't. Not right now. Outside? There a snack machine? Ice machine? Drink machine? Any kind of . . . machine?"

He clears his throat. "Yeah. Uh, yes. Go out the door, head left. It's in a little alcove just off the parking lot."

"Cool," she says, and opens the door.

"Are you okay?"

She shakes her head. "Not so much. I know it's cliché, but it's me, it's not you. I wholly encourage you to chalk this one up to 'bitches be crazy.'"

"Are you coming back?"

She answers honestly. "I don't know."

THE INTERLUDE

"It starts with my mother," Miriam says. "Boys get fucked up by their fathers, right? That's why so many tales are really Daddy Issue stories at their core, because men run the world, and men get to tell their stories first. If women told most of the stories, though, then all the best stories would be about Mommy Problems. Trust me on this. Daddies are great for little girls, unless they're Diddle Daddies. Mommies, though. That's a whole other bag of anger."

"So, you blame your mother for all this? It's her fault?" Paul asks.

Miriam shakes her head. "Not directly. But maybe not so indirectly, either. Let me lay out my family situation. My father died when I was very young, and I don't really remember him. He had bowel cancer, which from what I understand is the least pleasant cancer to have, because you're basically . . . shitting cancer. Some of life's best moments are during a good bowel movement, and to have that robbed from you, I can't even imagine."

"Girls don't usually like to talk about their bowel movements, do they?"

"I'm hardly typical" is her retort.

"You like being hardly typical, don't you?"

"I do. And don't psychoanalyze me. You're nineteen, for Christ's sake."

"You're only twenty-two."

She snorts. "Which makes me your elder, young man. Can I keep telling my story here? Your readers are going to be on the edges of their seats."

"Sorry."

"So, okay, Dad dies, young girl is left alone with her overly religious, practically Mennonite mother, Evelyn Black. Mother is a repressive force—you know how they always say The Man gonna keep you down? My mother is The Man. Her oppressive thumb makes a young girl into a Bible-reading teen who dresses a lot like a forty-year-old librarian, so much so that you expect her to smell like dusty carpets and old books.

"But that's hardly the truth of who she is. It's just what she thinks she *should* be. It's what her mother tells her is right, is proper. Chaste and charitable, prim and proper, mouth and vagina buttoned up so tight, the whole package threatens to strain and pop and take out someone's eye. Ah, but the girl has all these little secrets. To you and everybody else, it's hardly overwhelming, but to her mother, it's the motherfucking Apocalypse. The girl likes to sneak comic books. She likes to stand near other kids listening to their—gasp—rap albums and the Devil's own heavy metal. She gets a secret thrill watching the other kids at school smoke. And then she comes home and doesn't watch TV because they don't *have* a goddamn TV, and she reads her secret comic books and listens to her mother rant about morality, night after night, over and over, the end."

"The end?"

"Not really. Obviously. It's just the beginning. The young teenaged librarian—let's call her 'Mary'—is starting to suffer a breakdown. Not in front of anybody, but she goes back to her room at nights and cries herself to sleep, and she has these thoughts where she pulls out great bloody clumps of her own hair, or she knocks her teeth out with hammers, or other self-defacing horrors. She doesn't *act* on any of them, which in some ways is worse: It further tightens her, squeezing her until she's ready to explode.

"Thing is, it's not like the mother is exactly a bad mother. She's not physically abusive—she doesn't whip the girl with wire hangers or anything, doesn't smack her in the tits with a curling iron. She's not exactly *nice*, though. She insults the girl daily. Sinner, slattern, slut, whatever. The girl represents a constant disappointment. A big black smear. A bad girl, even though she's a good girl. Maybe the mother can smell the promise of sin. Maybe the mother senses the taint of buried evil."

"So," Paul asks, "what did you do? You did something. You couldn't take it anymore, and you did something."

"I had sex."

Paul blinks. "So?"

"Right. So what? You come from a world where twelve-year-old girls are texting—excuse me, 'sexting' to each other about how they gave some guy a blumpy—"

"A blumpy?"

"C'mon, really? A blow job while the guy is on the toilet doing Number Twosies? Blow job plus dumpy equals blumpy?"

Paul goes pale. "Oh."

"Yeah. *Oh.* Point is, you come from a place where kids do it and nobody's surprised. I come from a place where your mother tells you how your lady parts are really the Devil's mouth, and you don't feed the Devil, oh, no. Feed the Devil and he wants more, more, more."

"You fed the Devil."

"Just once. His name was Ben Hodge. We did the deed. And then he killed himself."

TWENTY

THE LIARS' CLUB

Miriam wants an orange Fanta so bad she can taste the chemical fake-fruit burn on the back of her tongue. But the machine is a Mello Yello, some kind of rip-off of Mountain Dew. She doesn't care. She wants what she wants, and she doesn't want to think about what she doesn't want to think about. Not that it matters, as she has no money for the machine. Oops.

She thinks, *I want an orange soda. And I want vodka to mix into the orange soda. And, while we're at it, I'd also like to stop being able to see how people are going to bite it. Oh, and a pony. I definitely want a goddamn pony.*

Her thoughts are so loud, she doesn't hear the car enter the parking lot.

Miriam presses her head to the machine. Then she sees it—a dollar bill.

"Bonus," she mumbles, reaching for it.

It's a ruse. A filthy lie. A fake dollar that, when opened, reveals a Jack Chick Christian tract. Some story about how playing games like Dungeons and Dragons is basically the same as suckling hell-milk from a demon's tit.

Miriam crumples it up, goes to throw it, and finds herself face-to-face with a gawky, bony Italian-looking dude in a trim black suit.

"Jesus Christ," Miriam says.

The Italian nods, though he is clearly nobody's Lord and Savior (despite a faint resemblance in the nose, which is so low and severe, it could be a fishing gaff). Miriam sees a small woman approaching, a short chubby thing with black eyes like hot coals and a set of bangs that look like they were cut with a hedge trimmer and a ruler.

"Evening," the woman says.

"Scully," Miriam says to the woman. To the man, she nods. "Mulder."

"We're FBI," the tall fucker says.

"I guessed that. That was the joke." She clears her throat. "Never mind."

"I'm Agent Harriet Adams," the woman explains. "This is Agent Franklin Gallo. We'd like to ask you a few questions."

"Sure. Ask away. If you're looking for Christian propaganda in cartoon format, I got some of that sweet gospel right here." She opens her palm and shows them the crumpled Chick tract. Her heart is leaping in her chest like a spooked gazelle—she can hear her blood in her ears; she can feel the pulse in her neck pounding like a kick drum. Is this it? Has her past caught up to her? She wonders, how many cigarettes would she be worth in the slammer? All those orange jumpsuits and unshorn women. Shit. Fuck!

What are her options here? Kick the tall fucker in the crotch? Slit the stubby bitch's throat with the Chick tract, hoping for a wicked paper cut?

She sees the woman's gaze flick to the left, then she hears feet on sidewalk. Heavy feet.

Louis's feet.

"Everything all right?" he asks, walking up.

The two agents size him up.

"We're looking for someone," the woman says, and holds out a photo.

Miriam's throat tightens. She's glad as hell they're not looking for *her*—but there Ashley is in the photo. Some party. Red Christmas lights. Laughing. That smug eyebrow. That mouth curled forever in a dickish grin. It's him.

Louis sees it. Miriam waits for him to give up the ghost. If they find Ashley, he'll roll over on her. Which means they'll find her. She can't have that.

"You know this guy?" the Italian asks.

The woman says, "His name is Ashley Gaynes."

"That's a dude, not a chick," Miriam says, verbally feinting left.

"He's a male, yes," the woman says, frowning.

"But his name's Ashley."

They stare at her like they want her dead.

She holds up her hands. "Oh. I just figured—never mind."

"Have you seen him? Or not?"

"Ummm. Nope. I see a lot of dudes. I haven't seen this dude."

The woman thrusts the photo upward, so that it's unavoidably in Louis's line of sight.

"And you, sir? Have you seen this man?"

Louis seems irritated. He tightens. "I'm sorry, who are you people again?"

Miriam leans in, and says in a Southern affectation to match his real one, "Baby, they said they're the FBI."

"Can I see some ID?"

The Italian rolls his eyes. The woman says nothing and shows hers. The man, exasperated, follows suit.

"No," Louis says. "I haven't seen him. Sorry, y'all."

The Italian steps in, cocks his chin, pops his knuckles. "You take one more look at that photo, and you think real hard about it—"

"Frankie," the woman says, putting her little mitt on his chest. "We can stop bothering these people. They don't know anything. Thank you for your time, folks."

The two of them turn and head back toward a black Cutlass Ciera parked a few spots down from the motel office. They seem an odd couple, Miriam thinks. Like a pair of pooches: a little bulldog tottering next to a bony Great Dane.

"They're looking for your brother," Louis says. He doesn't sound happy.

"My brother. Yeah. Thank you. Y'know, for not selling him out."

"I don't feel comfortable lying to the law," he says as they watch the black Oldsmobile exit the lot. It drives off down the avenue, an inky shadow lost to the darkness.

"That's because you have a handful of redeeming traits like honor and integrity and honesty and other positive qualities that are generally foreign to me. It means a lot to me. Really."

He takes a deep breath. "So, what happened back there?"

"These two FBI agents—"

"No. In the room."

She knew that; she just felt like avoiding it. "I don't know. I freaked out. I wanted an orange soda."

"An orange soda."

"Like I said, bitches be crazy."

"Any chance we can talk about it? Or just hang out, watch some TV?"

He's reaching, she thinks. It's sweet. But—

"I can't. I have to go. I have to tell my brother and go kick his ass for making me lie to a pair of federal agents."

"Can we do it again?" he asks.

His face is sad, pleading. This is a lonely man, she thinks; he must be, he wants to spend time with *her*. But then there it is, a flash, a shadow over his face—a pair of gouged-out eye sockets, four strips of electrical tape, blood pouring, maggots crawling, rust flakes falling from a shitty fish-gutter knife. She shudders.

"I'm an awful person," she declares. "I'm a hideous little

no-goodnik. I have horrible thoughts. I do horrible things. I curse, I drink, I smoke. I basically have shit in my mouth and my head, and it always comes pouring out of me—" *Like a stream of maggots,* she thinks. "And you don't need that. Louis, you're a genuinely nice guy. A *good person.* You don't want to be with me. You'll just get covered in shit. My shit. My problems, my emotions, my everything. I am like a bucket of sewage turned over your head. Go find a *nice* girl. Someone in a sundress. Someone who isn't so comfortable with the words *mother*, *cock*, *fucker*, and *sucker.*"

"But—"

"No but. This is it. You're sweet."

She gets on her tippy-toes and kisses his chin.

"Have a good life," she says, and she wants to tell him the truth. She wants to say that this is it for him, he doesn't have long—she wants to exhort him to go get a prostitute, go eat the nastiest and most expensive cheeseburger he can find, and for God's sake, stay away from lighthouses. But she says none of those things. A tiny part of her hopes that if she can stay away from him, that will be the secret. The trick. That will be what saves him. It's a lazy, passive theory—but since being proactive hasn't earned her a damn thing yet, it's all she has.

"Wait!" he calls after her, but it's too late. She's in the Mustang. She coaxes it to life.

And she sprays gravel peeling out of the parking lot.

"Another bust," Frankie says, rubbing his eyes. He yawns. "We're never going to find this little pecker. Ingersoll's going to have our balls for brunch."

"I don't have balls," Harriet says as she pulls the car over just past the motel entrance. She leaves the car running but dims the lights.

"What are you doing?"

"Waiting."

"For what?"

"For the girl."

"What girl? That girl we just met?"

"Yes. They were lying."

Frankie blinks. "What? Who? Paul Bunyan back there and his little snippy bitch?"

"Both of them. The girl lies better than the man. So much so that she almost had me. But she tries too hard. The man's lies, on the other hand, were utterly transparent."

"How do you always know this stuff?"

"The eyes. Ingersoll taught me that. They lie, so they blink. Or they look up and to the right, accessing the creative portions of the brain. Pupils shrink. An eyelid trembles. It's a panic response. I can sense it. Most prey animals respond by a twitch of the head, a sudden shift of the eyes. Lying is a fear response. Those two were scared."

As the car idles, they hear the popping of gravel.

In moments, a white Mustang comes racing past. Taillights twinkle.

"And the horse is out of the gate," Harriet says.

She eases the car back onto the road, silent and deadly as a shark.

THE INTERVIEW

"Ben Hodge."

Miriam says the name, lets it hang out there like so much dirty laundry on the line.

"Let's just get this out of the way: Ben was weak. Weak like I was weak. Here was this kid in school. Not ugly, but not a quarterback, either. Mop of dirty blond hair. Freckle-cheeked. Dull eyes but sweet. We had a lot in common. We were both loners, more by necessity than by any actual desire to be that way. We both were homely nobodies. Both had dead dads and oppressive moms—you know about my mother, but his? Ugh. A haggard, horrible woman. A *cave*woman. She was—no shit, get this—a *logger*. You know, climb up the trees, hug the stump with your thunder thighs, chainsaw spraying sawdust."

She pauses because she is remembering.

"Go on," Paul says.

"We weren't friendly, he and I. Never said two words to each other. But sometimes I'd catch him staring at me, or he'd catch me staring at him. We'd pass each other in the halls, stolen glances, all that clichéd crap. So, one night, it happened. My mother was not a drinker by and large. Condemned it like it was the milk of Satan. And yet, I knew that once in the bluest moon, she'd take a nip from this nuclear-green crème de menthe bottle she kept under her bed. I stole it, and I went right to Ben's house, and I did the stupid teen thing where you throw shit at the other person's window to get them to come out—I threw twigs because with my luck, I'd throw a pebble and break the window. His house was one of those country farmhouses with the old, warped glass. Fragile.

"He came out. I showed him the bottle. We went into the woods. We sat among the crickets there in the darkness, and we had a great time telling stories and making fun of people at school, and then—we did it. The rumpy-pumpy, the beast with two backs. Up against the tree, like a pair of clumsy, rutting animals."

"Romantic," Paul says.

"You kids and your sarcasm. You joke, but in a weird way, it *was* romantic. I mean, if you subscribe to this Hallmark fantasy that romance is all about the greeting cards and the dozen roses and the diamonds are a girl's best friend, no, this wasn't that. But it was an . . . honest connection. Two wayward idiots in the woods, laughing and groping and drinking." She pulls out her pack of cigarettes, sees that she's smoked them all already. She mashes it up and pitches it over her shoulder. "Of course, I went ahead and took a shit all over that beautiful human connection. As I'm wont to do."

"Oh? How so?"

"We get back to his house, and I'm feeling high and giddy and I'm grinning like the cat who killed the mouse, and his mother is waiting for him. For us. She's got one of the local cops with her, this bald prick named Chris Stumpf. Guy looks like an uncircumcised penis. So. Ben's mom starts reading him the riot act, and me, she tells me that if she ever sees me again, I'll be sorry, she'll get me, blah blah blah."

Miriam snaps her fingers.

"That's when it hits me. What we did in the woods. The kind-of-beautiful thing he and I shared turns ugly. Shame floods in. I'm like Adam and Eve, made to realize my own nakedness. My own mother wasn't there at that exact moment, no, but Ben's mom did the job well—a perfect stand-in. I could hear my mother's voice clear as the night sky, stripping me of all my dignity, shoving me toward the belching Gates of Hell itself. I suddenly felt like I was both *used* and *user*, a worthless lazy whore who gave her virginity to some sweet simpleton from down the road. And that was the end of mine and Ben's fleeting half-ass relationship—soak it in crème de menthe, light it on fire, and head home."

Paul shifts uncomfortably. "You never talked to him again?"

"I did, but only in passing." Miriam idly fingers the booze bottle, wishing she had more smokes. She wants to cut this short to go get some, but she can't. Things have to happen a certain way here. Order of operations and all that. "He tried to talk to me, but I wouldn't have it. I told him that what we'd done was wrong, but he still wouldn't take no for an answer. The dumb idiot told me he loved me; do you believe that? That's when the floodgates opened."

"What happened?"

"I let fly with some of the meanest shit you could imagine. I slung acid in his eyes, pissed in his ears. I called him a moron, a retard, even though he wasn't either of those things; he wasn't even slow, he was smart as a whip but just . . . came across the wrong way. I told him he had a limp dick, couldn't fuck, wasn't fit to lay a cripple or a coma victim. I mean, it was like I was *possessed*. I don't even know that I'd heard words like that before, and they came rocketing out past my tongue—I wanted to close my teeth and stop them from coming, but there it was. All that bile. Unstoppable."

Miriam takes one last look at the bottle in front of her. More than halfway empty now. She whistles low and slow, and then pulls back the bottle and drinks. And drinks. And drinks. Throat bulging with each gulp. She's already hazy. Her words, already slurring. Might as well go for broke, she figures.

Her throat burns.

But it goes numb fast.

She gasps, catching air, then pitches the bottle over Paul's head. He winces, ducks, and winces again when the bottle *pops* against the concrete.

"That night," she continues, stifling a little burp, "Ben goes into the bathroom, his head probably full of all the spew that came out of my mean-ass mouth, and he sits down in the shower stall and he peels the sock off of his left foot. Then he sticks the double barrels of a fuckin' shotgun between his teeth—the two barrels forming a sideways eight, what they call a lemniscate, a sign of infinity, what irony, right?—and then he curls his big toe around the double triggers. A tug of the toe. Boom. He was kind enough to do it in the shower so it required as little clean-up as possible for his mother. Nice guy till the bitter, blood-soaked end."

Miriam doesn't stifle the next belch. Whiskey breath. Her eyes water. She tells herself they're just watering because of the whiskey. It is a good lie; Miriam almost buys it.

"The real bite of it is, he left a note. Well, not so much a note as a, I dunno, a postcard. He wrote on a piece of paper in big black marker, 'Tell Miriam I'm sorry for whatever I did.'"

She stares off at nothing, uncharacteristically silent.

TWENTY-ONE

THE SUITCASE

She throws open the door to the motel (*motels, motels, always another motel, another highway, another stop on her coast-to-coast tour of nowhere*) and finds Ashley naked on the bed, his cock in his hand. Miriam can't see the television, but she hears a porny moan, the kind of moan women don't make in real life.

Ashley freaks out, tries to grab for his pants lying in a fabric puddle by the side of the bed. He fails and rolls off the bed, slamming into the floor shoulder-first.

"Shit! You ever hear of knocking? On the door?"

He doesn't put on his pants—he just ducks behind the bed, using it to cover up his nudity.

Miriam marches into the room and flips the blinds closed.

"I paid for this room," she says, then glances over her shoulder. Two blonde trollops with milk-jug breasts are wrapped in a sixty-nine on the tube. They're going at each other like frenzied cats. "And *apparently* I paid for lesbian porn."

"I thought you were on your date."

"Put on some pants. We have to go."

"Go? What? What did you do?"

Miriam's reached her boiling point. She feels like a cornered rabbit, ready to kick.

"What did I do?" she asks. "*Me?* That's a ripe one. What did *you* do is the question we should be asking ourselves, shithead. Why would the FBI be interested in *you*?"

His reaction surprises her: He laughs.

"The FBI? Please. Don't they have more important things to worry about, like pedophiles or terrorists? Or pedophilic terrorists?"

Miriam snatches the jeans off his lap, then throws them in his face.

"Hey, don't fuckin' laugh about this, Smiley McGee. Quit with the grins. This is serious. I was at the motel, or the motor lodge, or whatever the fuck they're called, and these two FBI agents walked right up like they could smell the stink of you all over me. Ashley, they had a *photo* of you."

Ashley's smirk melts away. It's the first time she's really seen him stunned.

"What? My photo? You're serious?"

"Asshole! Yes!"

He chews the inside of his cheek. "What'd they look like?"

"Tall, Dark, and Asshole was . . . well, tall. Italian, maybe. Dark suit. The other one was this mean little woman, this Napoleon in a turtleneck. Adams and . . . Gallo, I think. Like the cheap wine."

Ashley goes pale. "Shit," he says, quietlike. His eyes search the room. "Shit!"

He grabs the remote control off the bed and pitches it against the TV. The remote shatters. The TV flicks off—the lesbian porn fading to a bright dot, then to nothing.

"Now maybe do you get the gravity of the situation?"

Ashley grabs her wrists, snarls, "No, *you* don't get the gravity of the situation. Those two aren't FBI. They're not cops. They're not anybody."

"What? What the hell are you talking about?"

"They're demons, devils, ghosts. They're goddamn thugs. *Killers.*"

"Killers? You're babbling. Stop babbling."

Ashley isn't paying attention anymore. His mind works; she can see it. He starts to pace.

"Grab your shit," he says. He moves to the corner of the room, and he throws aside his duffel bag before lugging out the metal suitcase. Ashley grunts as he hoists it onto the bed.

"This is about the case." She says it matter-of-factly, because she knows it's true.

"Probably." He grabs Miriam's messenger bag from the other side of the bed and slings it at her. She catches it like a football, right in the breadbasket. She oofs. "Keys. Give me the keys."

"No."

"Give me the keys to the Mustang. Now."

"Not until you tell me what's going on."

"We don't have the time for this!"

Miriam grits her teeth. "Tell me."

"I swear to God." His hands ball into fists. "You give me those keys right now."

Miriam pulls out the keys, which hang from a fuzzy, dyed-green rabbit's foot.

"These?" she asks. She dangles them in front of him. "Go on. Take them."

He reaches in.

She whips him across the face with them. The keys cut a gash across his forehead. He staggers backward, pressing his forearm to the cut. Pulling his arm down, he sees the blood; an astonished look crosses his face. The *second* time now that he really looks spooked.

"You cut me," he says.

"Yup. You wanna get grabby again? Unclench those fists, buddy boy, and get to talking. Because if you don't tell me what the hell is going on, I will cut your fucking throat with these keys and stuff the rabbit's foot up your asshole for good luck."

Miriam watches him. He thinks about it. He's probably think-ing, *I can take her,* or *I'll lie; I can always lie.* But then all the gears and pylons and tumblers fall into place, and he makes his decision.

With nimble fingers, he works at the combination lock on the metal case.

The lock releases with a *pop.*

He opens the lid, and Miriam sighs.

Inside the suitcase are little Baggies, each piled atop the next, each no bigger than a coin purse or a snack bag. But these Baggies don't hold Oreos or spare change. In each is a baby's fist of little crystals, like broken quartz or shattered rock candy.

Miriam knows what it is. She hasn't tried it, but she's seen it.

"Meth," she says. "Crystal meth."

Numbly, Ashley nods.

"Tell me."

"Tell you what?"

"Tell me how this giant fucking suitcase of drugs made its way into your hands."

He sucks in a hard breath through his nose. "Okay. You want to waste time? You want to get us killed? Fine."

ASHLEY'S STORY

Jimmy DiPippo was my weed dealer in high school. He was a rich kid anyway, but the weed only made him richer. He had a used BMW, a nice watch, a couple gold rings. He was a nice guy, Jimmy, but rich or not, he was dumb as a bag of retards, and smoking all that weed didn't help. Well, last year I was . . . passing through my hometown . . . and I heard through the grapevine that Jimmy was still around, that he was still a dealer and still about as sharp as a tree stump.

Naturally, I figured we'd catch up, and I'd dick him out of some money.

I track him down at this party. Some girl's house at the end of a cul-de-sac in the middle of the suburbs of Scranton, which is about as awesome as it sounds. House party full of teenage assholes, for the most part—beer bongs and regular bongs and some kid with a superbong made out of a World War II gas mask, and bad techno music and dudes in sweet-smelling frat cologne. Just some shithole party, whatever, no big deal.

I find Jimmy out on the patio, smoking up this cute little hottie and her lunkhead fat-ass linebacker boyfriend, trying to sell them some weed, and I say hey, and he seems surprised to see me, too surprised, *nervous* surprised. But I don't think much of it, because Jimmy's always been itchy-twitchy. Sweaty, too—kid looked like a drowned rat in high school, and he wasn't much different now. Sweat was soaking through the band on his long-brim cap, the hat pulled cockeyed like he was some kind of hip-hop suburban hero, and I figured if you reached down the waist of his pants—which hung around the crack of his ass, thankfully covered up by his tighty-whities—you'd find his balls were floating in a swamp, too.

I let him finish his deal, then we stay outside and head to the patio furniture by the pool to play catch-up. He tells me he's still dealing, he's doing well for himself, and I tell him I'm a Wall Street broker in the big city, and I don't know why he believes me. I'm convincing, I guess. I was always convincing. Plus, him, dumb, you know the drill.

Thing is, he's getting more and more nervous by the minute. His foot's tapping. He keeps licking his lips and looking over his shoulder, and right then, I have no idea why. First I think, it's just because that's how he is. But this is something else.

"Whatever," I say to myself, I don't care about Jimmy. He sells drugs to kids, and more power to him, but we're not talking sacred cow-tipping here. I decide to get into the scam.

Scam's not a real complex one, and it's something I pretty much make up on the spot. I figure, if I'm playing the Wall Street broker made good, I can pretend like I have some cool insider trading secret. Some tip about a pharmaceutical company about to release a new antidepressant, some new concept car coming out of Japan. Whatever. I could've told Jimmy that Walmart was designing a new shock-absorbent anal tampon and he'd have bought it. I say to him, if he wants in, I can do him a solid like he did for me so many times way back when—and he did do me favors, free weed, lots of it—and I'd be happy to invest his cash without taking any cut for myself.

I have him interested, I can tell. But then he sees something out the corner of his eye, and he tells me he's gotta go meet some people, and he'll find me later. Then zoom, he's off like a bottle rocket. I trail him inside, and I lose him for a minute—some busty chick, busty because she's a little overweight but that's fine, she wants to do a shot with me, and that's okay, I'm good with shots. We slam back tequila shooters with the lime and the salt while the techno is doing its *thump*, *thump*, *thump* and the red Christmas lights are winking to the beat even though it's summertime, and yay, whatever. She takes a picture of me with her cell phone. Everybody's having a good time, and for a second, I forget why I'm even here.

Then I see Jimmy coming downstairs with a metal suitcase. Yeah. *This* metal suitcase.

I hang back and trail him—he's out through the kitchen and into a dark two-car garage. I follow him out there, and I duck behind a Range Rover and then, boom, the lights come on.

"Damn, man," I hear Jimmy say. "My eyes; that's bright."

From where I'm at, all I can see is feet. I see three pairs. I see Jimmy's high-tops. I see a pair of scuffed black loafers. And then I see a pair of white sneakers on small, stubby feet.

Nobody says anything, so Jimmy has to fill the space: "It's cool; you just surprised me, is all. Hey, what's up? I got your message; I brought the case. I don't know what the problem is; not like you guys do a recall on this product, right—" And he laughs, a nervous heh-heh-heh. "So, what's up? I'm good to go, in case you were—"

And then this woman speaks. Her voice is a monotone.

She says, "I hear you've made some new friends, James."

And it's weird, because I don't know that anyone has ever called Jimmy "James." Not even his parents. I always figured "Jimmy" was the name on his birth certificate.

He stammers something out, something like "Yeah, man, I'm a—I'm a real friendly dude; everybody knows Jimmy." But he knows something's up. I can't see him, but by now, I figure the sweat's pouring off him.

"Even the police," the woman says. It's not a question. It's an accusation.

"No," Jimmy says, but it's halfhearted at best.

"Oh, yeah," the dude says; got a Bronx or Brooklyn accent. "Jimmy, you been talking to the po-po. You been cozying up next to the pubic fuzz."

"The pubic what?" Jimmy says. He really doesn't get it.

And those were his last words. The worst last words ever, I might add. Whoever has the white tennis sneaks moves fast behind Jimmy, and then I hear choking, and Jimmy's feet do this epileptic dance on the cement floor of the garage, and I'm goddamn paralyzed with fear. I want to scream and run and piss myself and vomit, but I can't do any of those things. My mouth is open and my hands are frozen.

Then dots of blood hit the cement. *Pit, pat, pit.*

His foot kicks out, knocks the case back. It's not far from me. I could just reach out—

Something happens in my head. A switch flips. I don't know why I did it. It wasn't something I thought about in a conscious, "do this" kind of way.

There's a mop to my left. I grab it, and I stand up.

I see who's there now—the Italian asshole and this short, stocky bitch. She's got a wire around Jimmy's neck, a wire that dead-ends in two black rubber-ball handles, handles she's got tight in her pudgy grip.

The wire's biting into his neck. That's where the blood's coming from.

They all pause to look at me. They're shocked to see me. Even Jimmy, because right then and there, he's still alive, though not for much longer.

That gives me the time I need.

The dago reaches into his jacket, and I jam the mop into the lights. The fluorescents above our heads pop, throwing us back into the dark, and I grab the case and haul ass back into the kitchen. I slam the door behind me, toss a microwave cart under the handle, and it buys me enough time to get back out to my Mustang, throw this heavy-ass case into the passenger side, and get out of town. Only later do I even find out what's in it—it wasn't locked; Jimmy never did up the combination.

So now, here we are.

I never thought they'd find me. Never.

We're fucked.

TWENTY-TWO

EVERYBODY'S FUCKED

"No, *you're* fucked," Miriam says.

"We have to *go*," Ashley says. His smile is gone. She thinks back to the story he told, about how Jimmy the Dealer was on edge, itchy, twitchy—and that's Ashley right here, right now. He looks genuinely scared. The façade has cracked.

Miriam spins the keys in her hand. "Settle down, cupcake. They didn't follow me."

"You're sure?"

"I'm sure."

"We still have to get out of here."

"Fine. So we get out of here."

He shifts from foot to foot.

"The drugs," she says. "What were you planning on doing with them? That case looks heavy."

His gaze darts to the windows, the door. "It is heavy. Fifty pounds or so. It's worth it."

"How worth it?"

"I dunno. Ten grand a pound. Maybe more."

"Jesus. Ten grand a pound for meth?" She does some quick math. "You're looking at a half a million bucks in that suitcase. Why the hell do you need me, again? You're sitting on a fat bank account. You've got a high-stakes table, and you're dicking around at the nickel slots."

"I'm not a goddamn drug dealer!" he yells out—his patience and smiling charm have worn away entirely. "I haven't the *first clue* how to unload this much meth. Or any meth! Honestly? You really want to know? I figured you might be able to push it."

"*Me?* Are you kidding?"

"You look . . . like you maybe do meth. Or did."

"No," she seethes, "I look like I do *heroin*—and I don't do that, either. I have all my teeth and I don't smell like cat piss, so don't think I'm some basehead tweaker fuckface."

He throws up his hands. "Fine. Sorry to offend your delicate sensibilities. Can we go now?"

With a grunt of frustration, she tosses him the keys and shoulders her messenger bag.

"Go," he says, shepherding her toward the door.

Miriam is first out.

She doesn't see it—the car is matte black, and the darkness damn near swallows it whole. But then, *bam*, the headlights are on, right in her face: the Cutlass Ciera from the other motel is sitting there, right in the driveway. Shielding her eyes from the light, Miriam can't make out the shapes of the driver and passenger, but she knows they're in there. Waiting.

From behind her, she hears "Oh, no. Fuck. No no *no.*"

The car's still running when the front doors swing open. Harriet Adams and Frankie Gallo get out of the car. Neither hurries. Both carry pistols.

Miriam formulates the route—*go back inside, back through the motel room, kick out the bathroom window, escape through the field that hugs the back of the motel, or maybe the woods that sit off to the right*—and she turns around to enact her plan, but . . .

Ashley stands in her way, holding the metal suitcase. Their eyes meet.

She sees it click in his mind—the way the clock in Del Amico's motel room flipped over from one number to the next. *Your time is up,* a voice rings in her head.

Ashley gives her a shove and slams the door. The lock engages. She's alone out here. With *them.* With two loaded pistols.

Miriam screams his name. Her blood's a dull roar. She pounds on the door. Behind her, Harriet marches slow and steady, a serial killer, a terminator, an unstoppable and ineluctable force. Harriet waves the man, Frankie, around, yells at him to follow out back.

Miriam turns to run, but somehow, the woman is already on her.

Miriam thinks: *I can take her. Just look at her. I can outmaneuver this little human buttplug.*

Grunting, she hefts the messenger bag, swinging it like a weapon, but the woman leans back and the bag finds nothing but air. *Bam.* Miriam sees bright lights as the woman pistol-whips her, the barrel catching her hard—the gun's barrel sight cutting her cheek.

Miriam's heel catches on a hunk of broken parking lot. She falls backward, her tailbone slamming hard on asphalt.

Before she even knows what's happening, the gun barrel is pressed against her cheek, right where the weapon's sight sliced her. The business end of the pistol is cold. It stings as Harriet presses it harder into her face. Miriam winces.

"Stay a while," Harriet says, and Miriam sees a mad glint in the woman's eyes.

"Just let me go. I don't have anything. This isn't my business."

"Shh."

"I'm just a girl, just a stupid girl caught up with a stupid boy—"

Harriet shakes her head. "Do not attempt to appeal to my mercies, as I promise you that I have none. Now stand up. Slowly." With her free hand, Harriet reaches into her pants pocket and pulls out a thin white plastic cord: a zip tie. "We're going to walk over to the car, and you're going to get in, and we're going to go for a little—"

Bang, bang: two gunshots in quick succession from out back of the motel. Miriam knows that Ashley isn't dead—because Ashley isn't an eighty-year-old man in a nursing home missing a foot, yet—and she knows *she's* not dead, either, because she can still hear her heart punching her eardrums.

At the sound of the gunshots, Harriet flinches. It's barely that; her gaze narrows and her eyes dart: the look of a hawk who's spotted a mouse. It's just enough time.

Miriam's hand darts into the bag, finds purchase. She whips it back out, flicks her wrist—and sticks the butterfly knife into Harriet's thigh.

The gun goes off, but Miriam's head isn't there.

She palms a hunk of broken curb. Bashes it hard against Harriet's hand.

The pistol barks another shot. Miriam hears the bullet whine off the ground near her head, but it doesn't matter—the weapon flies from Harriet's grip, pirouetting through the air until it clatters against the parking lot some ten feet away.

Miriam doesn't wait.

She runs.

Her getaway sticks carry her forward even though she feels dizzy and sick and trapped. She leaves it all behind: Harriet, the pistol, the knife in the woman's leg, and her messenger bag. *Shit,* she thinks, *my bag. I need my bag. It's got the diary in it; it's got the rest of my life. Turn around, turn around and—*

Two more gunshots. Harriet's already retrieved the pistol. Miriam *feels* one of those bullets go by her head, just a whisper from her cheek. She can't stop. If she stops, she dies. She reaches the end of the L-shaped motel, the last room, rounds the corner, and sees the woods only ten feet away.

Another gunshot. As she ducks into the tree line, a bullet smashes into an oak by her head, coughing splinters.

Miriam crashes through the brush.

It's all shapes and shadows in the woods. Any moonlight she had is gone. A tangle of dark lines, whipped lashes of biting branches—she smashes through thorn and thicket like a spooked deer, barreling forth, almost falling forward as her escaping feet catch her.

She runs—she doesn't know for how long.

She thinks, *I'm safe, it's okay, stop running, take a breath, hide in the shadows—*

But another thought reaches her: *You're never safe. Run, you stupid girl, run.*

That's when something hits her in the face.

Her feet go out from under her, and everything spins into total darkness.

Footsteps. Crunching brush. Snapping twigs.

Miriam's eyes jolt open.

It's still dark. She feels across her head—the blood there is already crusting over. She sees a dark shape above her, a black line illuminated by the moonlight around it.

I ran into a tree branch, she thinks, still dizzy.

And now?

Someone's out here. She hears their steps. She hears them *breathing*.

Then they stop.

A breeze murmurs through the nighttime trees; leaves rustle against other leaves. Everything else is silent.

Sudden movement. Footsteps. Running, crashing through the brush—*toward her*.

Miriam clambers to her feet, grabs hold of a tree branch and launches herself forward, and now she's up and running, too. Her follower is in close pursuit; it can't be true, but Miriam imagines she can feel breath on the back of her neck, hands snatching the air just behind her heels, teeth biting into the meat of her shoulder.

It's Harriet, she thinks. *It's that awful woman. I'm dead meat.* But then the sound stops. It's gone. As if it never existed.

Which is a lot weirder, and a whole lot more disturbing.

Miriam stops. Waits. Looks around. Everything is back to shape and shadow—no movement, no sound but the leaves against leaves.

Did she imagine it?

Was it some kind of waking dream?

She smells soap. A whiff of it. Hand soap, like soap from a bathroom.

Miriam turns around.

A red snow shovel catches her in the face. As she drops to the ground, she hears the laughter of Louis, which becomes the laughter of Ben Hodge, which becomes the laughter of her mother—all of them above her head, a circle of moon faces cackling. Darkness returns, singing its cricket's song.

Frankie plods around the corner from the back of the motel, holding his forearm up to a busted, bloody nose. The blood runs down his chin, his arm.

He sees Harriet sitting on the front bumper of her Oldsmobile, her dark pants made darker by an oval of blood. The butterfly knife sits in her hand, slick and red.

"Prick hit me in the face," Frankie says, though it sounds more like *Prig hid bee in da vase.*

"With the case, I presume."

"Dat case is vuckin' heaby."

"The girl escaped. She stabbed me in the leg with this . . . flea-market knife."

"Gahdabbit."

"I'm calling Ingersoll. He's going to want to come here. He'll want to attend to this personally."

"Gahdabbit!"

"Let's go before the police arrive."

THE DREAM

She knows it's just a dream. It doesn't make it any better. Or easier.

Louis hangs on a dead oak tree like Jesus on the cross. He's illuminated by a single shaft of moonlight: God's own spotlight on the stage. His outstretched arms play host to a row of crows and blackbirds. One blackbird—a little one with a dab of red at the fore of its wing, like a drop of blood—hops over and clings to his collarbone. It pecks at the electrical tape pressed over his left eye.

Miriam stands at his feet, looking up. She falls to her knees. She doesn't mean to; it's what the dream demands she do. It's like she's lost control. No autonomy at all.

"I die for your sins," Louis says. In between the words is a throaty chuckle.

"You're not dead yet," she protests.

He ignores her comment.

"The cross. The crux. The horizontal line is the line of man. It's the temporal world, the world of matter and flesh and dirt. Mud, blood, stone, and bone. The vertical line is the divine line. The ascendant. It runs perpendicular to the world of man and is the axis of the otherworldly and unknowable."

"That's super. I want to wake up now."

"In a minute. I'm not done talking to you, little lady. The cross is also representative of the crossroads. A juncture of choice. Decisions, decisions. It's time for you to start making some choices, Miriam. It's time to rock out with your cock out. It's time to jam out with your clam out."

Louis grins. Earthworms play between his rotten teeth.

"Now I know you're just a manifestation of my own voice," she says, almost laughing. "No divine figure, no future ghost, would use the phrase *jam out with your clam out*."

Even crucified, Louis manages to shrug. "If you say so. Then how do I know so much about crosses? Did you take a comparative religion course that I missed?"

"Go to hell."

"Decisions, decisions, Miriam."

"I have no decisions. I'm fate's hand puppet."

"Remember. The cross—the crux, the crossroads—is about sacrifice. Jesus stands at the crossroads, and he chooses not the horizontal line of man but the vertical line of God."

"This is fascinating, but—"

The blackbirds and crows take flight. They screech and holler. Wings flap; all she can see is dark shadows fluttering. Talons claw at her eyes, tearing them out—

TWENTY-THREE

WHAT FATE WANTS

It's one of those mornings. Sky's just a Vaseline smear of form-less clouds—a bright, greasy layer of gray. Doesn't look like rain. Doesn't look like sun. Doesn't look like much at all.

Miriam's head pounds.

Tree branch. Bad dreams. A shitty combination.

The gash across her forehead pulses, but the cut on her cheek where the pistol bit her isn't taking the competition sitting down; it nibbles, like a hungry worm, with her face the apple.

Plus, her butt-bone still throbs.

And worst of all, she doesn't have any cigarettes. They were in her bag. A bag that is now God Knows Where. Probably in the hands of that horrible bulldog of a woman.

Sighing, she thunks her head against the door behind her.

She doesn't intend for it to be a knock, but that's how it happens. She hears shuffling inside. Louis opens the door, obviously surprised to find a battered girl sitting outside his motor lodge bungalow just past the ass-crack of dawn.

"Morning," she croaks. Even speaking a single word makes her body hurt.

"Oh, my God," he says. She can see it on his face: a very real look of pain, pain *possibly* worse than what she's experiencing. His large hands reach behind her, and he helps her stand with a gentle lift. Her legs wobble, and for a second, she's not sure if she's going to make it—but she fights back dizziness and takes a deep breath.

"Sorry. I would've brought donuts."

"What happened?"

She seriously considers telling him the truth. Something inside her wants to spray out of her like popping a raw, red zit. Festering pus. *Pbbtt.* Miriam wants to tell Louis everything: all about her strange ability, how she got it, how she saw him die a death that was coming way too soon, how Ashley isn't her brother, how they almost got killed over a metal suitcase filled to the brim with Baggies of crystal meth, *every last horrible nugget of truth*.

But she doesn't.

She convinces herself that it would only hurt him. It'd be selfish. He doesn't deserve that laid across his shoulders (*doesn't deserve to be crucified for your sins*), and it's not like he'd believe her, anyway. She's lied so much already.

"The boyfriend." *Keep on lying. You go, girl.* "He found me. I didn't think he would, but he's a talented asshole. He found out where I was staying and . . ."

She demos her blood-encrusted face like Vanna White showing a prize.

"Ta-da."

Louis's jaw sets. It's like a bear trap clanging closed.

"That sonofabitch."

"It's all right. I gave worse than he gave me. I stabbed her— sorry, *him*, my brain maybe got rocked around a bit—I stabbed *him* in the leg with a butterfly knife."

This actually seems to satisfy him, and she loves him for that.

"Well. He deserved it. What about your brother?"

Miriam waves it off. "Worthless shit. Sided with the boyfriend. Done with both."

"Good for you. You need to come on in here so I can get you cleaned up."

"I know. Faded black eye. Bloody head. Cut cheek. *America's Next Top Model*, right?"

The faucet runs. Louis has the washcloth wet with tepid water, and he runs it over her forehead. She's amazed at how gentle he is. He's huge. Those hands could crush her skull like it was a beefsteak tomato, and yet his touch is soft and slow—deliberate, delicate, a painter's grace. Like this is somehow art to him.

"You don't suck at this," she says.

"I'm trying to be careful. You might could use stitches for this cut on your cheek. It's not long, but it's deep."

"No stitches. Just the Band-Aids will cover me."

"It might scar."

She winks. "Scars are sexy."

"I'm glad you came back."

"Shouldn't have left in the first place."

With his teeth, Louis uncaps some generic brand Neosporin, blobs a little on his broad finger, and applies it to her forehead and then her cheek. She enjoys the touch. It's simple and it's intimate. It puts her in a Zen state; it's a mindlessness she embraces.

It does not embrace her, however. Not easily.

He's going to die, a nagging voice reminds.

She takes a deep breath, and she tells that voice, *I know*.

And it's true. She does know it. This is all one big roller coaster, she thinks. Everybody's buckled in for the ride; no getting off it early. The hills and valleys, the sharp hairpin curves and the long straightaways. The screams. The rush. The terror. The finality as it slows to a finish. Fate designed the experience. Fate's got its hands all over everything.

But, she thinks, maybe there's something fate *can't* touch. Maybe what's not yet decided is how you think about things, or more important, how you *feel* about them. Maybe fate doesn't control how easily you come to peace. She hopes that's true. Because she wants to find a little bit of peace.

Louis is going to die in a lighthouse in less than two weeks now.

She can't stop that. That's where he gets off the ride.

Maybe, she thinks, that's where she gets off, too. Because the truth is, she doesn't know what designs fate has for her. She's not privy to the map. Miriam can touch others and see how they die, but the same isn't true for herself—her demise remains a mystery. And it will until she meets that end, it seems. She likes to imagine it'll be a violent death. But now, with Louis's touch, she maybe thinks—or at least hopes—otherwise.

"I have a favor to ask," she says.

"Too hard?"

"Just perfect. You're leaving soon."

"On a run, yeah."

"Take me with you."

He pulls his hand away, surprised.

"You want to come with me?"

She nods. "I like you. I want to get away from this. Plus, I might be in danger. From the boyfriend. From the brother. Who knows? You're safe. I like safe."

Louis smiles as she lies.

"We hit the road in the morning," he says.

She kisses him on the chin. It makes her whole face hurt to move like that. It's pain she endures.

PART THREE

TWENTY-FOUR

THIS IS WHERE RANDY HAWKINS DIES

Nobody knows who Randy Hawkins is, because he is a big old nobody.

He's certainly not an attractive man: pig's nose, curly red hair, a denim jacket that was in style maybe two decades ago. His shoes are still on, but if one were to see his feet, one would note that they match his nose: pig hooves. They totally look like pig hooves.

His job isn't notable. Right now he works the meat counter at the Giant supermarket, but that's a pretty recent gig. Last job was as a gas station attendant, and his job before that was as a gas station attendant for a different gas station. Once he thought he could be a rock drummer, but he eventually puzzled out that it really helps to have drums and to know how to play them.

Maybe it's his attitude? He's mild, despite his habits. Quiet. In his own head, he's the furthest thing from boring, but to everybody else, he's dull as primer paint.

If he were a bagel, he'd be plain.

What is it, then, that makes Randy Hawkins special? Special enough to be hung by his hands in a meat locker, dangling next to cold slabs of beef?

Two things.

One, it's one of those "habits" mentioned previously.

Two, it's who he knows.

See, Randy does meth. Mostly, it's so he can stay up late and watch cartoons or bad movies. One might argue that Randy fears death and sleep to him is a neighbor of death—moreover, sleep wastes life, which only ushers one more swiftly toward death. Really, though, Randy isn't even aware of this fear of his. Besides, who doesn't fear death?

Problem is, Randy's meth habit—perhaps unconsciously meant to afford him a stay of execution—is only going to get him killed a lot sooner. Lately, Randy's dealer has been tweaking prices. The cost of crystal meth has ticked up, up, up. Randy's not the type to rock the boat, and he's definitely not the kind of guy to be *proactive* enough to seek out a new dealer . . .

. . . but what if a new dealer sought out Randy?

This new guy comes along. He says he has product. He says he's ready to sell, and for bargain-basement prices, prices lower than a worm's belly in a wheel rut. This new guy, he's smooth; he's smiling like he's come to wheel and deal. Even though Randy thinks the guy's a bit *too* smiley, like maybe this dude's been using his own product, that's fine. Randy likes low prices.

Randy stops going to his old dealer and starts hooking up with the new guy.

And that's where Randy's exceptional nature ends.

At least, as far as his captors are concerned.

The door to the meat locker rattles hard, then opens. It startles Randy, and he blows a snot bubble—a bloody one—and almost shits his pants.

The two people who kicked the crap out of him—the squat woman (who Randy can't help but find a little attractive) and the tall man—enter, but now they've got a third.

The third man is broad-shouldered but thin—too thin, like a skeleton used to hang a white suit—and weirder still, he's hairless like a skeleton, too. Bald head given a gleaming spit-shine. No eyebrows. No eye*lashes*. Every part of his skin—which has a faint, unhealthy tan, not chemical but more like the color of spoiled chicken—is smooth, slick, glistening as if oiled.

"Randy Hawkins," the man says, but his accent definitely isn't From Around Here, especially if "around here" is meant to include, say, the entire North American continent. Maybe the man is German. Or Polish. Or from some other nebulous Eastern European country. Randy Hawkins does not know the term *Eurotrash*, but if he knew it, he'd use it. The man points and asks, "This is him?"

Randy tries to say something but can't, because his own bloody sock is stuffed in his mouth and sealed there with electrical tape.

Harriet nods. "I worked him over."

Ingersoll nods as if admiring a painting. He runs a spidery finger up Randy's jawline, through the crust of blood there, to the ear that's swollen like a cauliflower, and then across the forehead where a number of horizontal hash marks (made with razor, not pen) line up.

He lifts Randy's head. Sees the chewed-up skin on the back of his neck.

"This is interesting," the thin man says. He rubs his fingertip across the scabby, abraded flesh. *Scritch, scritch.* "A new technique?"

"New tool," Harriet explains. "I went to Bed Bath and Beyond and picked up some items from the kitchen department. That's from a cheese grater. I also broke three of his fingers with a garlic press."

"Innovative. And culinary."

"Thank you."

Ingersoll looks Frankie up and down. "And what did you contribute?"

"Donuts."

Ingersoll gets a sour look on his face. "Of course." It is not an unfamiliar look.

"He's ready to talk," Harriet says. "I knew you wanted to be here for it."

"Yes. It's time I am involved fully. This has gone on too long."

Ingersoll pulls a small satchel from his pocket and kneels by Randy's feet. He presses his face against the beef slab hanging to the right, feeling the cool sensation against his forehead. Then Ingersoll opens the pouch and upends it onto the floor.

Little bones—most no bigger than marbles, some like long teeth—spill out. These are hand bones: carpals like driveway gravel, metacarpals like Lincoln Logs, phalanges like dog treats or the tips of umbrellas. All pale, bleached, clean.

Ingersoll does not touch them. His own finger drifts above them, as if he is following along with the text of a children's book or a Bible page. He nods and mumbles something in the affirmative. To everyone else, it's inscrutable, but to him, it's something as plain as day, no less clear than the big, white, fluffy letters of a sky-written message.

"Good," he says, obviously satisfied. He scoops the bones back up and places them in the pouch once more. He kisses the pouch the way he might kiss his mother.

He stands again and looks in Randy's red, raw eyes.

"You stopped buying from us," Ingersoll says. He licks his lips, shaking his head. "That is a shame. I like to think we offer a solid product for reasonable prices. But you can save yourself here, you know. You will whisper in my ear all you can tell me of your new supplier. If I am satisfied, if you tell me what I want to know, then I will spare your life and instead take only one of your hands. Are we clear?"

Whimpering behind his own blood-caked sock, Randy nods.

Ingersoll smiles, plucks out the sock between his delicate thumb and forefinger, and presses his own ear to Randy's mouth.

"Speak," Ingersoll says, and Randy spills it all.

+ + + +

Outside the meat locker, Ingersoll towels off.

The white towels, handed to him by Harriet, swiftly grow red.

Ingersoll hands over a plastic Baggie. Contained within are two hands severed at the wrists.

"Boil them," Ingersoll says, "till the meat falls off. Like osso buco. Once you have the bones free from the meat, bleach them. Purify them with sage smoke. Then give them to me. I will choose which ones, if any, belong in my satchel."

Harriet nods, takes the bag. Frankie has a look like he's already tasting bile.

"You," Ingersoll says, thrusting his finger against Frankie's sternum. The finger is thin, delicate, like an insect's leg, but it still feels to Frankie like it might punch through his breastbone and puncture his heart. "Dispose of the body."

Swallowing a hard knot of what might be puke, Frankie nods.

"Now we know where Ashley Gaynes lives," Ingersoll says.

But he knows now that Gaynes is only the secondary prize. The girl. She's the one he wants. He reaches in the pocket of his white jacket and gently runs his hands across the binding of Miriam's diary.

He has some questions he'd very much like to ask her.

THE INTERVIEW

It's a while before Miriam speaks again. Paul waits quietly, hesitant, pensive, as if any motion from him might shatter everything, might snap the fraying thread holding the sword that dangles above her head.

"I got pregnant," she finally says.

Paul blinks. "By who?"

"By whom, actually. You're a college student, learn your grammar. By Ben."

"Ben?" He looks puzzled.

"Yes. Ben? The one I had sex with? The one who shot himself? I'm sorry, did I tell that story to someone else just now? I admit, I fade in and out."

"No, sorry, I just thought, he's dead, how could he—"

Miriam snorts. At this point, she is three-quarters drunk. "We're not talking zombie sex; he didn't come lurching out of the grave dirt to fill my living body with his undead baby batter. We had sex one time, and that one time resulted in a pregnancy. That's the circle of life, Paul."

"Right. Got it. Sorry."

"Don't apologize; it's fine. I came back that night, escorted by the police, and my mom already knew what was up, and the weeks after that—and after Ben shot himself—were spent cloistered away in my room with the Bible. I'm surprised she didn't duct-tape it to my hands. She found all my comic books, which I kept under a loose floorboard with some CDs. She took it all away. If she could've stapled my vagina shut in the name of the Lord, I'm sure she would've."

"At what point did you know?"

She squints, thinks about it. "The morning sickness started . . . not quite two months after we did the dirty deed? Something like that. I woke up one morning and lost dinner from the night before, then ate some toast and lost that, too. I knew what it was because I'd been terrified of it. My mother's a big fan of consequence, always playing up how one's sins will be repaid by result, like poisonous fruit grown from a bad seed. Oh, you eat too much? That's gluttony, so here's some bowel cancer. What's that? You can't stop banging all those desperate housewives? Oops, looks like syphilis is rotting your cock off. Good luck!"

"That's an oddly karmic outlook."

"Don't tell her that. She'd put a knife to her own throat." Miriam mimes the slitting of her throat, her finger playing the role of knife. "Kkkkt! Kill the heretic."

"So, how'd she react to the pregnancy?"

"I hid it for as long as I could. I just said I was getting fat, and that was a lie I couldn't back up, because I was barely eating enough for one, much less two. My belly swelled but the rest didn't, and so I ended up looking like one of those African kids on TV with flies crawling all over their bloated bellies."

"So, she found out."

"She found out."

"And . . . what? She threw you out? She doesn't seem like the nicest mother."

Miriam takes a deep breath. "No. It was . . . totally the opposite. She changed, man. It's not that she became this sweet, adoring mother, but she really changed. She became more protective.

She stopped with calling me names and blaming me for everything. She'd come into my room, check on me, see if I needed anything. Christ, she even made me foods I really liked. It was strange. I guess she figured you can't put the snakes back in the can. All that time, she'd been treating me that way to stop me from making a mistake, and there I went ahead and made one anyway. Plus, maybe she really wanted a grandchild. Deep down, sometimes I wonder: Maybe that's how she had me. Maybe that's why she was the way she was. Not that I'll ever know, of course."

"But . . . ," Paul says. "You never had the child."

"Oh, I had him. He's been hiding behind your chair this whole time."

Paul actually looks.

"You're very gullible, Paul," she says. "No, I didn't have the baby."

"So, what happened? How did you lose the—" *Beep beep beep.* Paul's watch beeps. He lifts his wrist, and Miriam sees it's one of those old-school calculator watches.

"I didn't think anybody had those anymore," she says.

"I think I meant for it to be ironic," Paul explains. "Turns out, though, it's actually kind of useful. Who needs a Palm Pilot when you have an awesome calculator watch? Plus, it was, like, five bucks."

"Thrifty and practical, with a badass calculator watch. Good for you. So, what's with the alarm? Got a hot date?"

"Yeah," he says, lost in thought, but then he shakes his head. "Uh, though, it's totally not a hot date. I have to go to my mom's house, have dinner, explain to her for the thousandth time why I chose to go to college closer to Dad's house, even though it's only closer by, like, ten miles."

"Sounds like fun," Miriam says.

"Not really. We'll pick this up tomorrow?"

"Tomorrow," she lies. "Same time, same channel."

Paul clicks off his recorder and pockets it. He gives a wave, then an awkward handshake, and then he leaves Miriam alone.

She waits. Not long. Thirty seconds, maybe.

Then she follows out after him.

TWENTY-FIVE

STOREFRONT PSYCHIC

The entire meatball goes into her mouth.

"I'm still amazed," Louis says, watching her with a look on his face like he's watching a boa constrictor eat the neighbor's cat.

Around bulging hamster cheeks, Miriam asks, "Whuh?"

"The way you eat. I've seen it every day now, but every time, it's a unique experience."

"Mm," she mumbles, forcing the knot of meatball goodness down her throat. "Nothing wrong with a girl who enjoys eating a badass plate of spaghetti, sir."

Louis blinks. "Except it's ten o'clock in the morning."

"Not my fault this diner serves the whole menu all day."

"How do you stay so thin?"

She smirks, reaching across and taking his hand. "Looking for beauty tips?"

He doesn't pull away, but he doesn't look comfortable, either. Ever since that night in the motor lodge, he's been unsure. Hovering at her edges. He wants her. But he's afraid of something. Or maybe, she wonders, is she the one who's afraid? And he just senses it?

They haven't done it yet. The deed. The horizontal mambo. The King Kong climbing the Empire State Building. Miriam's not sure why. She almost banged his brains out before. Why not now? It's her way. It's what she does.

Louis is different. Or maybe she's different. Any time it crosses her mind, she pushes it back out. She's afraid that examining the experiment will somehow ruin it. As if that makes any sense.

"I have the metabolism of a coked-up jackrabbit," she explains. "Always have. I can eat whatever I want, whenever I want, and my body burns through it like tinder."

"Some women would kill to be you."

"Some women are stupid donkeys."

He laughs. "Okay, then."

That right there is a moment she enjoys, a moment worth embracing. Most men in her life—hell, most *anybody* in her life—would take a combative sentiment like that and throw their own right back at her. And thus, a spiteful badminton match would ensue, each sharply phrased comment whipping back and forth like a shuttlecock aimed at someone's eye. Louis, he just takes it. He smiles. He laughs. He doesn't feed her energy. He's got some kind of placating Tai Chi, some Zen-master redirection of her aggro spirit—and as a result, that spirit does not grow into a meaner beast but dissipates into naught but steam.

Miriam resists the urge to burp, quashing it behind a fist. She pushes the plate aside and grins. "So, where we headed to next, Big Poppa? And, actually, where the hell are we even at? I haven't exactly been paying attention."

They have been on the road now for a week and a day. A haul from North Carolina to Maryland (shipping paint cans), a haul from Maryland to Delaware (hoity-toity furniture), and now a haul from Delaware (paint again) to somewhere in . . . Ohio? This has to be Ohio. Flat. Blah. Trees. Highway. Meh.

"Blanchester, Ohio," he says, getting out a pocket map and unfolding it across the table. He points to it on the map. "Maybe forty, fifty miles from Cincinnati."

"*Blaaaanchester,*" she says, stretching it out like a zombie with a mouth filled with clotting brains. "Straight outta Blanchester, crazy emmer-effer named Chester the Molester."

"You're very strange."

"Get used to it, big guy. That's me, dropping science." She reaches across the table and kisses him. They haven't made the beast with two backs yet, no—but the kisses. She's been giving the kisses. It isn't like her. Usually, she doesn't like kissing the men she meets on the road. They push their sluglike tongues into her mouth, and her only wish is to bite the damn things off at the roots.

"Your science tastes sweet."

"I got an A-plus-*plus* in human anatomy and sexuality."

As she pulls away from him, Miriam looks out the window. Across the street from the diner, a pickup truck sits parked. Innocuous, nothing about it pinging her radar—but then the driver returns to his truck and drives off.

Behind the truck? Miriam sees neon glowing in the window. *Psychic. Palms Read. Tarot Readings.*

Louis peels off a couple bills and tosses down a generous tip—but Miriam just stares. She's thought about doing this for a long time, but she's never had the guts.

"Wait here," she says and stands up.

"Ladies' room?"

She shakes her head. "Nope. Psychic next door. I've always wanted to try it."

"I'll come with."

"No—you stay here. This is . . . private."

She can see his eyes scanning her, trying to put the pieces together. He's been periodically working away at the Miriam Puzzle the same way someone might come back to look at the Magic Eye poster to see if the image will finally resolve and reveal itself. Like usual, he gives up. No dolphins or sailboats to be seen in the chaos and noise. Not yet.

"Fair enough," he says, and while he's got one of his several envelopes of cash in hand (like Ashley suspected, Louis has several envelopes stashed around the truck—his "life savings," he told her), he peels off three twenties into her palm. "At least let me pay for it."

Miriam can't lie to herself. The money feels like it's about to burn off her fingers, like it's wet with blood. She looks down at it, and for a second, instead of seeing Andrew Jackson's ugly mug on the bill, she sees Louis, his eyes torn out, black Xs inked across the sockets.

She doesn't say anything.

She offers a wan smile.

Then exits.

Miriam knows what to expect, and this isn't it. She expects New Age foofaraw and pseudo-occult frippery: the crystals, the purple fringe, the chimes, the incense that irritates the eye, a fat cat lounging on a pillow. What she gets is fluorescent lighting in a shop for knitting aficionados (*Knit-wits*, Miriam thinks). Brown shelves holding afghans, baby hats, bundles of yarn. And no cat. Instead a fat-bellied beagle lies snoozing under a table. He looks gassy.

And the woman who sits at that table is less "Gypsy scammer" and more "notary public." Hell, she looks like the head of a church bake sale. Powder-blue cardigan. Poof of red hair. Reading glasses over the bridge of her nose.

"Okay, what the fuck?" is the first thing Miriam says.

The woman gives her a droll, dry look. "May I help you?"

"I . . . thought I was walking into the Psychics-R-Us store. Sorry." She turns to leave.

"I'm the psychic," the woman says. "My name is Miss Nancy."

"Miss Nancy, the knitting psychic?"

"I do knit and crochet, yes. A lady has to make money however she can."

Miriam shrugs. "Scream it so the cheap seats can hear, sister. Do I sit?"

"Sit. Please."

Miriam does. She drums her fingers on the table. "So, now what? What happens? How much will this scam cost me?"

"The fee is forty dollars, but I assure you, this is not a scam." The woman's voice is a bit gravelly. She smokes, or used to, Miriam thinks, and it only makes her itch for a cigarette—her smoke breaks have been few and far between since she started riding with Louis.

"Trust me, it's a fucking scam."

"Don't use that kind of language with me."

Miriam hears her mother's voice in there, somewhere. She nods. "Sorry."

"It's no scam; it's no sham. The psychic dimension is a real one."

"I know it is."

"Do you?"

"I'm psychic. Shouldn't you have known that?"

The woman clucks her tongue. "If you were a true psychic, you'd know it doesn't work that way and is rarely so simple."

"Well played, Miss Nancy. Well played. Fine, forty bucks it is." Miriam slides two twenties across the table. "And maybe if you're really good, I'll buy a knit cap or an ashtray cozy."

Miss Nancy takes the money, and in something of a surprise, tucks it into her cardigan, under her collar—essentially into her cleavage.

"What will it be, then? Tarot? Want your palm read? I read tea leaves."

"I usually just read the bottom of a shot glass. Out of those choices, I'll take none of the above, thanks."

Miss Nancy looks puzzled.

"I'm psychic," Miriam says. "Remember? C'mon, Nance. You don't need those things. Maybe the end result isn't a scam, but those items kind of are, aren't they? The pretty cards? The secrets supposedly inscribed upon my pretty palm? You just need skin on skin. Just a touch will do. Am I right?"

Miriam's not so sure she's right—she's out on a limb here because she's never actually met someone who claims to be a real psychic. But this is how hers works, and presuming that fate works a certain way, with certain rules, and demands certain things of its endlessly toiling workers, then she figures Miss Nancy is bound by the same proscriptions.

Below the table, the beagle murmurs, then farts.

"True enough," Miss Nancy finally says, her smile a pinched pucker. She opens her hand and taps it. "Put your hand in mine."

"I want you to be honest about what you see."

"I will, hon. I promise that."

"No fucking—er, no *screwing* around."

"Just put your hand in mine."

Miriam reaches over and lays her hand into the woman's grip. Nancy's hand is warm. Miriam feels cold.

They sit for a few moments. Silent. It hits Miriam suddenly— she's not seeing how this woman dies. No vision. No end game. *No death.* It's like the woman's a rogue agent, disconnected from the flow of fate and time, unbound by—

Nancy's fingers close like a flytrap around Miriam's hand.

"Ow, hey—" Miriam says.

The grip tightens. The woman's neck tenses until the tendons stand out. Miriam tries to pull her hand away but can't. Nancy's eyes snap open. The whites of her eyes start to bloom red from busted blood vessels. Her teeth grind so hard, Miriam is afraid they might crack.

Miriam tugs her hand again, but it's like being caught in a vice—and the woman's hand is growing warmer, hotter, like it might burn her.

Blood pops from Nancy's nose. It trickles onto Miriam's hand.

Pat, pat, pat. Miriam idly hopes the blood will lubricate the woman's crushing grasp and get her free. No luck.

Nancy begins to moan. Her head rolls and pivots.

Below the table, the beagle starts to bay along with her.

"Christ," Miriam says, genuinely scared. Is this about her? Is the woman having some kind of coincidental aneurysm? She puts her free palm against the table and shoves hard. The table slams into the woman's midsection, and she gasps.

The woman's fingers uncurl. Miriam jerks her hand back. The skin is red, and she can already see the bruises forming.

Nancy looks like shit. Sweat pours from her brow. She licks her lips and pulls out a small handkerchief to mop up the blood. Her eyes have gone totally red.

Miriam speaks in a small voice. "Miss Nancy? Are you okay?"

"What are you?" she hisses.

"What? What do you mean?"

"Something dead is inside you. A deep, black, shriveled thing, and it's crying out like a lost child for its mother. You are the hand of death. You are its mechanism. I can hear the wheels turning, the pulleys pulling." Nancy fishes into her shirt and withdraws the two twenties. She crumples the money into little boulders and pitches them back at Miriam. "Take it. I don't want your blood money. Death is following you, and you've got some monster—*some presence*—inside your heart and mind. I don't want any part of it. Get out of here."

"Wait," Miriam pleads. "Wait! No, help me, help me understand, tell me how to stop it, tell me how to close it all off and—"

"Get out of here!" Miss Nancy screams. The beagle joins her yowl with his own.

Miriam staggers to her feet and backs toward the door.

"Please—"

"*Go.*"

Her shoulders hit the door, and she backs out, dizzy.

+ + + +

Miriam spends fifteen minutes in a small alley by a dry cleaner's joint just a minute's walk from the psychic. She smokes. She trembles. Her mind wanders.

Then she composes herself and heads back to the diner.

"She tell you your future?" Louis asks.

Miriam offers a fake smile. "Total scam. She had nothing to tell me I didn't already know. Ready to hit the bricks?"

TWENTY-SIX

CUL-DE-SAC

The stink surprises Harriet. It is the smell of fresh-cut grass. It might as well be the scent of a fruiting body, of a corpse in a drain culvert left for days to the bugs and bacteria. For her, it's the smell of decay. The odor of utter stagnation. All her muscles cinch up like a too-tight belt.

Ingersoll, from the back of the Escalade (his presence upgrades them from the Cutlass Ciera, without question), sees her shoulders tense, and says, "This is familiar to you, Harriet."

"Yes," she says. The word lies there, gutted of emotion.

Around her, the suburban boxes. The whitewashed curbs, the bird baths. The solar lights, the clematis growing up around mailboxes. Pastel siding. Bright white rain gutters.

She wants to set fire to everything here, wants to watch it burn down to greasy cinder.

"I think I turn here," Frankie says, and then doesn't do what he just said. "No, shit, fuck, wait. *This* one. Here we go. These fuckin' little avenues all look the same. The houses, the lawns. Cookie-cutter, copy-paste bullshit." She can feel him eyeing her before, during, and after the turn.

"He doesn't know," Ingersoll says.

"He who?" Frankie asks. "He me?"

Harriet shifts uncomfortably. "No, he doesn't."

"How long has it been since I partnered you two?" Ingersoll asks.

Frankie has to think. Harriet doesn't. "Two years, three months."

"What don't I know?" Frankie asks.

"Nothing," Harriet answers.

"Everything," Ingersoll says.

"Tell me," Frankie says. "I wanna know. You know everything about me. I'm an open book over here. I don't keep nothing from you."

"Will you tell him?" Ingersoll asks as Frankie pulls up into a cul-de-sac, a suburban dead-end of same houses. Frankie looks to her.

She feels ill.

Odd, given that Harriet rarely feels anything. Does she enjoy the feeling, just because it's a sensation? Is torturing herself as much fun as torturing others?

She chooses not to answer Ingersoll's question or her own.

Instead, she says, "We're here," and gets out of the car.

"He does not kill them?" Ingersoll asks, his nimble fingers looking through a wicker mail holder hanging in the foyer.

"No," Harriet says. "He's a con artist. He cons them out of it."

Frankie yells from the other room, from a den office. "Nobody's here. He's gone."

Ingersoll nods. "Not unexpected. He will have left some trace. Some sign of his passing. More important, I want a sign of the *girl's* passing. You will find it. I will wait for you to find it."

He goes and sits at the breakfast nook in the kitchen and steeples his hands, sitting perfectly still and perfectly silent.

Harriet and Frankie continue to put the pieces together.

The house—at 1450 Sycamore, in Doylestown, Pennsylvania, a suburb of Philadelphia—is owned by a Dan and Muriel Stine.

Dan loves fishing, the stock market, and, despite his apparent conservative sensibilities, the glam metal bands of the 1980s—Poison, Mötley Crüe, Warrant, Winger.

Muriel also plays the stock market with her own money from her own accounts. Beyond that, the house doesn't contain nearly as much information on Muriel. It's because they are divorced. Six months now. They have a daughter, an eight-year-old named Rebecca. Frankie finds the papers in the office.

"Dan still lives here," Harriet says. "Muriel has moved on to greener lawns."

"This place really gets to you," Frankie says.

"It does no such thing."

"You're lying to me."

"Keep looking. Ingersoll will want useful information."

Gaynes's modus operandi isn't that he cons people out of these houses, just that he cons people into telling him where they live. He meets them at a convention, a restaurant, a bar. They're working. They're away from home. Ashley comes, breaks in, lives here until they come back, and that's that. That's his trick. On the one hand, it's simple. On the other, it's *too* simple. Ashley thinks himself better than he is, perhaps.

Harriet cannot find out where Dan—the owner of a local sporting goods franchise—has gone. Maybe to visit a mistress. Maybe to find out how soccer balls and Pilates equipment are manufactured. Harriet doesn't really care. This place is like a crime scene, but the fingerprints she seeks aren't those of Dan Stine.

Harriet decides to check upstairs.

Halfway up the carpeted steps, she smells it.

Decay.

Real, this time. Not metaphorical.

She calls to Frankie. Like dogs, they sniff around.

Master bathroom, second floor.

The shower curtain is closed. The toilet seat is down. A little glass pipe, its bulb end darkened with carbon, sits atop it. The stink is terrible in here.

"Fuck. He's dead," Frankie says, mumbling behind the arm he's got pressed to his mouth and nose. Harriet doesn't bother. The smell doesn't disturb her. Not like the smell of cut grass. Or potpourri. Or a roast in the oven. "Stupid prick got into the product and fucking ODed. Holy shit."

Behind the shower curtain, a shadow. Harriet pulls it back.

A body lies in the tub. Plastic bag over the head. Dried blood clinging to the inside of the bag at the back of the head.

Frankie blinks. "Someone killed Gaynes."

"It's not him," Harriet says. "It's Dan Stine."

"How do you—?"

"I just know." She holds her breath, then tugs the bag off the head. The back of the head is a ruined mess. "Gaynes hit him with something. A pipe, a bat, a crowbar. I didn't see any blood, but I bet you'll find it downstairs. Or outside. But the hit didn't finish the job. Hence, the bag. While Stine was down, Gaynes suffocated him with the bag. Maybe he did it in the tub, or maybe he just brought the body here."

She stands up.

"Ashley Gaynes is now a murderer."

"C'mon," Frankie says, stopping her as they walk down the stairs. "I want to know."

"No."

"We're up here doing all the work, Ingersoll's downstairs . . . I dunno what. Receiving important instructions from the devil, probably."

"Ingersoll doesn't take orders," she says.

"Whatever. I'm just saying you can tell me. You don't have to tell me in front of him. That's what he wants. He wants to see it unfold. He likes putting things in motion, seeing how they play out. So, tell me what's up. Right here. Right now. He doesn't have to have the satisfaction."

Harriet stares.

"You ever notice that Ingersoll looks like a praying mantis?" Frankie asks.

Harriet pushes past him and heads down the stairs.

"Ashley Gaynes has gone off the reservation," Harriet explains to Ingersoll as Frankie catches up, frowning.

"Oh?" Ingersoll asks, idly drumming his fingers on an issue of *Field and Stream*.

"He's consuming the product, as Hawkins suggested. And he's no longer conning people out of their homes. He's simply murdering them and taking their places."

"That is a dark turn for our amateur con artist."

"Yes."

"I like it. Good for him. Any news of the girl?"

Harriet hesitates. "No."

"Any idea where they're going?"

"No."

"So, you've found very little of value, then."

Frankie shrugs. Harriet says nothing.

A thin smile spreads across Ingersoll's face. With his lack of eyebrows, it's difficult to tell whether the smile shows genuine amusement of some sort or is sour and sarcastic.

He takes a napkin from the napkin holder and unfolds it.

Then he pulls a pen from his pocket.

Ingersoll lays the thin napkin over the issue of *Field and Stream*, then gently runs the pen in a diagonal arc over the napkin.

Like a child holding up a school-made snowflake, he pinches the napkin at each end and holds it up. On it is revealed a company name and a phone number.

Harriet reads it aloud: 321 Trucking, then the number.

"I don't get it," Frankie says.

Ingersoll stands. "I found the only piece of actionable information in this house, and I never left this table."

"That's why you're the boss," Frankie says. Harriet hears the exasperation in his voice.

Ingersoll hands the napkin to Harriet. "Call this trucking company. This will lead us to him, to our case, and to the very special girl. Time is wasting, my friends."

THE DREAM

She's peeing.

That's not unusual, since it seems like she has to go every thirty seconds, what with the baby doing his little Irish step dance on her bladder. The doctor told her that the pressure would relieve during the second trimester, but her mother said it was a lie, and her mother was right. Big lie.

Miriam looks up. Someone has carved a message into the stall's wall—odd, because around these parts, girls are pretty girly and don't go carving messages into bathroom stalls on habit. Maybe a swirly ink message, *I Love Mike*, but always with marker, never with a knife.

The message reads: *Merry Christmas, Miriam.*

She finds that strange. Yes, it's almost Christmas, but how does the bathroom stall know that? She sees another message below it, and it reads: *She's coming for you.*

Miriam thinks little of it.

Somewhere in the distance, she hears: *clomp, clomp, clomp.* The plodding of boots.

She's about to pull a few squares of toilet tissue (and here in this bathroom, it's about as sturdy as an angel's whisper, so she needs more than a few lest she dampen her hand) and she sees that someone's in the next stall, someone who wasn't there a minute ago.

One foot ends in a ratty sneaker.

The other foot is missing below the ankle. It drips black blood on the tile.

"Merry Christmas," says Ashley's voice. "Don't you miss me?"

She finds that in a weird and horrible way, she does. But she shakes it off, and now the feet are gone, and the blood has been cleaned up, and she leaves the stall to wash her hands.

She's washing her hands.

She's looking at her hands, not her face, because she doesn't like how the pregnancy has bloated her cheeks, her chin, her everything. She's poofy like those puffy bubble stickers she collected when she was nine. Unicorns and rainbows and all that.

The sound comes again: *clomp, clomp, clomp*.

She's done washing her hands.

She looks up.

Her face is pale. Her hair, chestnut—her natural color—and pulled back in a ponytail.

Something moves behind her. A blur of dark blue, then a flash of red.

"You killed my son" comes a haggard, horrible whisper.

Mrs. Hodge stands behind her. Snow galoshes tracking wet footprints into the bathroom. A navy-blue snow jacket, dirty and old, sitting awkwardly on her thick torso. The woman's hair is stringy, dark, unwashed, and it hangs like jungle vines across her ruddy face.

The woman's holding a red snow shovel.

Miriam grips the porcelain sink—

The shovel slams into her back.

Miriam's feet skid out from under her, and the sink clips her on the chin, and when her face hits the tile, she bites her tongue. She doesn't just taste blood; it fills her mouth.

She reaches out and tries to pull herself away, but the floor is freshly wet and gives her hands no purchase. Her palms squeak and slide across tile.

"You little poisonous whore," the woman says. "You don't deserve what Ben put in you."

Wham. The shovel comes down hard between her shoulder blades and then again against her head and again against her back, and the flat metal keeps slamming into her, harder and harder, until she feels something inside of her—like a little glass snowflake between pinching fingers—fracture, crack, and shatter, and she feels a warmth between her legs, a rush of wetness, and her hand reaches down between shovel blows and comes back with the palm wet with red, and she plants one bloody handprint on the floor to pull herself up—

But it doesn't matter, because the shovel comes down again.

Miriam hears a baby crying, a hard echo in the bathroom, coming from the hallway. The squalls are suddenly drowned, like the baby's choking, gurgling in its own fluids, and then the screams are cut short entirely and all goes dark.

She hears Louis's voice whisper in her ear, "Six more days, then I'm dead."

TWENTY-SEVEN

END OF THE ROAD

The whisper, harsh in her ear, lingers as she jolts awake.

"I'm sorry," Miriam blurts.

Louis looks over at her as he wheels the truck off past the exit ramp and through a tollbooth. "Sorry for what?"

For letting you die, she thinks. Her hair is stringy, sweaty. It clings to her forehead.

"Nothing. I thought—I think I was snoring."

"You weren't."

"Well. Good."

She rubs her eyes. It's night. The windshield is wet from recent rain, but in the jaundiced streetlights, it looks like someone pissed all over the glass.

"Where are we?" she asks.

"Pennsylvania. Headed toward a truck stop in Coopersburg. I got a buddy up there who's real good with trucks. Has a gift. I like him to do all my maintenance, and whenever I swing through this area, I always pay him a visit."

She smacks her lips together. Her tongue rasps against the roof of her mouth. A case of total cottonmouth. *Cigarette. Coffee. Booze.* One of those three would be nice right now.

"Pennsylvania. Weren't we just in Ohio?"

"We were. But then you fell asleep."

"Shit. That's a long trip, isn't it?"

He shrugs. "Not really. About eight, nine hours. That's the name of the game. Go as far as you can, fast as you can—we get paid by the mile."

"So that's why most truckers drive like a bull in a china shop."

"Yup. They're trying to feed their families, so they pop NoDoz or worse and push it. Sometimes beyond the breaking point." His voice gets quiet. "I don't have a home, don't have a family to feed, so I can take it easy. Even taking it easy, I make about thirty-five cents a mile, and today we did a five-hundred-plus-mile haul—that's darn near two hundred bucks. I pull in about sixty grand a year, and I don't have a mortgage, don't have many bills."

"Does it bother you? This life? You're basically . . . a nomad. You have no home."

"Neither do you."

"I know. And I love it . . . sometimes. I love that I'm just a piece of garbage floating down the stream—wherever it takes me, it takes me. But I also hate it. I never feel connected to anything or anybody. No anchor. No roots."

"I feel connected to you," he says.

"I feel connected to you, too," she responds, and yet she marvels at how feeling connected to him also makes her feel more distant. A paradox, an impossibility, but there it is. She's close to him, but between them lurks a great and monstrous gap: the yawning abyss betwixt life and death.

He feels it, too. She knows he does, because he's quiet then. He doesn't *understand* it like she does. He doesn't know what's coming. But she figures, somewhere inside of him, he feels it. The way spiders can sense a thunderstorm, or the way honeybees can signal an earthquake.

The lights of the local highway strobe into the cab.

She breaks the silence. "We crashing in the truck tonight?"

"No," he says. "The truck stop has a motel and a diner attached to it."

"That's my life. Motels. Diners. Highways."

"Mine, too."

Then the silence returns, and the truck rumbles on.

The tables at the diner are clean, the eggs are good, and the coffee neither looks nor tastes like urine from a diseased kidney. The motel next door, too, is clean. Doesn't stink of puke or cigarettes. No roaches doing a kick-dance on the sink. The motel's doors don't lead right to the parking lot, either. The place has a goddamn genuine hallway. It's like the Four Fucking Seasons, she thinks. Is that what separates a motel from a hotel? Is this actually a hotel? she wonders. Has she ever stayed in a hotel?

Miriam should feel happy. This is a step up. Louis is a step up.

She paces outside, smoking, unhappy.

"You don't know what you're doing," she mumbles to herself.

It's true. She doesn't.

She's just been going with it. Garbage in the stream. Be happy. Find bliss. Let it work. Make Louis happy. Don't worry about tomorrow. And that was working fine, just fine.

"But then, dumbass that you are, you have to go and visit a bona fide psychic who erupts like a goddamn blood geyser and tells you that you're the human equivalent of the Enola Gay. Meanwhile, Louis is going to die in *five days* and what are you going to do about it? Nothing? Let it happen? Sit back and watch and smoke your goddamn cigarettes?"

As if angry at the cancer stick, she pinches it and pitches it—

And Ashley ducks as the glowing cherry whirls over his shoulder.

"Talking to yourself?" he says.

It's like seeing a ghost. As if he emerges out of nothing. Miriam can't help but wonder if he's even real. He doesn't sound the same. A tremor quivers below his voice. He itches at his side. His stance is off, even—his confidence is tilted, like his body.

Miriam pats her jeans pocket. The knife isn't there. Of course it's not there. She had to leave it behind in that woman's thigh when this cocksucker bailed on her.

"You fucking shitcock asshole."

"That a way to greet an old friend?" He chuckles. It's not a healthy sound. *He's not a ghost.*

"Old friend. That's a good one. You come near me, and I bite. I'll bite off your fingers. I'll bite off your nose." To emphasize, she snaps her teeth together: *clack clack*.

Ashley comes closer anyway. He steps into a halo of bleak light. His smooth face is dotted with patchy beard growth. His eyes, hollow. His hair is messy, and not in the purposeful way he once favored—it's now just a greasy tangle.

"I need your help," he says. He *pleads*. "I need you."

"You need a bath. You smell like—" She takes a whiff. "Cat piss. Jesus, Ashley. You're using. You're actually *using* that stuff."

"I'm on the run."

"Then get the hell away from me."

"They're following me. Dogging my every step. I gotta stay sharp. It's just for now."

She laughs. *"Just for now. I can quit anytime. I didn't know she was fourteen, officer."*

"Fuck you, you alcoholic, nic-fit freak."

"Those are legal." As if to demonstrate, she taps a cigarette out of the pack and grabs it with her lips. "They also make me smell like a bar, not an overturned litter box."

"We can go somewhere. We can go anywhere. Just get on a plane and go."

"Where's the case?"

His eyes dart to and fro. "I've taken care of that. But I can get it when we need it."

"You can't take a metal suitcase full of crystal meth on a plane, dumb fuck."

"Then we'll take a bus."

"Oh, heck, I *love* the bus," she says. "Nothing better than a twelve-hour ride in an oven-baked casket with unwashed schizophrenics. *Supersweet.* Understand something: I'm not going anywhere with you. You're on your own. You left me to die out there, paired up with a gun-toting Annie Wilkes wannabe. She could've killed me." *Probably should've.*

She takes the unlit cigarette out of her mouth and pops it behind her ear. Heel pivots to toe, and then she's turning away from him and heading inside the motel.

"Wait," he says, coming in after her. The motel clerk—a bald guy in one of those translucent green poker visors—regards their conversation with sleepy eyes. She doesn't plan on giving him a show. She hits the hallway, passes the ice machine.

Ashley dogs her.

He puts his hand on her shoulder. She thinks seriously about biting it, but she doesn't know where those hands have been over the last week.

Instead, she shoves him back.

He reaches for her again. She grabs a fistful of his shirt and hurls him backward.

"I'll tell him," he says, staggering.

She stops. Over her shoulder, she asks, "Tell *what* to *whom*?"

"Your truck-driver boyfriend. I'll tell him everything."

Her feet carry her forward, away from Ashley. She heads toward their room. The key is in her hand before she knows it, and she suddenly recognizes that this was a bad move. But she doesn't know where else to go or what else to do, and the quiet, scared little girl inside of her just wants to go to Louis and curl up in his lap and let him protect her from her mistakes.

She opens the door and calmly walks in.

She closes the door behind her and locks it.

She sits on the bed, trembling.

Louis is already up and alert. He looks concerned.

"What was that? What was that in the hallway?"

Miriam stares forward. She bites her lip. She tries to say something and can't find words.

Then: a pounding at the door.

"What is that?" Louis asks. "Who is that?"

"Don't answer the door," Miriam says.

"Don't—what? Why not?" He moves toward the door.

She grabs his hand as he passes. "You don't have to. You can just ignore it. *Ignore it.* Please."

Then he asks the question. It's telling. It tells what he really thinks about her, or more accurately, what he *fears* about her.

He asks, "What have you done?"

"I . . ." The words don't trail off so much as they never manifest to begin with.

Louis goes to the door and opens it.

Ashley shoulders his way into the room as if Louis isn't there. Arms crossed tight in front of him, rocking back and forth like he's some kind of mule-kicked simpleton, Ashley stands in front of Miriam. "I need to know how I die. Tell me how I die. They don't kill me. Tell me they don't kill me. I know they're coming, Miriam. You can help me; I need you to help me—"

"Hey," Louis barks. But then he sees who it is. "Is that your brother?"

Ashley laughs. "I'm not her brother, *bro*."

"What? Miriam?"

"Don't look at her. Look at me. We're here to rob your ass. This is a scam. A con."

Miriam says nothing.

Louis frowns. "You'd better tell me what's going on, son."

"We know you've got bank. All that money in envelopes. Hand it over. Or else."

"Or else what?"

Ashley pulls a gun—really just his thumb and index finger shaped into a gun. "This, motherfucker. Now stick 'em up." He cocks his thumb back like he's ready to fire.

Louis lays Ashley out with one punch. *Bam.*

It's like a wrecking ball. Ashley topples backward onto the bed. He starts to get up, dizzy—the punch should have put him down for an hour, but whatever meth is still crawling through his system is happy to animate his body like a puppet on strings.

With his meaty hands, Louis picks Ashley's entire body up and pitches him backward into the bedside table. A lamp spins off and crashes into the ground, casting that corner of the room into darkness. Louis then grabs Ashley by the ankle and drags him back around the bed toward the door, with Ashley's head hitting the table legs on a crummy desk, the corner of the dresser and TV stand, and even the rubber doorstop.

Louis throws Ashley out of the room, then slams the door.

A sense of mad elation fills Miriam's heart. He saved her. He did so without asking any questions. He saw the threat and eliminated it. She feels protected. She feels safe.

Miriam leaps to her feet and throws her arms around Louis's prodigious torso.

He doesn't return the embrace.

Gently, he pushes her back.

"Is it true?" he asks.

Her heart sinks.

"Louis—"

"Just tell me, is it true? He's not your brother? Were you planning on robbing me?"

"Not at first, but then—then maybe—but not now, not now, I ditched him, that's why I ditched him, you have to believe me, I never wanted—"

But Louis moves away from her and starts throwing his items back in his bag.

"Where are you going?"

"Away," he says. "Away from you."

"Louis, wait."

"No. My truck's not in the shop yet, not until morning. I'm just going to leave. Room's yours for the night if you want it. I don't much care. But I can't abide liars."

She grabs his wrist, but then he grabs hers in return. His grip is gentle enough, but she knows that with a twist of his wrist, he could snap her arm into brittle bits.

"You were right. You are poison. You tried to tell me. I should've listened."

He takes a deep breath, then says the word that is a knife that goes right through her heart:

"Good-bye."

Bag over his shoulder, he pushes his way out of the room, steps over Ashley's supine body, and moves silently down the hallway until he's out of sight.

Miriam hasn't cried in a long time, but she cries now.

Hard, wracking sobs. Her eyes burn. Her ribs hurt. She cries the way a child cries: gasping, hitching, keening.

Over her cries, she can hear his truck rumble to life.

The sound grows to a growl, then fades.

Louis pulls his truck out of the lot and back onto the highway.

He doesn't think much of the black Escalade that passes him, going in as he goes out.

TWENTY-EIGHT

SHOCKING DEVELOPMENTS

It doesn't take long for Miriam's sadness to crystallize into a sharp spike of anger. Her tears become acid. Her frown a curved blade. Her trembling hands like reciprocating saws, ready to vibrate messily through offending flesh.

She's up. She stands in the doorway. Ashley sits like a piece of windblown trash against the wall, a bleary, almost drunken smile smeared across his face. One sleepy lid half closed.

"Can we go now?"

She kicks him in the mouth.

The back of his head cracks into the wall. Her heel knocks one of his bottom front teeth out, and it hops across the carpet like a jumping bean before coming to a rest.

A trickle of red wets his lip.

"Ow," he says.

A few rooms down, a door opens and a pale man with jowls like a slobbery dog's muzzle peers out. Miriam tells him if he doesn't put his head back inside his room, she's going to tear it off and piss fire in his neck hole.

He turtles swiftly back into his room.

"The trucker. He left, didn't he?"

Miriam says nothing. She is a smoldering volcano.

Ashley wipes his lips. "That's going to be a problem, then."

"Go to hell."

"You love me," he says, spitting blood.

"Keep dreaming."

"You need me."

"That might've been true before. It's not true now."

He grins. Red teeth, like he's been eating raspberries. "You *want* me."

"I pity you."

She hawks up a gob of phlegm. She's about to spit it into his smiling mouth.

Then—

Down the hall, they appear. Like two shadows. Two demons.

Frankie in his black suit. Harriet, not in her turtleneck but in a dark red blouse, a Christmas blouse, even though it's almost July.

They have pistols.

Miriam sees them, and Ashley doesn't, not at first. But his eyes follow her eyes, and when he finally realizes—

"We're dead," he says, a hoarse, panicked whisper.

Miriam is not prepared. Normally, she'd have this place cased out. She'd know her exits. Her corners. Her safe places and vulnerabilities. Being with Louis made her slow, lazy. When she was a child, her mother used to walk her through the store holding her hand, gripping it so hard, Miriam thought her knuckles might break. But she eventually learned not to fight, because that way her mother would relax her grip—and then, oops, Miriam could slip her grasp and run off to the candy or cereal aisle. This is like that. She relaxed her grip.

Right now, she has only one real option: the emergency exit to her right, at the end of the hall. While they stalk down the hall, she'll flee into the open lot.

Everything seems to move in slow motion, like she's got chains around her arms, legs, waist, pulling her back, halting her escape.

She pivots—

Ashley tries to lurch to his feet, but he's weak, beaten—

Miriam's running, but behind her the two killers move without hesitation, hands up, pistols up—

They're twenty feet away now and closing—

Ashley can't stand. He's on all fours, scrabbling like a panicked animal trying to clamber up a rocky escarpment. He's crying out—

Fifteen feet now, maybe less. She can't tell; everything seems wrong—

Miriam feels something dart by her ear; she jerks her head left as a wire with two metal probes on it *tinks* against a faux-gold wall sconce. She doesn't know what it is until—

Ashley cries out, a stuttering wail through closed teeth; his body seizes, goes rigid, eyes wide like a pair of headlights—

Taser, she thinks, not pistols. *Tasers, they missed me—*

Her shoulder crashes into the emergency exit, throwing it wide. No alarm goes off; no alarm ever goes off, no matter what the warnings say. In places like this, they never seem to be hooked up to a goddamn thing. She tastes the evening air; she sees the highway ahead of her—

Wham.

An arm in a white sleeve clotheslines her trachea. Her heels go out from under her. Her back cracks hard into the exit door, slamming it shut behind her.

She looks up, gasping for air.

"You," she wheezes.

The man seems taken aback. A smile plays at the edges of his lips.

"We have not met," he says.

Bam. Someone—Frankie, Harriet, both—hits the emergency door from the other side, but whoever it is doesn't expect Miriam to be leaning back against it, and they don't make it through the first time. She feels like a bird in a net, wildly flapping its wings. She knows she has to get away, has to *get free*, lest they—well, she doesn't know what they'll do to her, but she knows it can't be good.

Miriam lurches to her feet, clearing the door just as Frankie slams into it thinking he needs all his weight and momentum. He comes tumbling out like a cascade of brooms from an over-crowded closet.

Frankie stumbles and stands between Miriam and the tall, hairless man.

She shoves Frankie hard into Hairless Fucker. They both go down, and a tiny voice inside her is thrilled that the sonofabitch might get his bright white suit dirty.

Like a deer fleeing the hunt, she bolts across the lot toward the highway.

It's a fast highway. Two lanes each way.

It's all rushing metal, glaring headlights. A stampede of steel at 70 mph.

Miriam doesn't think. She just runs. Straight into traffic.

Her foot hits the median before she even realizes it. Behind her, the delirious effect of honking. Brakes, screeching.

She's out in the other lane—a car whips past her, the mirror nearly clipping her outstretched hand clean off just before spinning her like a top—when she hears the hard crash of metal on metal, glass on glass, airbags and gravel and screaming. She hears someone from *this lane* say "Holy shit!" when they see whatever's going on in *that lane*, and Miriam knows she just caused a car accident, maybe a bad one, but she doesn't look back, because looking back means slowing down and slowing down means getting dead.

You're a bad person, she thinks.

You just caused a car wreck.

And a tiny part of you is happy about it, because it's a distraction for them, a slow-down, an obstacle.

You're a user. Even when you don't mean to be.

People might be hurt. You could stop and help—

But another voice reminds her: It is what it is, fate gets what it wants, this has already been written, so move, move, *move*.

Her foot hits the highway shoulder on the other side. An umpire's voice in her head yells, *Safe!* A car behind her drones its horn. Endlessly. She pictures a body slumped over, head on the wheel, but she hopes that's not what it is, that it's just the car.

The umpire in her head is wrong, though. She knows she's not safe. That's just an illusion.

Miriam keeps running.

Ahead of her, a storage lot. Row after row of orange storage units.

It's a twenty-four-hour facility, but it's got a gate and a keypad, and it's closed up tighter than a choirboy's asshole with a perimeter fence topped with a row of barbed wire. But that's a feature, not a bug. Miriam jumps. Hits the fence like a shark.

She climbs.

The barbed wire is old. Hasn't been maintained. No tension. It bows under her hands. But it still bites her, still tears ragged claw marks in her jeans and the skin beneath. She reminds herself that she hasn't had a tetanus shot lately, and wouldn't that just be the bee's knees, escaping her killers but dying of fucking *lockjaw*? But she's up and over and landing hard on the other side.

The impact goes up her shins and into her knees and the pain is bad (*maybe you broke something*), but she doesn't stop. The fact that she can run, even with pain, means nothing is broken, right? (*Says the girl who is not a doctor.*)

The storage units are bathed in sodium light, but pockets of shadow remain.

Miriam darts into the heart of the storage unit. Seven rows deep. Five units in.

The stink of rotten fast food hits her, but she doesn't care;

she hunkers down behind a trash can, makes herself as small as she can between the two storage units.

She waits.

That was him.

The hairless fuck with the fillet knife. The one who cuts out both of Louis's eyes and stabs him in the brain to kill him.

Proof positive, yet again, that Miriam is the one who causes this. The chain of events replays out, a cruel and taunting film-strip, flip, flip, flip, a cascading series of *what ifs*: If she didn't get in that truck with him, if she didn't get hooked up with Ashley, if she didn't *go back* to Louis . . .

But still, it isn't coming together. She doesn't understand. Not yet. Louis is gone. They're here. He's not. Why would they connect with him? Unfinished business?

It doesn't make any sense.

One thing she knows, though, is that fate never shows its hand early. It always waits till the last possible moment to turn the cards.

The show ain't over yet.

She's spotted.

The only weapon she's got is a broken stick she found on the ground behind her, and she thinks, *I'm not going out without a fight.* She'll stick it in someone's eye. For payback. Some kind of first-strike retaliation where the revenge comes before the act committed. Vengeance of the time traveler, vindication born of prevision.

"You all right?" comes the voice.

It's a man. Not Frankie. Not the Hairless Fucker.

Midthirties. Light beard. Glasses. Hair lacquered to his forehead with sweat, baseball hat in hand. He peers over and around the trash can.

"Miss?"

She stands. She doesn't know how long she's been here. A half hour? An hour? Longer? Sirens have come and gone from the accident. All's been quiet but for a couple-few cars coming in and out of the facility (and with each car, her heart pauses, her breath waits).

The guy's eyes widen when he sees her.

"You're bleeding," he says.

Miriam doesn't know how to respond. She remains sandwiched in the space between the two units; exposure could mean death. It's not death she's worried about. It's what comes before.

"Yes," she says. Dumb. But it's all she has.

"Were you in that accident?"

"Yes," she lies. Though maybe it's not a lie. She was certainly present for it.

"Do you need help?"

She fires back with a question of her own: "Do you have a car?"

"Yeah. I was here just putting a few more things into a storage unit before our move to the new house, and—sorry. You don't really need to know this. My Forester is parked around the corner."

"Will you take me somewhere?"

He hesitates. He's not sure, and he's right to be uncertain. Miriam knows that elements don't add up. No glass in her hair. The cuts on her legs aren't from a car accident. He hasn't asked the right questions in his head yet, but he will. She only hopes by the time he comes up short, they're already in the car, driving far, far away from this place. *You're going to get out of this—a rat through a bolthole, almost there, just a little farther. . . .*

"Yeah," he says finally. "Absolutely. Here, this way. My name's Jeff—"

She moves to step out.

The man, Jeff, flicks his gaze left.

Then his body jerks sideways, accompanied by a spray of blood and a pistol shot.

Miriam kicks over the trash can and turns to run the other way, to duck between the storage unit and come out the other side.

That doesn't happen.

Instead, she comes face to face with Hairless Fucker. He nods. "How easily we are sidelined by distractions," he says.

And then he takes a step back and fires the Taser into her stomach. Every cell in her body lights up like a Christmas tree. Hot and cold. Stinging fire ants. A string of firecrackers. Her bones feel like they might break. Everything is white, bright, and terrible.

THE INTERVIEW

Paul's body sits crumpled at the bottom of the stairs. His head is turned at a bad angle, the chin up over the shoulder and pointed at ninety degrees. The eyes, open and glassy. The mouth, closed, as if posed forever in thought. His bag lies a few feet away. A cell phone, a few feet past that.

Miriam descends the steps.

A minute ago, she watched him leave the warehouse.

Philly's chemical stink—a dull, acid perfume that rises with steaming manholes and drifts down with spitting rain, calling to mind a mixture of sewer gas and pesticide—burns her nose and burns her eyes, and she feels herself tearing up, and she convinces herself that's all it is, the stink of the city.

When he left, Paul crossed the road.

He checked that calculator watch from a bygone era as he did. No cars struck him. No heart attack claimed him.

He stepped up on the curb. His cell phone rang.

A set of concrete steps waited for him, and he took his call, and said, "Hi, Mom," and maybe the phone was enough of a distraction, but his foot took the step at a bad angle, more heel and less toe, and he started to fall.

He would have been fine, but the body and brain don't always play well together. The body would have fallen in a way that was natural, the blow cushioned. The brain freaks out. Fight or flight.

Panic response. That's what happened to Paul. He tried to save himself. Stiffened. Tightened. Twisted.

It didn't save him.

His body tumbled the rest of the way, and at the bottom, his neck twisted. The bone broke. Miriam will later read that sometimes that's called an "internal decapitation." It was over quickly.

Miriam didn't need to be there to see it. She'd already seen it play out. This was his hour.

She walks down the steps. Pauses over his body.

You could've saved him, that voice says. It always says that. As if on cue, a shadow passes overhead—a balloon, she thinks, a Mylar balloon. But when she looks up, it's just a cloud passing over the sun, not a balloon at all.

"I'm sorry, Paul. I wouldn't have minded you telling the world about me. They wouldn't have believed you, of course. Nobody ever does. But it wasn't meant to be, pal."

Miriam looks through his stuff. She takes the recorder. She goes through his wallet, like a vulture picking meat off bone. Paul is a wealthy kid, that much is obvious, and he has a couple hundred bucks plus a few gift cards, a couple credit cards.

With nimble fingers, she undoes the sweet, sweet calculator watch and slides it up over her hand, tightening it too tight against her wrist. The bite of the band will always remind her where the watch came from.

She sits there for a little while longer. She gets something in her eye, and she wipes it away. Pollen or dust. Or just the stink of the city.

TWENTY-NINE

BACKSEAT DRIVER

"I am a businessman."

These words wake Miriam.

The voice belongs to Hairless Fucker.

He's not talking to her. He's talking to Ashley.

They're in a car. No—an SUV. Cream leather interior. Uppity; it's got DVD screens in the backs of the seats, and USB jacks, a glowing GPS and backup camera in the console up front.

Miriam's in the back-back seat. She doesn't know what is covering her mouth, but she wouldn't be surprised to learn it's two strips of black electrical tape in a wide X.

Her hands, zip-tied. Feet, too. She feels groggy. The world swims. This is more than just the Taser. A faint memory flits through her brain—hands holding her, a pinprick, a syringe, a warm and fuzzy undertow. Pine trees pass outside the car. Dark green against a gray sky. They pass fast; they blur. Whatever the drugs were, they're still not out of her system.

Ashley is in the seat ahead of her, facing forward.

Hairless sits next to him.

Way up in the front, Harriet drives. Frankie's in the passenger seat, cleaning his gun. The smell of gun oil—heady, rich, mechanical—fills the vehicle.

"Business," Hairless continues, "is a kind of ecology. It has its hierarchies, its taxonomies. It has a food web, a pecking order. It is a natural thing."

Ashley's mouth is taped shut. Miriam can't see his hands or feet, but the way he struggles tells her he's bound, too. Hands behind back, like her.

"We think of nature in a certain way. We think of it as balanced. We think of it being fair, in its own way. Nature is not fair. It is not balanced. It is weighted in favor of what we would think of as evil. Cruelty is rewarded. You see? Harriet knows."

Harriet speaks. She sounds excited. The monotone is gone. The flavorless cardboard drone has been replaced by a bloodthirsty, giddy tenor rising in pitch, growing in sheer delight.

"Penguin mothers are kind to their children. Wolves are honorable. Chimpanzees are noble and wise. All lies, lies to comfort us. Man wants nature to be noble because it forces *him* to be noble. Man knows that he is above the beasts, and so if beasts can be noble, then man *must* be noble, too. Such a moral, honorable benchmark does not exist," Harriet says. Her words drip with *nyah-nyah-nyah, I told you so* contempt. "Animals are vile and cruel. Cats rape each other. Ants enslave other insects, including other ants. Chimps fight in massive gang wars—they kill wantonly, they piss and shit on the corpses of their enemies, they take the babies of their genetic foes and dash them against rocks. They steal the females and force them to breed. They sometimes eat the defeated males."

Harriet looks back at them, and Miriam sees in her eyes a manic gleam.

"Nature is brutal and grotesque. That is the only benchmark. That is the precedent. We are animals, and as part of nature, we too must be brutal and grotesque."

Miriam thinks she sees Harriet's shoulders shake with a tiny paroxysm of pleasure.

The woman returns to driving.

Hairless offers a golf clap. Miriam growls against her tape-gag.

The Hairless Fucker turns to her and extends a long finger against his lips.

"Shh. Your turn will come. For now, let me speak with your friend." He turns back to Ashley, who is pale and sweaty like a bottle of milk left out on a warm counter. He's staring at something Miriam cannot see, something near him on the seat. "This, Mister Gaynes, is how our time together will work. I have two questions for you. If you answer both of my questions honestly and swiftly, I will not kill you."

Hairless fidgets with whatever it is that Miriam cannot see. She hears a metal squeak, the squeak of hinges.

He holds something up.

This, she can see.

A twelve-inch, all-metal hacksaw. Brand-new. Still has the sticker on it.

Hairless flicks the blade with his fingernail. *Ting, ting, ting.*

"I am a businessman, as noted, and to be successful I must be cruel, so forgive me this. My first question is about the girl." Hairless turns and gives her a look. She can't read it. Maybe it's because he can't read her—and that puzzlement shows on his smooth, bone-white face. "Is it true, what she can do? Is it for real?"

Ashley moans against the tape.

"Oh," Hairless says, chuckling. He plucks the tape off Ashley's mouth. *Rip.*

"I think so," Ashley blurts, gasping for air with a mouth ringed by red, raw skin. "I think it's real. She believes it's real."

Miriam struggles. She wants to boot him in the face. She wants to bite through her gag and scream for him to shut up, it won't matter, don't give in to these assholes. If given half a chance, she'd bite his tongue off. She'd kick him through the window. Something. Anything.

Hairless continues with his questioning.

"Now, my product. My case. My drugs." He pauses, takes a deep breath. "Where are they? What have you done with that which is mine?"

Ashley spills like a drink.

And when he does, Miriam's heart goes cold.

"It's in the truck," Ashley says. "The trucker. Louis. I hid it in his truck."

Next to Miriam sits Louis, Ghost Louis, *Xs-for-eyes* Louis. He smiles, bites his lower lip like a girl about to be given a pony.

Miriam's head has been like a box full of puzzle pieces rattling. Now the pieces fall into place.

Miriam feels warmth on her cheeks. She realizes she's crying.

Hairless lets out a breath.

"That was so easy," he says, smiling. "I always worry that it will be difficult. And so often, my worries bear fruit. I thank you for your cooperation."

Ashley gasps, laughs a little, nods. But then he sees. His eyes dart back and forth, and he starts to stammer—"No, no, c'mon, no. No!"

Hairless Fucker has the saw. He moves scary-fast.

This is how it happens: Hairless gets atop Ashley, his back against Ashley's chest. He drives his elbow up into Ashley's jaw, smashing it shut and closing the door on any protests Ashley might make. Hairless keeps that elbow there, like a chair under a doorknob.

With his free hand, Hairless hoists Ashley's leg so that the foot is propped up against the headrest of the driver's seat. Harriet doesn't seem to mind.

Hairless tugs back Ashley's pant leg.

Ashley thrashes, screams, but Hairless is a fucking pro, and he rides the flailing con artist like a rodeo cowboy.

"I told you!" Ashley shrieks through his bloody mouth. The

words are sloppy, bubbly, and flecks of blood spit up onto the back of Hairless's bald head. "I told you want you wanted!"

"And I told *you*," Hairless declares through gritted teeth, "that nature was cruel. Chimpanzees, dolphins, wolves. Red in tooth and claw! They understand revenge. This is that. This is revenge! You hobble my operation—"

Hairless presses the saw blade to the flesh of Ashley's ankle. "So I hobble *you*."

Hairless begins to cut. Bearing down, elbow back.

Ashley makes a sound like Miriam's never heard before. It's a high-pitched animal sound, a mammalian dirge.

Harriet drives as jets of blood arc up over her shoulder.

Frankie blanches, turns away. "This is a rental," he says between screams.

The saw moves. It eats with metal teeth.

Miriam can barely parse what's happening. The blurred motion. The splashes of red. Louis's ghost next to her, whistling that faux innocent, "I knew all along" whistle.

Do something, her brain yells.

Her body lies frozen. Like it's disconnected, gone off-line.

The saw grinds—now against bone. Ashley's eyelids flutter.

Good, part of her thinks. Fuck him. This is all his fault. (*This is all* your *fault,* another voice reminds her, a voice that sounds suspiciously like Louis's.) But she knows when Hairless is done with Ashley, it's on to her. What parts of her will he cut off? What parts is she willing to forsake? The hot tears burn streaks down her cheeks, and her mind lights up.

Do something.

Do something!

She does something.

She props her chin on the seat in front of her, uses it to get leverage. Bound feet under her, she pushes up, shoulders herself over into the same seat as Hairless and Ashley. She almost slips off the bloody leather but manages to get her back against the seat, her legs up.

Hairless regards her with nothing but idle curiosity.

"A survivor," he says. "I like that."

She aims her bound feet toward his head. But precise control isn't on the cards when her body's been relegated to the movements of a fat grub or clumsy inchworm.

She kicks Hairless in the chest.

The blade slips from his hand, but not before making one last dig. Ashley's foot swings by a strip of skin and ankle hair that looks like a stretched Band-Aid.

Miriam kicks again, both feet into Hairless's sunken chest.

The door behind them opens. Maybe Ashley opened it on purpose or by accident. Maybe it was never closed properly. Miriam doesn't know and doesn't care.

What she knows is that Ashley tumbles out of the car. His body is a shuddering shape, a shadow, and then it's out the door and gone. The space where he was is now nothing but passing pine trees, dark needles against a steel sky.

Hairless, looking more than a little bemused, leans back, holding onto the oh-shit handle above his head with his bony, almost feminine fingers.

In his other hand, he holds Ashley's severed foot.

He regards it the way a teacher might regard an apple from a student.

Miriam knows she only has seconds to act.

She tries to push back with her legs. If she can get to the opposite door, if she can press her back up against it, her bound hands can grab the handle, pop it open, and she can escape. But the blood—there's too much of it. It's slick. It's like trying to run in a nightmare: feet jogging through wet cement. Grunting, she pushes back again and again, flexing her legs, hoping her feet will offer her some purchase. . . .

It works. Her back hits the Escalade door. Her fingers work like blind worms, feeling for the door handle.

"No," Hairless says, as if by saying it, he commands reality.

"Fhhh mmmuuu," Miriam screams through the tape just as her fingers find the handle.

"Lock the door!" Hairless cries out—but it's too late.

The door flies open, and Miriam flies backward.

She knows it's going to suck. Hitting asphalt? At sixty? It'll be a like a bug jumping on a belt sander. Gravel will eat the back of her skull. It's suicide, probably.

The idea doesn't make her uncomfortable.

But her head doesn't hit the passing blacktop.

A pair of hands has her by the calves. Hairless Her head dangles out the car door, her hair brushing the highway zooming by beneath her. The rush of wind fills her ears. She can smell saltwater, car fumes, pine trees, the cloying chemical curdle that is the state scent of New Jersey. It's freedom she smells and hears, and it isn't long for her world—

—which reverses, like a tape rewinding.

Hairless drags her back into the car. His face floats above her.

She thinks to headbutt it, but it's like he knows what she's thinking, because he presses a blood-slick hand against her forehead.

The other hand pulls a syringe.

Miriam struggles. A bead of clear fluid oozes from the tip of the needle, and caught in the wind from the still-open door, it trembles and dances away toward oblivion.

"We'll talk soon," Hairless says.

He jams the needle into her neck.

"Nnnngh!" she shouts against the tape gag.

The world shudders and breaks apart. Its pieces float toward an uncertain darkness.

THIRTY

THE BARRENS

The world oozes. Everything is wet paint on a canvas, clumps of color sliding down.

Miriam feels hands under her armpits. Her feet drag along sand. Bleary late afternoon light pokes through the gray above. Mosquitoes fly. Pale pines cast long shadows, shadows that seem to have fingers, that seem to want to pluck her skin from her bones.

Ahead of her, Hairless walks. His white blazer is peppered with red.

Ashley's blood.

Ashley's severed foot sloshes along in a clear zip-top freezer baggy in the Hairless Fucker's hand, swinging this way and that.

Time contracts. Then dilates.

They're nowhere. More trees. An overturned claw-foot tub leans against a mound of moss, the lower half given over to some kind of black mold.

A tire swing rotates on a heavy-gauge chain. Atop the tire, a big black crow sits, turning with the swing as if he's enjoying the ride.

She steps on seashells. Brittle. They break underfoot.

Miriam tries to say something. Her mouth is still taped. It comes out a soggy mumble. She breathes through her nose: a low, dry whistle.

Ahead, a small cabin. White siding, the bottom fringed with moss.

At least it's not another motel, she thinks.

She fades out.

Rip.

Miriam's eyes jolt open. The world rushes in with a windy *whoosh*: a river of blood in her ears, an undertow pulling her back toward full-bore consciousness.

Miriam finds herself hanging in a shower with faded tiles the color of sea foam.

Her hands are bound above, draped over a shower head.

Her feet, also bound, barely touch the tub beneath her. She has to stand on tippy-toes. She has no traction, only the ability to wriggle like a worm on a hook.

Frankie stands in the doorway, too tall for it. He stoops to fit himself in.

Hairless relaxes on the toilet. Streaks of dried blood—the mascara of a weepy girl—mar his cheeks. In his lap rests Miriam's diary. Gently, he shuts it.

Harriet flaps the electrical tape she's just yanked from Miriam's mouth in front of Miriam's face—a strange taunt—and backs away.

"I have read this book," Hairless says, tapping the notebook against his leg.

"Fuck you," Miriam mutters.

Hairless shakes his head as Harriet squeezes her hand into a black glove. "Such a boring refrain from you. Fuck this, fuck that, fuck me, fuck you. Such a crass little girl. Harriet, I see the ghost of a bruise around this girl's eye. Please, will you wake the dead?"

Harriet steps up onto the rim of the tub and pops Miriam in the eye with the gloved fist. Miriam's head rocks backward, hits the wall. *Wham.*

"There we go, yes," Hairless says. "That will remind you to be polite when you are in such esteemed company. Now, speaking of the dead. You have an intimate connection with the dead, do you not?"

"The dying," Miriam croaks. "Not so much the dead."

"Yes, and we're all dying, aren't we?"

"We are. Well put."

"Thank you. See? That is the politeness I was hoping you might offer. Good." Hairless holds up the book and gestures with it. "I believe what you write in this book is true. I do not think it the fantasy of a deranged girl, deranged as you may be. May I tell you of my *oma*, my grandmother?"

"Go for it. I'm not going anywhere."

Hairless smiles. A fond remembrance flashes in his eyes.

THE WITCH WOMAN

My grandmother, Milba, was a witch woman.

Even as a little girl picking cranberries out in the bog, she could see things. Her visions did not happen unbidden, but by her studying the world around her. She would touch things, things of nature, things of the bog, and those things would show her what was coming.

If she found the bones of a snake, she could handle them, let them roll around in her small fingers and watch how the bog water ran off them, and therein she might see what would happen to her father later that day when he went to market, or how her sister might suffer a splinter under the nail of her toe.

She could smash the berries in her palms and read the red guts. They might tell her what weather was coming. By running her hands up the bark of a tree, she might learn what birds nested there, and by breaking the neck of a rabbit kit, she might learn where the rest of the rabbits had their warren.

Later, when I was a child and we had come to this country, my *oma* would sit out on the front stoop of our house, sharpening her knives across the sidewalk and steps. She would hull peas or break beans and close her eyes to see what they might tell her. By old age, Oma was small and withered, a bent stick with arthritic claws and a nose like a fishhook, and the neighbors thought her strange, the way she babbled, and so they called her a witch.

They called her a witch as an insult. They did not know she had visions. They did not know the truth of it.

They would come to learn it.

There came a day when I had been abused at school again. I was a thin child, sickly, and it did not help that I had been born without a single sprout of hair on my worm's body. It also did not help that my English was not particularly good at the time, and I often had trouble speaking as well as the other children.

The boy who bullied me, a boy named Aaron, was a Jew. He was fat in the stomach and had big muscles and curly hair, and he said he hated me because I was a German, a "fuckin' Nazi," even though I was not German. I am Dutch, I would tell him, Dutch.

It did not matter. At first, the abuse was what you would expect. He would hold me down and beat on me until my nose bled and bruises covered my body.

But as the days went on, he did worse things.

He burned my arm with match tips. He pushed things into my ears—little stones, sticks, ants—until I suffered from infections. He grew more brazen, crueler. He had me pull down my pants and he did things to me—he cut my inner thighs with a knife, and stabbed at my buttocks with it.

So, I went to my grandmother. I wanted to know when this would all end. I said to her, show me, show me how it ends. I knew what she was, what she could do, but I had always been too afraid of it—too afraid of *her*—to ask. But now I was desperate.

Oma told me she would help me. She sat me down and said, "Do not be scared of what I can see, because what I can see is part of nature. It is natural. I read natural things, like bones or leaves or fly wings, and they tell me what is coming. The world has its strange balance, and what I can see is no more magic than how you look down the road and see a mailbox or a man walking—I simply see how everything will balance out."

Oma had a jar of teeth, teeth she had collected from many

animals over many years, and she emptied that jar in front of me. She had me open one of the scabs on my arms from the burning matches, and she took some of my blood on her fingertips and ran them across the scattered teeth.

Oma told me, "Your suffering will be over soon. Tomorrow night."

I was excited. I said, "That soon?"

And she said yes. She had foreseen it. Aaron would meet his end.

"He will die?" I asked.

She nodded. I was not sad about this. I was not conflicted. I felt happy.

The next night, I waited in my bed the way that a child might wait for Christmas morning. I could not sleep. I was too excited, and a little scared.

I heard a sound outside. Scraping. Metal on stone.

It was Oma. She took one of her kitchen knives, sharpened it on the stoop, and then went to Aaron's house—which was only down the street by less than a mile. A withered shadow, she crept into his room. And while he slept, she stabbed him. A hundred times.

She came back to my room and told me what she had done, and she gave me the knife.

"Sometimes, we must choose what we see down the road," she said.

And then she went outside to wait.

They came for her in the early morning hours. She made no mystery about what she had done—her gown was covered in the bully's blood. I do not know what they came to do to her, maybe kill her, but it was too late.

She had died there on the stoop.

A bent little shape, a weeping willow, dead.

I wept for her.

I did not weep for Aaron.

THIRTY-ONE

HAIRLESS FUCKER DIES

"That's a great story," Miriam says. "I really like the way it proves nothing about your grandmother's magic powers, the way she says something's going to come true and then she goes and stabs a little boy to death to make it true. That's super. I *totally* see why you believe this stuff."

Hairless's smile fades. His tone is sharp, steely.

"You watch your tongue, or I will bite it off. Oma was a true spirit. She saved my life when I was too weak to do so."

Miriam says nothing. She just feels the pulsing ring from where Harriet hit her.

The small, stocky woman paces back and forth in front of the tub, fist still tightened.

"She also taught me that the universe has rules. Rules that are hidden from men, unless one is willing to look deeper, to kick over the log and see what squirms underneath."

Hairless pulls out his satchel and shakes it. Something that sounds like dice clatter together. "I collect bones. It is what I read."

Miriam coughs. "Great, you've got the voodoo, too."

For a moment, the Hairless Fucker says nothing. Then he nods. "Yes."

Miriam's not so sure. She thinks he's lying. Maybe he convinced himself of it, or maybe he's just hoping to convince others.

"Still," he says, "you have abilities far more precise than most. You have abilities on par with my *oma*. That impresses me. It *thrills* me."

"Happy to be entertaining."

"I always need good people in my organization."

"And what organization is that?"

"Acquisition and distribution."

"Drugs, drugs, guns, drugs, sex slaves, drugs."

His eyes twinkle.

"I can't help you," she says.

"You can. You have vision. You're not a moral person."

"That stings," she says. And it does. She says it all snarky, but it genuinely stings. An evil man like this thinks he's found a bird of his feather? "I'm a bad girl, not a bad person."

"There is a difference?"

Miriam's eyes are two knife-holes, out of which pour hatred.

"I did not think so," he says, stroking her diary with long fingers. "You will work for me, then. Welcome to the team. The organization appreciates your unique skill set."

"I'd like to discuss my benefits."

Hairless chuckles. "Oh?"

"I don't need health benefits, because I drink too much, and I smoke even more. In fact, right now I'm kind of ready to gnaw my hands off for a cigarette. So, in return for saving you some money with those health insurance companies—they're vampires, don't you know—I propose that you simply let my friend, Louis, be. Just let it lie."

"But what of my suitcase?"

"I can get it for you. Let me go to him. I can get the case, no questions."

"You're offering this to me? As a negotiation?"

"I am. I'll work for you if you spare him."

She sees him consider it. The offer passes before his face like a shadow. He cups his chin. He rubs the flat of his hand against his Hairless Fucker head. But then she realizes: He's just putting on a show. Hairless is mocking her.

"Hmm," he says, dragging out the consonance. "No."

"Fine, then I don't work for you."

"You are not in a negotiating position. The lowest, sickliest wolf in the pack does not negotiate with the alpha for a bigger bite of the kill. It is not done. You would not respect me if I gave in to your wishes. I sense you are a, how to put it? A *get an inch, take a mile* kind of girl, yes? I give a little now, and you walk all over me. I am not your father."

"No shit. Your dull, Eurotrash seed couldn't father a donkey. Though I'm sure you've tried, you froufrou piece-of-shit donkey-fucker skinhead."

"Besides," Hairless says, ignoring her. "You obviously care about this man in the truck. That is a no-no. I must take away those things you care about, so all that is left is me."

He approaches the tub after setting her diary down on the closed lid of the toilet.

He puts one foot on the tub's edge. He floats his hands above her hips—he does not touch them, but his fingers hover. They hover up over her stomach, her tits.

"I am all that you need to care about. My approval. My smiling face. They know."

Harriet and Frankie—the "they" in question—shoot looks to each other. Frankie looks uncomfortable, but Harriet's dull eyes dance for a half second; they flash like mirrors.

"Your first task for me—" His nimble fingers, each pointed like it's nothing but bone sharpened to a narrow tip, drift over her collarbone and neck. Miriam has a tiny daydream in which her hands break free and (like she's the Bride of the Incredible Hulk) she brings the shower head down out of the wall, burying it into the Hairless Fucker's shiny dome. "—is to tell me how I die."

She hawks a looger, spits it at his eye. Bull's-eye. "No."

He wipes it away with the back of his hand.

"I know that all it takes is skin on skin," he says.

Then he grabs her chin with vice-grip fingers—

Reggaeton bangs a dull Dem Bow beat from the back of a nightclub; the alley is awash in long shadows and the fringe glow of neon from the street. Hairless emerges from those long shadows alone, no Harriet, no Frankie.

Pastel pink suit, black shoes, mirrored shades despite the midnight hour.

His face is marked by deeper lines. Even his scalp is starting to tighten with time, as this is seven years—almost eight, really—into the future.

His steps onto a set of metal stairs heading to the back door of the club.

Hairless's gaze flicks imperceptibly: A big black sonofabitch, skin as dark as volcanic glass, emerges from behind a Dumpster. Mister Midnight's got a black vest on, open to the front, showcasing an oiled, sweat-slick chest with little afro-puffs of hair dotting the obsidian flesh.

The door at the top of the stairs opens a crack but no more.

Mister Midnight walks without a sound. He's on the steps. One tremendous foot after the other, coming up behind Hairless.

Hairless pretends not to notice.

When Mister Midnight makes his move, the Hairless Fucker is ready.

The big sonofabitch pulls a curved blade, a kukri, out of nowhere. It comes down on Hairless, or that's what it's supposed to do. Instead, it kisses air as Hairless deftly pivots and presses himself back against the railing.

A flash of metal. Hairless's hand dances (a painter's hand).

A straight razor in his grip draws quick Xs across Mister Midnight's exposed chest.

But the big sonofabitch isn't taking it. His elbow crashes against Hairless's wrist. The straight razor spirals away, hits the metal steps, clang, and is gone.

At the top of the steps, the back door to the club creaks open. The beat grows louder.

With his two long-fingered hands, Hairless grabs Mister Midnight's head the way one might hunker down to eat a too-big burger. And eat he does. He bites the big sonofabitch's nose, the cheek, the jaw. He wrenches his head side to side. Blood spatters the wall and steps.

Mister Midnight screams.

Then two gunshots.

Someone has emerged onto the top of the steps. A spindly drug addict with a knit cap pulled low and meth craters pocking his cheeks.

A .38 snubnose in his hand blows lazy smoke. Two roses of blood bloom on Hairless's back as he lets go of Mister Midnight. The big sonofabitch, clutching his raw-meat face, starts to go down—and, as he does, Hairless effortlessly snatches the curved kukri from the man's failing grip.

Hairless turns on the addict, blade raised high.

His face is a grinning, crimson rictus. A skull with bloodstain lipstick.

Hairless lunges at the addict.

The blade cleaves the addict's head right down the middle.

The gun goes off.

Hairless's brains fly like someone tossing out muddy washwater.

Blood zigzags down his face. He looks around. He sits down on the steps as the addict comes tumbling down next to him. The red stuff drips past his nose to his lips, and he licks them and makes a look like he's pondering the taste, seriously thinking about becoming a cannibal. And then he slumps to the side, dead.

—and he presses her cheeks so hard that her teeth bite into the inside of her mouth.

He holds her there like that, staring into her eyes.

"You saw," he whispers. "You saw how I die."

Miriam nods, as much as his grasp will allow.

Beaming, he lets go. He's eager. Excited. "Tell me. Tell me, now."

Miriam grins a rueful grin.

"I kill you," she lies. "Me. I shoot you *right in the fucking head.*"

Hairless searches her face. His gaze is panicked. *You can make me have my vision,* she thinks, *but you can't make me tell you the truth.*

"She's lying," Harriet says. "I can see it."

Hairless steps away.

"You'll tell me," he says, still unsure. "You'll tell me so I can beat it. I will beat fate. I will sidestep death with your help, one way or another."

"Doesn't work like that," Miriam says, tasting the bloody penny tang from where she bit into her cheeks. "You can't beat the system. The house always wins."

"I am different."

Hairless's phone rings. He holds it up, looks at the number, then snaps his fingers at Frankie. "You. Let our new employee have her rest."

Hairless answers the phone as Frankie ducks through the doorway and comes back with another syringe.

Miriam struggles, hoping to bring the shower down, maybe the whole house.

Frankie sticks the needle in her neck.

"Yes?" Hairless says on the phone.

The world hems in from the edges. Rimmed with blur and shadow.

"You have the location?" she hears Hairless say, but it's like hearing him through the glass of a bubbling fish tank. His words slow. Honey, molasses, black tar. "You know where the trucker is, then?"

Louis, she thinks.

Once more, she tongue-kisses darkness. Lights out.

THE DREAM

Miriam's mother sits at a table but doesn't notice her. Can't notice her, probably. That's the frustrating part. Miriam hasn't seen the woman in eight years, and this doesn't even count because it's a dream, and she knows it's a dream.

Her mother is a pinched woman, shrunken and dry like a shriveled apricot. She's not that old, not really, but she looks it. Time—fake time, dream time, the time in Miriam's own crazy head—has taken its toll.

"It's almost over now," says Louis behind her.

The tape over his eyes shifts and bubbles, the way soft drywall rises and falls with a tide of hidden roaches.

"Yeah," Miriam says.

"What are we looking at?" Louis checks his wrist like he's looking at a watch, even though no watch is there. "Twenty-four hours or thereabouts."

Her mother opens a Bible, studies the pages.

"But if the sacrifice of his offering be a vow," her mother says, "or a voluntary offering, it shall be eaten the same day he offereth the sacrifice, and on the morrow also the remainder shall be eaten. But the remainder of the flesh of the sacrifice on the third day shall be burnt by fire."

Idly, lost in thought, Miriam nods. "That what it is? Funny how you know that, because if *you* know that, it means *I* know that, and yet—I didn't know that. I haven't seen the time since the . . . car ride."

"Could be that the subconscious mind is a powerful little booger."

"I suppose so."

"Or maybe I'm something bigger, meaner, something outside of you. Maybe I'm Death himself. Maybe I'm Abaddon, Lord of the Pit, or Shiva, Destroyer of Worlds. Or perhaps it's that I'm just a bundle of thread cut from the mean, uncaring scissors of Atropos—I'm just the tangled skein of fate lying on the floor at your feet."

"That's great. Thanks for fucking with me in my own dream."

Her mother speaks again: "For every kind of beasts, and of birds, and of serpents, and of things in the sea, is tamed, and hath been tamed of mankind: But the tongue can no man tame; it is an unruly evil, full of deadly poison."

"Shut up, Mom." To Louis, Miriam says, "That's her telling me I have a filthy mouth."

"It's you telling you that you have a filthy mouth."

"Whatever."

"What happens next?" he asks.

"Nothing, I guess. Last I checked, I was hanging from a dirty showerhead in a moldy cottage found somewhere in the approximate middle of New Jersey's sandy asshole. As such, I'm not really making any plans."

"So, you're done with trying to save me?"

"Well, looking at my options—"

"Give, and it shall be given to you," her mother interrupts.

"I'm talking, Mom."

Her mother continues: "For whatever measure you deal out to others, it will be dealt back to you in return."

"As I was saying!" Miriam barks, hoping to jar her dream

mother out of her Bible-quoting reverie. The woman doesn't budge. She's like a kidney stone lodged in the urethra—not going anywhere. "As I was saying, I'm out of options. I'm done trying to play savior, done thinking I can make a difference."

"That's awfully fatalistic."

"Fatalistic. Fate. Fatal. Would you look at that? Ain't language a crazy bitch? Stupid me, never drawn the connection before. Fate and fatal. That tells you something, doesn't it? It tells you that all our lives are a donkey-cart ride over a cliff's edge. Everybody's fate is to die, and why try to stop it? We all tumble into darkness with the donkey, braying and hee-hawing, and that's that; game over. I see the fatalities of people. I see how their fate plays out. And I haven't been able to do dick about it before, have I? It's like trying to stop a speeding train by putting a penny on the tracks."

"That actually works."

"It does not; shut up. I'm fucked here, which means you're fucked, too."

"He stabs out my eyes."

Miriam's heart goes cold. "I know."

"I call your name before I die. Isn't that strange?"

"No," she lies.

"I'm going to die."

"Everybody dies."

"I die badly, painfully, tortured to death."

"It is what it is."

"You did this to me. You have to undo it."

"Fate gets what fate wants."

Her mother turns to her.

She looks into Miriam's eyes. Even though she's sitting, she reaches up with arms made long, so long they stretch across the room, and pulls Miriam to her. The world shifts, drags, smears in long blurs and streaks of light.

Her mother says, "And thine eye shall not pity, but life shall go for life, eye for eye, tooth for tooth, hand for hand, foot for foot."

Miriam stammers, "I don't understand—"

And then the dream is rudely ended.

THIRTY-TWO

AIN'T TORTURE GRAND?

Rudely ended by a fist, actually.

Harriet's fist. Right in Miriam's solar plexus. The air sucks out of her lungs. She'd double over if she could, but she can't, so instead, she just coughs like she's trying to expel a squirming knot of angry weasels from her chest cavity.

"Awake now?" Harriet asks.

Miriam blinks away the haze from whatever drugs Frankie stuck into her. She notices that Harriet is wearing black gloves. *So I don't see how she dies? Is she really that much of a control freak?*

"In a manner of—" She wants to say *speaking*, but she only wheezes and hacks, trying to find breath to fill her windbags.

"The solar plexus is an excellent place to hit," Harriet explains. "At least, it is if your target is untrained. It's a massive bundle of nerves. Fighters know to toughen and tighten that area. They strengthen the muscles there to form a braid of armor. For everybody else, though, it's a beautiful and easy target to strike."

Miriam draws one last gasp, feels like her body has caught up with itself.

"Thanks for the MMA fighting lesson, Tito Ortiz."

"I don't know who that is."

Miriam licks her dry, cracked lips. "Not really a surprise. So, hey, thanks for waking me up out of my dream. It was getting a little too creepy in there for me; my head is no longer a safe place to visit, I think. To what do I owe the pleasure?"

Harriet's hand forms a flat hatchet blade, and she chops it right into Miriam's neck.

Miriam gags and gasps anew. Her face goes red. Her eyes feel like they might suck back into her brain, or pop out and roll across the floor.

"The throat," Harriet clarifies. "Hit it too hard, the windpipe collapses, the target dies. Hit it just hard enough, and you can stimulate the gag reflex; an instant limiter in a fight. The body in panic state, offering the attacker critical advantage."

When Miriam can breathe again, and when she's curtailed the urge to dry-heave the dust and acid that's probably lining her stomach, she speaks.

"Why the"—*hack, cough*—" play-by-play?"

"Because I want you to know that I know what I'm doing."

"Again, why?"

"So your instinct will be to fear me. Eventually, my very presence becomes torture. If a man abuses a dog enough, soon the dog fears all men. The dog becomes weak. The creature exists in the *flight* mode of *fight or flight*, always ready to piss itself and turn tail."

Miriam almost laughs. "Trust me, I fear you. I fear the unmerciful shit out of you. Though, truth be told, I also fear that haircut of yours. It looks like someone cut it with a fire ax. Jesus, you could probably slit somebody's throat with those bangs."

Harriet just delivers three hammer punches to Miriam's armpit.

Miriam's body is a switchboard of pain. She cries out.

"Armpit. Another major bundle of nerves."

"What do you want?" Miriam shouts. "You want to ask me something? I'll tell you! Just ask. Stop it, please. Just stop."

"Begging. That's new for you."

Miriam almost weeps. "I like to remain versatile. Like a shark, swim forward or die. So, just ask me what you want to ask me. I'm an open book."

"I have nothing to ask you."

"You're not trying to find out how Hairless dies?"

Harriet shakes her head.

"Then why are you doing this?"

Harriet smiles. It's a scary sight. Her teeth are small, tiny white pebbles in that ankle-biter mouth. "Because I really enjoy it."

Shit. She's going to kill you.

Miriam has to find a way out of this. To forestall it, then stop it.

Miriam reaches: "Hairless wants you to torture me endlessly? Seems strange that you're just going to abuse your new coworker into bloody, babbling uselessness."

"He doesn't know. This isn't his desire. It's mine." Harriet's eye twinkles. "Sometimes a girl has to take a little time for herself."

"And a mani-pedi just wouldn't do?"

Harriet puts one foot up on the tub's rim.

"You and me," she says, "we're alike."

"That's true," Miriam says, going with it. But she thinks, *On Bizarroworld.*

"We're both survivors. We both do what we have to do to make it to the next day. But even more important, you and I enjoy what we do. You're a monster, and I'm a monster, and we embrace it. I embrace it more than you, of course. You still pretend that you're troubled, tortured, a little drama queen with the back of her hand pressed to her head—*oh, woe is me.* I've moved past that."

"Nothing about you is troubled or tortured?" Miriam asks.

"Nothing that bothers me anymore. I've let it all go."

"How'd you manage that?"

"Ingersoll showed me the way."

"Hairless? And how's that? I bet it's a real interesting story."

Harriet tells her.

HARRIET'S STORY

I chopped up my husband and ran him through the garbage disposal.

THIRTY-THREE

SHORT, BUT NOT SWEET

Miriam waits to see if there's more.

Harriet stands firm-jawed, flexing her fists.

Somewhere, crickets are chirping. Tumbleweeds are tumbling. Between Miriam and Harriet sits a giant gulf, a wide-open space occupied by a howling wind and not much more.

As a delaying tactic, this does Miriam little good.

"That's it?" Miriam says.

Harriet seems confused. "What do you mean?"

"That's not a story. That's the end of a story."

"It suits me fine."

"I just figure," Miriam says, "that there's more to this tale. You don't just one day up and chop up your husband and stuff him down the—garbage disposal? Really?"

"It's doable," Harriet says without inflection. "Not the bones. But the rest."

"Your husband."

"My husband."

Once more, silence. The house around them settles: creaking, squeaking, a quiet cracking like the sound of a spoon hitting the burnt-sugar crust of crème brûlée.

"I just—I just feel like a story is hiding in there somewhere."

Harriet steps up over the tub's lip and elbows Miriam in the face. In the jaw, actually. Miriam sees a burst of white light followed by a sucking vortex of outer space, like a black hole coming for her on a galloping horse. Once more, she tastes blood. Her tongue idly searches out a wiggly tooth toward the back of her mouth.

Miriam turns her head and spits scarlet sputum against the faded tile. *Spat.* She thinks first about hawking it into Harriet's eye, but at this point, she can't imagine that would be productive. Maybe later.

"Oooo-kay," Miriam says, already feeling her lip going fat and numb, "so you just one day up and decided to hack up your husband and shove him into the garbage disposal."

"It was deserved, if that's what you're asking."

"It's not. But it sounds like, contrary to what you were suggesting earlier, there's more to the story." Miriam blinks. "I think I'm drooling blood."

"You are."

"Oh. Good to know."

Harriet's cell phone vibrates. She opens it, looks at the screen so that Miriam cannot see. Her face shows no emotion, but she does pause and seem to consider.

Then, finally, Harriet shrugs and tells her story in full.

HARRIET'S STORY, THIS TIME WITH FEELING

Walter never made sense to me.

I married him because it's what you did. It's what my mother did. My grandmother. It's what all the girls in my neighborhood did. They found men, and they supported those men through thick and thin. In my life, women were crutches. Stepping stools. Vacuum cleaners with breasts.

My husband never had any sense of elegance, no grasp of sequence or consequence.

When a storm rides up the coast, it leaves debris. Loose boards, paper cups, flotsam, jetsam. Nothing but discards and broken things.

That was Walter. He'd come home from work—sales manager at a pigment plant, where they sold dyes and pigments to cosmetic manufacturers, mostly—and his process was a casting-off, a dismissal of the order I'd created.

That's what I remember most about Walter. The signs of his passing.

He'd have pigment on his shoes, and there'd be blue footprints on the carpet.

He'd kick those shoes off under the coffee table and leave them there.

Dirty handprints on a shirt, a curtain, the armrests of his chair.

A tie hanging on a doorknob or the headboard to our bed.

A greasy highball glass on the corner of the nightstand.

His very touch was like cancer. He'd take a good thing—organization, cleanliness, perfection—and subvert it, diminish it, dirty it up and dry it out.

Our intimate life was no different. He'd lie atop me, grunting and thrusting. Always with that grotesque slapping of skin, like the sound of a chorus of frogs or toads forever applauding.

His hands were always so sweaty. His hair, too, by the end of it. I felt drowned in the stuff. He ate submarine sandwiches during the day. Oil, vinegar, onion, garlic. It came out in his sweat; wherever he touched me, he left that odor behind. I felt greasy. Pawed. Molested.

Walter was a clumsy ape.

Three years into our marriage, Walter wanted to have children. He told me so right after dinner. We never ate together; it was always him at the coffee table and me in the other room, at the breakfast nook, waiting for him to be done so I could go try to clean up his messes before they left a permanent mark.

That night, I'd made rigatoni in pink sauce, a vodka sauce. I remember this as plain as day. One of the noodles had jumped the edge of his plate—he was always so sloppy with his eating—and sat there on the carpet. It was like a worm, burrowing in. The melted Parmesan cheese had already stuck to the fibers. The pink sauce had already soaked in. I thought, I'll need to steam-clean the whole carpet. Again.

That's when he said it.

He stood up, put his hand on the small of my back as I bent over to pick up the fallen noodle, and said it so matter-of-factly.

"Let's have kids."

Three words. Each word a clump of dirt. Each a dirty noodle on the carpet.

I stood up and I had my first moment of rebellion.

I said, "We'll have children when you stop acting like a dirty little baby."

Walter had a chance there. He could have saved himself. He could have said something nice or just said nothing.

But he opened his mouth and said, "You watch your goddamn mouth."

And he did this . . . thing. He grabbed my wrist—the wrist that led to the hand that still held that stupid rigatoni noodle—and he gripped my wrist tight, so tight it hurt. He meant for it to hurt. I saw it in his eyes.

I pulled my hand free.

"That settles that," he said.

Then I walked into the kitchen.

I went to the blender. It was old, an Oster two-speed with the beehive base and the heavy glass pitcher.

I picked it up by the handle, and I marched back into the living room.

Walter had slumped back down in his chair. He looked up at me as I stood there.

"What are you doing with that?" he asked.

And I bashed it over his head.

It didn't knock him out, but it hurt him very badly. He fell out of the chair, bleeding, and couldn't stand up, no matter how many times he tried.

I pulled him into the kitchen.

I got out the block of kitchen knives, plus a meat tenderizer, plus a meat cleaver.

I cut him apart. Starting out and moving in, so he was alive for much of it. Fingers whittled down. Toes. Fillets of calf, thigh, bicep. Two hundred pounds of flesh. And buckets of blood settling into the grout lines of the kitchen tile.

I put his bones in trash bags. I put his meat into the garbage disposal.

The disposal was a good one. It only jammed at the end, with his scalp hair. It broke it, actually. Smoke drifted up from inside the drain's mouth.

I didn't know what to do, then, so I called the police and waited.

They arrested me. I didn't resist.

No bail for me. The community was apparently quite shocked at the turn of events. Our neighborhood was quiet, middle-class; the most that ever shook the sheets was a domestic abuse charge, or maybe some kid setting off car alarms.

A wife chopping up her husband was a big deal.

It made national news for a while—just a blip, but an important blip.

It attracted Ingersoll to me.

They went to transfer me to the courthouse for trial, but it's not like they had me under intense scrutiny and security. I was an early-thirties housewife who had quietly gone along with everything they asked.

They didn't expect a truck to broadside the van.

They didn't expect me to be extracted and whisked away.

But that's what happened. Ingersoll found my story and believed that something very important—something very useful to him—could be found in me.

He was right. He's been spending the better part of ten years grooming me. Cultivating my cruelty the way you might prune a bonsai tree. It's more about what you cut away than what you leave behind, I assure you.

That's where I'm at today. I owe him everything. That's why what I'm going to do today, with you, pains me so very much. The last thing I want to do is disappoint him.

But this is what he instilled in me.

I do not enjoy competition. Too many mouths and not enough food. You see?

THIRTY-FOUR

SUICIDE IS PAINLESS

Miriam's blood is an icy slush. Its sluggish passing beneath her skin leaves a trail of gooseflesh above.

"I get it," she says, quiet.

"This organization doesn't have room for the both of us."

Miriam tilts her head and wipes her bloody, drooly chin on her hyperextended shoulder.

"This book," Harriet says, picking up the diary off the toilet lid. "I read everything you've written in here. You and I come from a similar place. Small-town suburbs. Repressive family life. A yearning to do and be more than what your life allows. With just the right push, you could come to love the things you can see and do as a result."

"I'm not cruel. I'm not like you."

Harriet raps her knuckles against the diary's cover.

"One difference does exist," Harriet notes. "Even Ingersoll's steady hand and my life experience would not—could not—pull you out of this nose dive you've created for yourself."

"Nose dive."

"Yes. I know how to read what's on the page and what you've written between the lines." Harriet's eyes are now alive, alive in a way they weren't when she was physically hurting Miriam. This hurt, the hurt that's coming, is going to cut way deeper.

"And what did I write?"

"You're planning on killing yourself."

Miriam says nothing. The only sound is her breathing—labored, whistling through dry nostrils, sucked in through bloody lips.

"I never wrote that in there," she finally says.

"Not a convincing denial."

"It's true. I never wrote that. Don't know where you get the idea."

"You make it as clear as possible without ever coming out and writing it. You note the number of pages left in nearly every entry. You even hint that you're counting down to something. That it could be all over. That it's the end of the line. Pair that with the fact you hate yourself, hate what you can do and *see*, and the conclusion isn't a hard one to reach. Am I right?"

"It's bullshit."

"Really? I think your suicide is one last grab for power. You talk a lot about fate in here. But you still don't know how you die, do you?" Harriet grins. "Suicide is you taking that power for yourself. It's your way of saving that little boy with the balloon."

A pair of tears runs down Miriam's cheek, warm over the bruises and blood.

"It's okay," Harriet says. "I understand."

It's true, Miriam thinks. This has been her plan all along. The end of the diary is an easy target. Any time she visits someone's death—and steals from them like a thieving magpie or chewing maggot—she writes an entry in the diary: one more page down, one page closer to the finale. She never knows how it will happen. When the time comes, she'll do it by whatever means are at hand. The world offers its residents a billion ways to die: knife, gun, pills, fire, step in front of a car, fall backward over a cliff, swim out to the center of a frozen lake, kick a gang thug in the junk. She can grab a fistful of gravel on the side of the road and eat it. She can steal a cop's gun and run into a Gymboree full of kindergarten kids. Dying is easy.

She has no specific scenario in mind, because it feels smarter that way, like she's surprising fate, sneaking up on it with tiny footsteps. It's the same reason she never comes out and says it in the book. If she never says it aloud, never writes it down, fate can't know.

Silly logic, she thinks. But some part of her wonders.

Harriet opens her cell phone and thumbs a button a couple times.

Then she lifts the phone and shows it to Miriam.

It's a blurry camera-phone image. It shows the back of a tractor-trailer.

Miriam knows whose it is before Harriet tells her.

"They found your friend. They're trailing him right now. It'll all be over soon."

Eyes. Brain. Rusty fish knife. Lighthouse.

Miriam blinks away the tears, but those fuckers keep on coming.

Harriet holds up the diary. "Nine pages left."

Then she tears out the blank pages, one by one.

Each is like a knife-slash across Miriam's heart. Each *rip*—which Harriet draws out, accentuates as if for its beautiful music—cuts deep.

Harriet flips the blank, ragged pages over her shoulder.

She comes to the last page.

"Dear Diary," Harriet says, as if reading real words on a real page. "This is my last entry. My trucker boyfriend died a painful death at the hands of my new employer. Life is very hard. Fate is fate and blah, blah, blah."

She tears out that page.

It's stupid, but Miriam can't bear to watch.

Miriam hears, but does not see, the flap of the page as Harriet throws it into the air. Then the sound of the book dropped to the floor.

She opens her eyes. Harriet's right in her face, holding a gun and a small lockback knife.

"What are you doing?" Miriam asks.

"Time to get docile."

In one swift motion, Harriet reaches up and cuts the zip tie binding Miriam's hands above the showerhead. Miriam's not ready. Her still-bound feet—on tiptoes, always on the tiptoes—can't get balance. The way her muscles ache, the way they've been stretched and tingle from the lack of blood, doesn't give her enough feeling or movement for her to stop her fall—

Wham.

The back of her head cracks against the faucet. She tries to stand, but the tub is slippery, and she pitches forward, belly-down. Her eyes go blurry. Dark spots float in her vision. She feels her feet lift up, not of her own volition, and something tugs at them— *snick.* Then her feet hit the porcelain, the zip tie between them cut in twain.

"I—" Miriam stammers. "I don't unner-understand."

She hears Harriet's voice at her ear: "I said, I need you docile."

The butt of the pistol cracks down on Miriam's collarbone. Pain explodes. Harriet flips Miriam over and starts hammering her with the gun—literally. Harriet's got the gun barrel in her pudgy doll's hand, and she brings the butt down again and again like she's trying to bash nails through boards. The gun butt slams into Miriam's ribs, her stomach, the side of her neck, everywhere. Her body is a thousand nodes of agony.

Blood back in her hands, she does it before she realizes it—

She punches Harriet right in the ear.

The little Napoleon stumbles out of the tub, clutching the side of her head. Miriam struggles to clamber over the lip of the porcelain and falls to the tile floor shoulder-first.

"Maybe you're not clear," Harriet growls, "on the definition of *docile.*"

She grabs Miriam by the hair, slams her head into the side of the tub.

Miriam's world rings like a goddamn bell. It barely even hurts anymore. It's mostly a dull *thudding*, like she's just a bag of sand that someone keeps hitting with a cinderblock. Part of her thinks, *The pain is over, at least*, but it turns out that this is an entirely inaccurate sentiment.

Before she knows what's happening, Harriet's got her on her wobbly feet, and Miriam wonders why she sees herself standing in front of her. *Is this a near-death experience? An out-of-body moment?* She stares into her own eyes for a moment, blinking.

Then she rushes to meet herself, like maybe she's going to give her own lips a drunken, sloppy, blood-bubbled kiss—

Crack.

Her skull feels like an apple that's been split with a camping hatchet. It occurs to her: *Harriet just slammed my head into the mirror.*

Sure enough, she sees herself fractured into a thousand little shards, the spider in the center of a jagged web. Pieces drop away. Blood soaks her face.

Harriet—now surprisingly gentle—rests Miriam on the floor, face up.

"There we go," Harriet says. "A docile little girl."

Miriam tries to say something, but she only blows bubbles of red spittle. Her wet lips smack together. Sound reaches her ears too late, or distorted, like she's in an oil drum. And every time her heart beats, it's like someone pounds on the outside of that oil drum with a sledgehammer. Miriam's a piece of ruined meat. She feels raw.

She tries to push herself up, but her hands won't even get underneath her. They just slide away, spread-eagled, fingers curling in like the legs of a dead bug.

Her head tilts, cheek against the tile—an act that occurs not of her own volition.

The floor is cool, and she wants just to lie there and close her eyes and curl up there forever. *Maybe I'll die here,* she thinks, and not far away she sees one of the blank pages from her diary half curled against a radiator. *Maybe this is the end of the line.*

Maybe that's okay.

A heavy weight suddenly rests on her chest.

Groggy, she tilts her chin and sees Harriet above, smiling.

The gun is on her chest. Every time her heart beats, the pistol trembles.

"Consider the gun a present," Harriet says. She sounds like she's speaking to Miriam from the other side of a burbling fish tank. "The diary is done. Your trucker boyfriend will be dead by dusk. You hurt all over. Make the pain go away."

Make the pain go away.

The words echo.

Harriet smiles and retreats from the room, softly closing the door behind her.

The gun sits on Miriam's chest like a boat anchor.

Her hand—numb, feeling like a giant pillow—flops up onto her chest and feels for the weapon. She tries to curl her finger around the trigger, but it's hard, too hard for such a simple action. Instead, the finger lies across the trigger guard, a worm on a sunbaked road.

It's over, she thinks.

Louis is dead soon. She can't see the time, but she can feel it in her every thundering pulse-beat that the hour is nigh.

The diary is done.

She's been privy to so many deaths.

Why not her own?

This is her power. This is what she can take from fate. She can take her own life in her own hands, snatch it out of destiny's grip.

Her finger curls around the trigger.

Her mother's voice from the dream reaches her, floating to her like a distant song carried on a slow breeze:

"And thine eye shall not pity, but life shall go for life, eye for eye, tooth for tooth, hand for hand, foot for foot."

She hoists the gun.

Harriet listens, ear pressed tightly to the door.

She hears the stupid girl moving around, slow and sluggish. The brush of her arm against the floor. A moan. The faint rattle of the pistol's mechanisms in an unsteady grip.

Harriet smiles.

This really will be her crowning moment.

She's made people hurt before, but not like this.

Part of her feels bad. That strikes her as disturbing. Yes, she felt some sympathy toward this girl, but guilt? She hasn't felt a pang of guilt since . . . Well, when *was* the last pang of guilt? Has she ever had one?

A sour feeling strikes her gut. Guilt. No use for that.

A sound interrupts the tiny song of remorse inside her: the sound of the gun's hammer being pulled back.

Good girl, Harriet thinks. It makes sense. Pulling the hammer back is easier than just using the trigger. The girl's been worked over. Probably barely has the strength.

She'll hardly have to lift the pistol. Just a pivot, a counterclockwise turn until the barrel is up under her chin, and then—

Right on cue, the gun goes off.

Bang.

Harriet's smile broadens.

As the pistol fires, the door shudders—probably the girl's leg kicking out. Soon will come the awful odor of voided bowels, a smell that is only pleasant due to the associations Harriet has with it, really.

Harriet takes a step away from the door and feels a sharp pain in her head.

She staggers, almost falls, when reaching for the doorknob.

She tries to ask aloud, "Why is my shoulder wet?"

But the words don't form. They can't. Her mouth won't response to her brain's wishes.

Harriet smells something like burning hair.

A small *O* sits in the middle of the door. Smoke drifts up through the pencil-sized hole.

Harriet reaches toward her ear and pulls away a wet, red hand.

She says something—something meant to be a vile expletive, a wild diatribe against the stupid girl in the stupid bathroom who just shot her in the stupid head—but really, her wires are all tangled up now.

All she manages is an exclamation of relative nonsense: "Carpet noodle."

Then she tumbles to the floor.

THIRTY-FIVE

CHOOSING LIFE

For Miriam, choosing life is nothing so grand as seeing the vast reservoir of potential that a continued existence would allow. Her mind's eye does not play movies of kids on swings and a dog in a yard and the warm glow coming off a golden pond.

No, as it is so often with Miriam, her decision to live is one based on spite and anger—a mouth full of vinegar that drives her once more to sabotage her own plans.

She really was going to kill herself.

It made sense. Harriet spoke true.

Her life was shit. She was fate's bitch. She was a fly munching on a turd, or mold consuming a perfectly good banana.

It was time to die, she decided.

Lying on the cold, bloody tile, Miriam felt the gun on her chest. With tiny pushes, pushes that took far too much effort, she spun the weapon so that the barrel was nestled right under her chin.

She thumbed back the hammer so that the trigger pull would be nothing at all, just a little tug, the barest whisper of movement. Just to be sure, she pushed her chin down on the barrel.

But then she saw—

Two shadows underneath the bathroom door.

Two shadows that equated to two feet. Harriet's feet.

She's listening at the door, Miriam thought.

And that pissed her off.

This was her moment. *Her* death. Harriet had lent it a poetic veneer, but now the twat was standing on the other side of the door, snickering like she had stuck Miriam's hand into a cup of warm water while she slept?

She raised the gun. It felt like her muscles were about to tear from their moorings along her arm bones and go slingshotting against the broken mirror.

She didn't aim, didn't try to imagine where it was that Harriet was standing. It was all automatic. A total reflex.

She fired, *bang*.

Seconds later came a mumbled statement (*carpet noodle*) and a thump.

Miriam steps over the body. It takes her a while to get there, what with her body feeling like hammered shit. She sees herself in the mirror before she leaves the bathroom—her face looks like a gray pillowcase stuffed with softballs, and her already-pale skin makes a terrible contrast with the endless streaks of drying red.

She looks like a murder scene.

But she's alive, she thinks, as she stands over Harriet's body.

The stocky woman lies with her mouth open, her blood and brains emptying onto the carpet and soaking in real good.

Miriam looks down at the gloves on Harriet's hands.

"Guess we know how you die after all," Miriam says. It sounds like she's got a mouth full of rocks and molasses. She tries to laugh, but it pains her too much. She coughs. She's afraid her rib cage is going to come up her throat or out her ass. Every square inch of her body throbs.

She nudges Harriet, half expecting Little Napoleon to lurch up and start biting at her Achilles' tendons, but the woman experiences no such miraculous resurrection.

Now: Louis.

Miriam doesn't really believe she can save him. But she knows she's there when it happens. The vision showed her that.

The question is: Where?

No. Wait. The first question is: *When?*

Miriam bends over—*ow, ow, ow*—and finds Harriet's cell phone in the pocket of the dead woman's black pants.

4:30 p.m.

Louis dies in three hours.

Cell phone in hand, Miriam staggers through a moldering kitchen in 70s décor and out through a half-cocked screen door. Outside, gray skies pass above an endless vista of bent and meager pines, each a bleak needle, each a Charlie Brown Christmas tree.

A gravel drive circles the ramshackle cottage, cutting through the pines.

Nearby, on a crooked fencepost with no fence, a fat crow sits staring.

"I don't know where I am," she tells the bird. The crow takes to oily wing. "Thanks for the help."

All right, think, she thinks. *The New Jersey Pine Barrens. That's like, what? Only about a million acres of scrubby pineland and sandy loam. And Louis dies in a lighthouse. New Jersey doesn't have too many of those—ohhhh, only maybe two dozen. I'm sure I can hit all of them in the next three hours, right after I make a beeline for civilization. Which is assuredly right around the corner, and by "right around the corner," I mean "miles from this place."*

This is an impossible task.

It can't be impossible! she thinks. *I'm there. I somehow manage to show up. What fate wants, fate gets, and fate wants my ass in that lighthouse. Think!*

But she can't think. Her brain hits a dull wall, a dead end— and it keeps hitting it, like a bee against a windowpane. Maybe it's the pain that's blunting her brainpower. Maybe shock and trauma are merrily skipping in tandem to drag down her thought processes.

She's looking for a sign. If fate wants her to show up, fate will have to give her a ride.

The cell phone in her hand rings.

It vibrates, too, and it scares her so bad, she almost throws it into the woods like a live hand grenade.

Luckily, she bites back that impulse. She looks at the phone.

Frankie.

Her heart seizes.

She answers the phone.

"What?" she asks, trying to mimic Harriet's matte tone. Her sore throat and swollen lip seem to help.

"How's the girl?" he asks. The signal's weak, but she can still hear him.

"No trouble," Miriam says. She embellishes a bit: "That cocktail kicked her ass."

Frankie pauses.

Shit! Dummy. Don't embellish. Harriet wouldn't embellish.

"You okay?" he asks, suspicious.

"I'm fine."

"You sound different."

"Said I'm fine."

Another pause. "You sound like you wanna do something to that girl. Hurt her, maybe."

"Don't push me."

"Okay! Okay. Jesus, don't get creepy."

Miriam winces, and decides that this is her only shot.

"Where are you at?" she asks.

"We got the trucker. I forgot that he was a big boy. Needed two of the cocktails to put him down, but it worked. Ingersoll's got him in the Escalade, and I'm going to take the truck and go burn it."

"Where you taking him?"

"Ingersoll's got a bug up his ass for somewhere with a little verticality. He says a storm is coming, and he wants to harness its power and, uhh . . . How'd he put it? 'Read the skies.' We got a line on a lighthouse under construction. I guess they're putting in a new . . . big giant light, or whatever the fuck it is you need to replace on a lighthouse."

"Where's the lighthouse?"

"Why?"

Fuck! I don't know why!

She clenches her eyes shut, and tries: "I don't answer to you."

"Sorry," he says. "Uhhhh. Barnegat, I think. Long Beach Island. Wherever it is, it smells like dead fish and medical waste."

"I have to go. The girl is waking up."

"Give her a kiss for me," Frankie says.

"Don't be cute."

Miriam hangs up.

She holds the cell phone in her hand. The pain is still present in her body—it's beating her like a drum—but it no longer bothers her. Miriam feels alive. Present in the moment. In the deep distance, thunder clears its throat with an acid rumble.

Taking a deep breath, Miriam strides out to the driveway.

She gets about ten feet, then turns around.

She's in the cottage for thirty seconds.

When she emerges anew, she has the pistol in one hand, her diary in the other, and the cell phone nestled in her pocket.

She starts walking.

THIRTY-SIX

THE FIRST HOUR

Miriam feels like she's been walking for hours. She checks the phone, and every time it feels like it's five minutes forward, sometimes less.

The gravel road—"road" being the most optimistic term possible for this long stretch of sunken pits and limestone scree—is a straight ribbon through leaning pines and anemic bramble, a ribbon that seems infinitely unrolled. Her steps appear to take her no farther. The adrenalin rush is gone; her muscles stiffen with every step, and a small voice inside her head wonders, *Did I actually die? Maybe this is rigor mortis setting in.*

The trees have grown over the road, a canopy of skeletal hands. Sparrows and starlings flit from branch to branch. Thunder continues to rumble in the distance.

"Thatta girl," Louis says, walking next to her. "I knew you had it in you. Such a *buck-up* spirit. This time, you're embracing fate. You know you show up when Louis dies. So you forge ahead. I like the new you. Be a fountain, not a drain, I always say. Be the leaf in the stream that goes with the waters, not the dam that stands against them. Am I right?"

Miriam has little patience. She offers the hallucination no more than a passing glance and a throaty grunt.

"No glib commentary?" Louis asks. A yellow jacket pushes

its way out from under his eye tape and orbits his head before zipping off into the trees.

"I need a cigarette."

"That's not very glib. I'm disappointed."

"I'd like a drink."

"Still not impressed. This really *is* a new you."

"Choke on a turd."

"Then again," Louis says, "maybe not."

THIRTY-SEVEN

THE SECOND HOUR

She hears the highway before she sees it.

That familiar Doppler rush of cars. The passing growl of a motorcycle.

Miriam staggers to the edge of the seemingly infinite gravel drive, alone. (Louis's future ghost has long left her behind, though from time to time, she sees him passing through the trees as she stumbles forth.)

The road ahead is two-lane. Gray macadam. A crusty, broken dividing line like a spattered stripe of golden piss.

She blinks and tucks the gun away in the back of her waistband.

She's been here before. Countless times. Standing on the highway shoulder, thumb out, hoping to catch a ride the way a remora fish wants to cling tight to a swiftly moving shark (a shark swiftly moving toward food, since the remora is like the vulture, which is like the crow, which is like Miriam herself—scavenger, carrion feeder, and all-around lazy fuck).

Once more, she seeks a ride to somebody's death.

The thumb-out hitchhiker trick won't do it this time. It's too slow. Most people know what they're getting when they pick up a highway drifter: an addict, a crazy person, a serial rapist, a big giant question mark that isn't worth answering.

Miriam just doesn't have the time.

She sees a car coming. Subaru Outback station wagon, a couple years past its prime.

Miriam steps out in front of the speeding hunk of Japanese automation. Late, too late, the gray glare on the windshield passes and Miriam can see that the woman is on her cell phone, probably not paying attention to something so insignificant as, say, the road.

Still, Miriam doesn't budge.

The car bears down. Doesn't stop.

Then, last minute, squealing brakes. The car's ass end starts to wobble like the hips of an old dog, but it's too little, too late.

The car hits Miriam.

Luckily, by the time it does, it's only going a couple miles an hour.

It still hurts (right now, the *breeze blowing* hurts every micrometer of Miriam's skin; even her hair feels pain), but it's more jarring than anything else.

Still, it gives Miriam a second wind, a boot-kick of adrenalin.

The woman behind the car is dumbstruck. She's an older woman, maybe in her midfifties, with a white-blonde drill-instructor haircut that suggests she's either a lesbian or just one of those women who no longer gives a shit or the time to fix her hair in the morning.

The phone slides out of her hand, but the hand stays held to her ear. It'd be comical if Miriam had a sense of humor left.

The woman seems to get her bearings and reaches for the steering wheel, and Miriam sees that *panicked rabbit* look.

Sighing, she pulls the gun, points it at the windshield.

The woman's hands go up.

"Good lesbian," Miriam murmurs, then comes around to the passenger side and eases her screaming bones into the seat.

The woman gapes. Miriam holds the gun in an unsteady hand.

"Barnegat Light," Miriam says.

The woman's mouth moves, but no words come out.

"Sorry," Miriam says. "I meant it as a question. Barnegat Light?"

"Whuh-what about it?" The woman's voice is raspy, like she's talking through a coffee grinder. Obviously a smoker. Miriam wonders if that's what she'll sound like in twenty years.

"Where is it?"

"Luh-Long Beach Island. At the northern tip."

"How do I get there, and how long?"

"You go that way," the woman indicates the direction opposite of the way she was going, "until you reach the Garden State Expressway. Then you take that south—no! North, north, sorry, until you can get onto Seventy-Two, and Seventy-Two will take you east over the causeway to LBI. Only one muh-main road on LBI, so just head north till you see the lighthouse. It's maybe a forty-five-minute trip, maybe uh, an hour."

"Last question. You smoke?"

The woman nods, hasty, shaky.

"Give me your cigarettes."

The driver fumbles a box of Virginia Slims from the cup-holder in the door.

"Uck. You smoke these?" Miriam asks, then waves it off. "Whatever."

Miriam takes the pack, and her finger touches—

It's twenty-three years from now and the woman steps off her porch. She's a bag of bird bones, and she trembles her way out the driveway as a light snow drifts around her, carried on whorls and corkscrews by a cold wind. The woman goes to the mailbox, gets the mail, and then takes one step on a shoe-sized patch of black ice. Her leg kicks out, her head hits the mailbox, and she lies there. Hours pass. Evening comes. Snow builds up on her face, but she's still not dead, and she manages to pull out a slim little cigarette from her pink robe and light it up before finally succumbing to the slow, dragging hands of hypothermia.

—the woman's finger as the pack passes between their grips.

Miriam blinks. Shakes it off, then thumbs in the cigarette lighter, gets it warmed up, and plugs one of the thin little pipe-cleaner cigarettes into her mouth.

"Now," Miriam mumbles around the unlit cigarette, "get the fuck out of this car before I hit you in the face with the gun and break all the tiny bones in your ear. Keep on smoking, by the way. Good for you."

The lady throws open the door and scurries out of the car like a cat that just got shot in the ass with a pellet rifle.

Miriam lights her cigarette, slides over the seat divider, and throws the Subaru into drive.

Her lungs fill with magic nicotine. Her foot stomps on the pedal.

Movement. Sweet movement.

THIRTY-EIGHT

THE THIRD AND FINAL HOUR

No movement.

Shitty, dead-fish-floating-in-the-water lack of movement.

Miriam was cooking with gas. Then she reached the causeway crossing the Barnegat Bay and traffic locked up tighter than a handful of tampons crammed up a nun's asshole.

Now it's car after car. Kayaks and boat trailers and pale yuppies and kids watching *SpongeBob SquarePants* on DVD screens in the backs of the front seats. Even this late in the day, people are desperate for a taste of the beach, a whiff of sand and surf (the surf smelling like rotting mollusks and the sand home to old hypodermic needles and clumpy, filth-caked condoms). The sun has long faded, just a bleary smear against the dark clouds hovering above the island. It's like a line of tourists driving toward the Rapture.

Miriam lays on the horn.

The last cigarette from the pack is down to its nub. She grits her teeth and flicks it out the window, and it bounces off the hood of a silver minivan next to her.

The mother in the passenger seat—a blimpy hippo already sunburned so badly, it looks like she's been wandering the desert for forty days and forty nights—shoots her a sour stare.

Miriam thinks of shooting the woman back, with bullets.

Miriam elbows the horn again. She's feeling claustrophobic.

This is coming down to the wire. She's been sitting in traffic for far too long now.

She needs a sign.

"I need a sign," she says, panicked.

"Here comes one," Louis says in the back seat. He peels up his electrical tape and reveals not a gaping socket as usual, but a ruined eye that looks more like a thumb-squished grape than anything else. For added effect, he winks.

Then he's gone.

Miriam desperately looks around to see what he's talking about.

Sour, sunburned lady? No.

Carload of dogs and screaming children in front of her? Probably not.

A small plane flies overhead. But since she doesn't have any kind of Batman grappling hook on her belt, she thinks that plan is pretty much fucked from the get-go.

Then she sees it.

A biker—no, a *cyclist*.

He's lean and ropy, dressed to the nines in red-and-blue spandex like he's the Superman of the bicycle crowd.

As he whizzes past on the side of the causeway, Miriam throws open the passenger-side door.

His front tire meets unyielding resistance.

The cyclist flies over the open door. She hears but does not see his head hit the pavement. At least he's wearing a helmet.

Miriam's up and out of the car and on the bike before she even thinks about it. The front tire's bent a little from where it smacked into the Subaru's door, but even wobbly, it's locomotion.

She checks the cell phone.

She has less than an hour now.

"My bike!" the cyclist cries.

Miriam steers unsteadily past.

THIRTY-NINE

FRANKIE

The Barnegat Lighthouse—old Barney—stands ahead.

The winding sandy path is hemmed in by a rickety post-and-rail fence, which is itself hemmed in by black shrubs with yellow flowers.

Gulls cackle and complain overhead, where black garlands of clouds look like distant bands of blackbirds.

The tides rush in, rush out, an outlying murmur.

Miriam steps over the yellow police tape that's meant to block people from going in, and she steps past the sign announcing UNDER CONSTRUCTION and another sign explaining that soon the lighthouse will be home to a new lantern and state-of-the-art polycarbonate windows.

It feels like she's on a roller coaster ride—cresting the hill, though no hill awaits. Her stomach is home to squirming eels. It expands and contracts. Sinks and swims.

Her feet fall on sand that shifts beneath them. She sucks in a breath and kicks off her shoes. A sense of the inevitable precedes her, running ahead like an eager dog. She feels like she's a little girl forced to approach a mother who waits with a leather belt in hand.

She walks.

It feels like she's not approaching the lighthouse, but that it's approaching her.

You can't change anything. Her own voice, not Louis's, chiding her in her head. *Just remember that. You're not here to change anything. You're just here to bear witness. It's what you do. It's what you are. You're the war crow on the battlefield. The chooser of the slain.*

She reaches the end of the hedges. The sand path continues toward the lighthouse. The lighthouse has a white base, a brickred top.

Frankie mills about outside. He's a tall drink of motor oil on the bright beach, a dark shape on an illuminated X-ray, a long dark shadow in sympathy with the sky above. He paces. Rubs his nose. Itches his ear.

Hairless, the man Harriet called Ingersoll, is nowhere to be seen.

It's almost time. Miriam doesn't have to look at the cell phone to know it.

But she pulls out the phone anyway. Gun in one hand, phone in the other, and diary tucked in her pants, she thumbs the redial button on the phone.

Then she starts walking.

Frankie's phone rings. It should. She's calling it.

He answers, and she hears him in stereo—his voice on the phone and his voice ahead: "Harriet?"

Miriam wings the phone at his head like a fucking boomerang. It whips hard across the bridge of his not-insignificant nose, and he staggers, blinking back tears.

She thinks to shoot him, but—*No. Ingersoll will hear the shot. Don't do it.*

Instead, she hurries up and drives the barrel of the gun deep into Frankie's solar plexus.

"The solar plexus is a massive bundle of nerves," Miriam hisses.

Frankie fumbles for his gun, but Miriam's knee to his wrist knocks it from his hand.

As he wheezes, his face turning red, she chops him in the neck with the butt of the pistol.

"Mastoid process triggers your gag reflex."

True to her information, he doubles over, gagging. He doesn't dry-heave; he vomits what looks like a half-digested hoagie.

She wonders how she's going to kill him. Hunched over in a sumo position, puking on himself, he's trying to crabwalk backward.

Fuck it, she thinks. *Strangle him to death.*

Miriam gets behind him and takes her gun arm and brings the crook of the elbow up under his throat. She pulls back hard enough to choke a pony—

Frankie's an old man forty-two years from now, and he's sitting in a darkened theater with his grandson, and the boy is held rapt as his face is lit by whatever it is that's on the screen. The boy is beaming, and Frankie sees it, and then he lays his head back and rests his eyes and lets the heart attack that's been attacking him for the last six hours, working him over with dull pipe and crushing grip, finally take him. His mouth opens, gasping one last breath, and the boy doesn't notice; he just keeps watching.

—and she lets go. Frankie, gasping, stumbles forward into his own hoagie bile.

He tries to stand, but Miriam presses the gun to the back of his head.

"You're going to be a grandfather someday," she says.

"Okay," he croaks, blinking back tears.

"You don't really like this life, do you?"

"No. Christ, no. I hate it."

"You have the keys to the Escalade?"

He nods.

"Take them. Go to it. Get away. You don't want to be here."

Another nod.

"I see you again," she says, "I'll make sure you never get to be a grandfather."

She moves past him and heads into the lighthouse as thunder tumbles over thunder, not far away now, but very close.

FORTY

OLD BARNEY

The lantern room is encased in glass—or, rather, some windows are glass, some have already been replaced with polycarbonate panes.

They haven't yet replaced the lantern, though.

Louis is bound to a wooden chair next to it. The lantern is a bulbous thing, like a giant insect's eye. Louis is held there by brown extension cords over hands and feet. His head is affixed to the base of the lantern by what seems to be a whole roll of electrical tape.

Ingersoll plays with the rusty fillet knife.

He stole it from a fisherman asleep on a nearby jetty. Broke his neck and let the poor fool crash into the surf—though not before snatching the knife from beneath his chair.

Ingersoll rolls the bones that he empties from his satchel. They clatter across the lantern-room floor at his feet, and he sorts through them the way one might sort through dried beans, looking for stones. His finger shifts the bones this way and that. Like he's reading them.

He's not, of course. He can't read them. He does not possess his grandmother's gift of vision, not like he wants to. He pretends, sometimes, and this act of pretending is sometimes so good that he convinces himself.

This time, he tries as hard as he can to see what will happen here.

265

One of the windows above his head is broken. Wind keens through it.

"A storm is coming," he says.

His target, Louis, is still bleary-eyed, beaten, and half drugged. His head lolls as he stirs to some greater semblance of alertness.

Ingersoll sighs. The bones are telling him nothing. Once more, as always, he must invent his own truth and direct his own future.

"Why would I kill you?" he asks aloud. "You are meaningless to me. But you've seen my face. And my new employee, Miriam, is awfully fond of you, and this I cannot have. You will forever cloud her vision. She is mine, my friend. Not yours."

He twirls the knife between gaunt fingers. "Besides. I enjoy causing you pain, and I am fond of the fact that Miriam has already seen this scene play out, hasn't she?"

Ingersoll admires the knife. He smells the rusted, pitted blade.

"Get away from me," Louis stammers. "Who are you? Who are you people? I don't have what you want!"

"That no longer matters," Ingersoll says with a shrug.

He moves fast—a coiled spring unsprung. He stabs Louis in the left eye with the knife. It does not go to the brain and only ruins the eye, a choice the hairless man has made. Louis screams. The attacker withdraws the knife. It makes a sucking sound as he extracts it.

His thin lips form a mirthless smile.

The Barnegat Lighthouse has 217 steps.

Each is an agony. Each a troubled birth, an expelled kidney stone, a black widow's bite.

The steps are corrugated steel painted in flaking yellow. They wind in a tight spiral through a channel of black brick.

It is like ascending the throat of some ancient creature.

What she's going to behold plays out in Miriam's mind again and again like a song set to repeat. The broken window. The wind through the gap. The stick of the knife. The sound of an eye being ruined. Her name, spoken by Louis in sadness and surprise.

Again and again. An endless circle of steps and visions.

Thunder again, outside. Muted through the brick. She wonders, *Am I late? Is that the thunder that plays in my vision?* When she witnesses a death for real, she often looks for these clues, these cues—visual, auditory, whatever. The honking of a car horn. A commercial on the television. Something somebody says.

When she finally comes upon it, when she finally staggers into the lantern room to witness this tableau of horror, this shoebox diorama of death, she doesn't expect it.

It takes her by surprise and steals her breath, even though she feels like all her life has been rushing toward this moment in one vacuum gasp.

Ingersoll doesn't hear her coming, but when she arrives, he offers her little more than a flick of his gaze and the hint of an admiring smile.

By the time Miriam steps into the lantern room, the knife is poised above Louis's other eye. It's not buried to the hilt. Not yet. That's a killing blow. That comes next.

It's good that she's here, he thinks. So she can see. She'll have the proof. It strikes him; he should have had her come here all along, to stand as witness to his glory and his cruelty.

Louis sees her with his one good eye.

Perfect.

"Miriam?" he asks, but Ingersoll is already ready with the killing blow.

It happens so fast. After all this, it feels like it should happen leisurely, in slow motion.

Things don't seem right.

The gun in her hand feels warm.

She smells something bitter, acrid. Smoke stings her eyes.

Ingersoll holds the knife tight. His hand starts to shake.

He turns and reaches up to touch the hole in his temple. A thin rivulet of blood dribbles down from the entry wound, like rusty water from a busted spigot.

Louis blinks his good eye.

He's not dead, Miriam thinks.

This isn't how it happened in her vision. This isn't how it's supposed to play out.

Her heart skips a beat. She feels sick. Woozy. Queasy. Greasy.

The gun is in her hand. Her arm is extended.

She drops the gun and it clatters against the floor.

"I—" she starts to say, but she's truly at a loss for words.

Ingersoll teeters.

And then he lunges like a tiger, knife in hand.

He's on her, his one hand closing on her throat with fingers like mandibles, and she's carried backward with the momentum. She slams against the metal steps, and she feels him go up over her, and then she goes up over *him*, and the world goes topsy-turvy. Black bricks and white lines smear into an abyssal spiral, and again and again she's greeted by a faceful of hard yellow metal—

Her muscles cry out, her bones feel chipped and cracked, and she thrusts each limb out from her body as hard as she can, and it slows her tumble—

She comes to a stop about thirty feet down.

Fresh blood marks the wall next to her.

Beneath her, Ingersoll's eyes stare up.

His head is cocked at an impossible angle, the chin tucked over the shoulder, the vertebrae pressing so hard against his hairless flesh that it looks like his neck will split like an overripe fruit. His dead gaze seems affixed to her. A painting whose eyes always watch.

Miriam almost laughs.

But laughing—even almost laughing—hurts. Real bad.

She looks down and finds a rusty fishing knife sticking out of her chest. It goes clean through her left tit, right to the hilt.

Miriam tries to draw a breath. It's like sucking in a lung full of fire.

"Shit," she says.

Darkness takes her, and she continues her tumble down the lighthouse spiral.

THE DREAM

"Do you get it now?" Louis asks, walking alongside her.

Together, they cross a black sand beach, each granule catching the sun in a way that makes it shimmer. The sand is warm beneath Miriam's feet. A tide licks at the shoreline. The air smells salty, but not briny or fishy.

"I get that I'm dead, and thank Jesus this doesn't look like Hell."

"You're not dead," Louis says, itching at one of the black Xs across his eyes. "Though I should note that you *are* dying."

"Great. So this is some kind of midsurgery fever dream. Just show me the light already so I can go running toward it."

"You're missing the point."

"I am?"

"You are. Think about it. What just happened?"

She really does have to think, because she'd rather not look back. She'd rather just be here, in the now, on this beach. In the bright sun.

It doesn't take too long, though, for her to remember.

"I beat the game," she says.

"You did," Louis answers.

"For once, it didn't happen like it was supposed to. It almost did. But I changed it."

"You sure did. Spectacularly so. Good job."

"Thanks." She smiles then. For real. Not a half-smile, not a bitter smirk, not a snarky grin, but a real, can't-stop-it-from-spreading smile. "I don't know what I did differently. I sure tried real hard. Maybe it's because I love you. Or him. I guess you're not him."

Louis's smile fades. "I'm not him, and you're still not getting it. You know why it happened. You know how you broke the cycle."

"I don't! I really don't."

"Want a hint?"

"I want a hint."

She blinks, and Louis is now her mother. Pinched face, small, puckered body.

"And thine eye shall not pity, but life shall go for life, eye for eye, tooth for tooth, hand for hand, foot for foot."

Then, poof—back to Louis with the *X*-eyes.

"I still don't—"

No, wait. Yes, yes she does.

"I killed somebody."

Louis snaps his fingers. "Ding, ding, ding. Give this girl a panda."

Miriam stops walking. Clouds drift in front of the sun. Somewhere out over the water, a storm brews, and rain clatters against the tides.

"I'm usually just the . . . the messenger. The vulture picking at the bones. But not this time. This time, I . . . I changed things. I killed Ingersoll."

"You balanced the scales. The scales always want to be balanced. You want to make a change, a big change, a change *so cosmic* you're unwriting death and kicking fate square in the face, then you best be prepared to pay for it."

"With blood," Miriam says, her mouth dry, her bones cold. Lightning licks at the ocean way out there under the steel sky.

"With blood and bile and voided bowels."

"Who are you?" Her voice is quiet.

"Don't you mean, what am I?"

She doesn't respond.

Louis again becomes her mother. Then he becomes Ben Hodge, the back of his head blooming like a bloody orchid. Then Ashley, hopping in place on one foot.

Then back to Louis.

"Maybe I'm fate," he says. "But maybe, just maybe, I'm the opposite of fate, the way that God has His opposite in the Devil. Maybe I'm just you, just the voices in your head."

He grins wide. His teeth are each little skulls.

"One thing I do know, though. We've got so much more for you to do."

"We?" she asks, her heart frozen—

FORTY-ONE

FATE'S FOE

She gasps awake, feeling like she's tangled in seaweed. She starts tugging off the choking weeds—the ones that wormed their way down her throat, the ones that have burrowed into her arm and chest—and suddenly there's all this beeping, some fast, some slow, some a steady drone, and the world swims into view just as an antiseptic stink crawls into her nose, nests there, and has babies.

Louis is on her, holding her down.

"Whoa," he says, "Hold on, bucking bronco, hold on. You're okay. You're okay."

A white cotton pad sits over his left eye, held there by a yellow elastic band.

"Fuck you," she hisses. "You go to hell. Answer my question. Who are you? What do you mean, *we*? Get out of my head. I want to die or wake up. I want to die or wake up!"

"You are awake," he says, and strokes her hair. "Shhh."

She blinks.

This Louis smells of soap.

And he has one working eye.

And her chest hurts like someone just stabbed her there. Which, last time she checked, is exactly what happened.

"I'm not asleep?" she asks in a small voice.

"Nope."

"This isn't a dream?"

"I don't think so, though I can say it still sometimes feels like one."

Miriam doesn't know what to say. She blurts, "I'm sorry."

"Sorry?"

"This situation is . . . complex. And it's my fault."

He sits down in the chair next to the bed. "It's complex, all right. Not too sure it's your fault, though."

"You can't really understand, and you wouldn't believe me if I told you—"

"I read your diary," he says.

She stares.

"What?"

He pulls it out from the back of his waistband and rests it on her lap. "I'm sorry. I know that's not a real nice thing to do, but you left me needing some answers. I hope you understand that. I thought you were just trying to rip me off—and maybe, once upon a time, you were—but next thing I know, I'm in a lighthouse and some bald weirdo is trying to cut out my eyes, and then you're there, and you're half dead at the bottom of the lighthouse and the bald weirdo is *all* dead in the middle, and . . . I needed to know what was going on. You were gone from this world, so I couldn't ask you anything. All I had was this book—it had fallen out when you took your tumble."

Miriam draws a deep breath, and it hurts like hell. "So you know. You know what I am. What I see."

"I do."

"Do you believe it?"

"I reckon I do. Either that or you just performed the longest, weirdest con in the history of con-jobs."

"Do I see a hint of a smile?"

"You might. Even after all this, you might."

She hesitates, but she's never been known before for traipsing around touchy subjects.

"Did they save the eye?"

Louis bites at his thumbnail. "Nope."

"I'm so sorry."

He waves it off. "Things happen in this life. Sometimes they're good things, and sometimes they're bad things. You have to come to terms with the bad things, especially when you can't change them."

"And when you can change them?"

"Then you do your damnedest to make those changes."

An image of Ingersoll, blood bubbling up out of the bullet hole, flies before her eyes.

"I guess you do," she says.

"Heck," he says, leaning back. "At least I got this cool eye patch."

"That you do. If they don't let you drive a truck anymore, maybe you could be a pirate."

"It's the pirate's life for me."

She laughs.

"You going to stick around?" she asks. "I know you probably have places to be, but I'm guessing that they're going to keep me here a little while longer."

"They are. At least another week. You fractured some bones, and there was this funny thing about a knife sticking out of your lung."

"It's just, I think I need somebody right now."

He nods. "I do, too."

"So, you're not going anywhere?"

"Only wherever you're going. You saved my life—kind of. For that, I figure I owe you my time."

She smiles. "Can you do me one more favor?"

"Name it."

It hurts to do so, but she picks up the diary and pitches it at him like a Frisbee. He almost doesn't catch it, but he fumbles it a few times before getting a grip.

"Still working on that depth perception thing," he says.

"Oh. Sorry."

"What's the favor?"

"Throw that away," she says.

"How about I just throw it in the ocean?"

She frowns and makes an *uck* noise. "I wouldn't do that to the poor fishies. Plus, I always hate that scene in the movies. Throw it in the ocean, it's always out there. Or it'll wash up on the shore for someone to find. Get rid of it. All the pages are used up. It tells a story I don't want to tell. Find a trash can and throw it out. Better still, a Dumpster, and better than *that*, a giant belching furnace, the kind that burns up bodies."

He stands and kisses her. His lips are dry, but that doesn't stop them from being soft, or it from being the best damn kiss she's ever dreamed could be kissed.

"I'll throw it away," he says.

"I hurt."

"I know."

"I think I need to sleep."

"I know that, too. You going to be okay for a while? You look a little sad."

Miriam shrugs as much as she can manage. "It is what it is, Louis. It is what it is."

ACKNOWLEDGMENTS

Thanks to my wife, my family, my friends. Thanks to my agent, who helps these books stay alive. Thanks to Lee Harris, for giving this book its first chance at life, and to Joe Monti, for its lifetime home. Thanks most of all to the readers, without whom Miriam Black would never have made it this far.

AN EXCERPT FROM
MIRIAM BLACK:
BOOK TWO:
MOCKINGBIRD
CHUCK WENDIG

SHIP BOTTOM

Boop.

Suntan lotion.

Boop.

Pecan sandies.

Boop.

Tampons, beach towel, postcards, and, mysteriously, a can of green beans.

Miriam grabs each item with a black-gloved hand. Runs the item over the scanner. Sometimes, she looks down and stares into the winking red laser. She's not supposed to do that. But she does it anyway, a meager act of rebellion in her brand-new life. Maybe, she thinks, the ruby beam will burn away that part of her brain that makes her who she is. Turn her into a mule-kicked window-licker, happy in oblivion, pressed up against the walls of her Plexiglas enclosure.

"Miss?"

The word drags her out of the mind's eye theater and back to checkout.

"Jesus, what?" she asks.

"Well, are you going to scan that?"

Miriam looks down. Sees she's still holding the can of green beans. Del Monte. She idly considers braining the woman standing there in her beachy muumuu, the worn pattern of hibiscus flowers barely covering a sludgy bosom that's half lobster red and half wood-grub white. Two halves marked by the Rubicon of a terrible tan line.

Instead, Miriam swipes the can across the scanner with a too-sweet smile.

Boop.

"Is something wrong with your hands?" the woman asks. She sounds concerned.

Miriam waggles one finger—a jumping inchworm dance. The black leather creaks and squeaks.

"Oh, these? I have to wear these. You know how women at restaurants have to wear hairnets? For public health safety? I gotta wear these gloves if I'm going to work here. Rules and regulations. Last thing I want to do is cause a hepatitis outbreak, am I right? I got hep A, B, C, and the really bad one, X."

Then, just to sell it, Miriam holds up her hand for a high five.

The woman does not seize the high-five opportunity.

Rather, the blood drains from her face, her sunburned skin gone swiftly pale.

Miriam wonders what would happen if she told the truth: *Oh, it's no big deal, but when I touch people, this little psychic movie plays in my head and I witness how and when they're going to die. So I've been wearing these gloves so I don't have to see that kind of crazy shit anymore.*

Or the deeper truth behind even that: *I wear them because Louis wants me to wear them.*

Not that the gloves provide perfect protection against the visions. Nobody but Louis is touching her anywhere else, though. She keeps covered up. Even in the heat.

Behind the woman is a line seven, eight people deep. They all hear what Miriam says. She's not quiet. Two of the customers—a doughy gentleman in a parrot-laden shirt and a young girl with an ill-contained rack of softball-sized fake tits—shimmy out of the queue and leave their goods on the empty checkout two rows down.

Still, the woman hangs tough. With a sour face, she pulls a credit card out of nowhere—Miriam imagines she withdraws it from her sand-encrusted vagina—and flips it onto the counter like it's a hot potato.

Miriam's about to grab it and scan it when a hand falls on her shoulder.

She already knows to whom the hand belongs.

She wheels on Peggy, manager here at Ship Bottom Sundries in Long Beach Island, New Jersey. Peggy, whose nose must possess powerful gravity given the way it looks like the rest of her face is being dragged toward it. Peggy, whose giant sunglasses call to mind the eyes of a praying mantis. Peggy with her gray hair dyed orange and left in a curly, clumsy tangle.

Fucking Peggy.

"You mind telling me what you're doing?" The way Peggy begins every conversation, it seems. All in that Joisey accent. *Ya mind tellin' me what y'doin'?* The lost *R*s, the dropped *G*s, *wooter* instead of *water*, *caw-fee* instead of *coffee*.

"Helping this fine citizen check out of our fine establishment." Miriam thinks but does not say, *Ship Bottom Sundries, where you can buy a pack of hot dogs, a pack of generic-brand tampons, or a handful of squirming hermit crabs for your screaming shitbird children.*

"Sounds like you're giving her trouble."

Miriam offers a strained smile. "Was I? Not my intention."

Totally her intention.

"You know, I hired you as a favor."

"I do know that. Because you remind me frequently."

"Well, it's true."

"Yes. We *just* established that."

Peggy's puckered eyes tighten to fleshy slits. "You got a smart mouth."

"Some might argue my mouth is actually quite foolish."

By now, the line is building up. The woman in the floral muumuu is holding the green beans to her chest, as though the can will protect her from the awkwardness that has been thrust upon her day. The other customers watch with wide eyes and uncomfortable scowls.

"You think you're funny," Peggy says.

Miriam doesn't hesitate. "I really do."

"Well, I don't."

"Agree to disagree?"

Peggy's face twists up like a rag about to be wrung out. It takes a moment for Miriam to realize that this is Peggy's happy face.

"You're fired," Peggy says. Mouth twisted up at the corners in some crass facsimile of a human smile.

"Oh, fuck you," Miriam says. "You're not going to fire me." It occurs to her too late that saying *fuck you* is not the best way to retain one's job, but frankly, the horse is already out of the stable on that one.

"Fuck me?" Peggy asks. "Fuck *you*. You bring me nothing but grief. Come in here day after day, moping about like someone pissed in your Wheaties—"

"Do people even eat Wheaties anymore? I mean, seriously."

"—and I don't need a grumpy little slut like you working in my store. Season's over after this weekend anyway, and you're done. Kaput. Pack up your crap and get out. I'll send you your last paycheck."

This is real, Miriam thinks.

She just got let go.

Pink-slipped.

Shit-canned.

She should be happy.

Her heart should be a cage of doves newly opened, the free birds flying high, fleeing far and away. This should be a real the-hills-are-alive-with-the-sound-of-music moment, all twirling skirts and wind in her hair. But all she feels is the battery-acid burn of rage and bile and incredulity mingling at the back of her throat. A rising tide of snake venom.

Louis always tells her to keep it together.

She is tired of keeping it together.

Miriam yanks her nametag off her chest—a nametag that says "Maryann" because they fucked it up and didn't want to reprint it—and chucks it over her shoulder. The muumuu lady dodges it.

She goes with an old standby—her middle finger thrust up in Peggy's juiced lemon of a face—and then storms outside.

She stops. Stands in the parking lot. Hands shaking.

An ocean breeze kicks up. The air brings with it the smell of brine and fish and a lingering hint of coconut oil. Serpents of sand whisper across the cracked parking lot.

A dozen gulls fight over bread scraps. Ducking and diving. Squawking and squalling. Drunk on bread crust and victory.

It's hot. The breeze does little for that.

People everywhere. The *fwip-fwip-fwip* of flip-flop sandals. The miserable sob of somebody's child. The murmur and cackle of endless vacationers smelling a season drawing to a close. A thudding bass line booms from a car sliding down the slow traffic of Long Beach Boulevard, and she can't help but think how the beat sounds like *douche-douche-douche-douche* and how it echoes her hammer-fist heartbeat dully punching against the inside of her breastbone. And Walt the "cart boy," who's not really a boy but in fact a developmentally handicapped fifty-year-old man, gives her a wave and she waves back and thinks, *He's the only one here who was ever nice to me.* And probably the only one she was ever nice to, too.

She thinks, *Fuck it.*

She peels off one of her gloves.

Then comes the other.

Miriam pitches both over her shoulder—her hands are freakishly pale, paler than the rest of her body, the fingertips wrinkled as though she's been in a long bath.

If Louis wanted her to keep it together, he'd be here. And he's not.

Miriam goes back inside the store, cracking her knuckles.

AN EXCERPT FROM
MIRIAM BLACK:
BOOK THREE:
THE CORMORANT
CHUCK WENDIG

NOW

"And the Lord said, let there be light."

A flutter of black fabric, and the hood is gone.

Miriam winces. Blinks. A white wave bleeds in from the edges. The world presses through the blur: Shapes emerging from a puddle of milk.

The fat man who spoke sits across from her. Behind him walks the brittle woman, his partner—a boozy, tilted smile stitched between the moorings of two sharp cheekbones. Her hand is bandaged.

"You look like shit," Grosky, the fat one, says after a low whistle.

"You look like a track suit wrapped around a bunch of trash bags," Miriam answers. Her voice feels raw. *Sounds* raw. Like bare feet torn on broken shells, abraded by sand, stung by salt.

Ragged, ruined, roughed-the-fuck-up.

Grosky just shrugs. Laughs a little. He's got a soft voice. Though she knows he can turn the volume up when he needs to. The booming timpani in the barrel well of his chest.

He's got the box. *Her* box. Right there in front of him. He drums his sausage-link fingers on it. The lid rattles. The padlock judders.

The scarecrow—Vills, Catherine Vills—paces like she's nervous. Like she's got something to hide, which Miriam knows she does.

Miriam feels it in her feet as much as she hears it: The tide coming in. Not far away. The hush-and-boom of waves crashing. She looks around. This is just some ramshackle beach hut. Wood walls, leaning against one another as if for emotional support. Thatched roof overhead. Cobwebs hang and sway as a fishy breeze creeps in through open windows.

"Where are we?" Miriam asks.

Grosky doesn't answer her question. "You want anything?"

"Cigarette."

"You shouldn't smoke."

"You shouldn't mainline lard and melted cheese. Do you even eat the cheeseburgers anymore, or do you just inject them right into your man-tits?" She tries to mimic said injection, but remembers that her hands are cuffed in front of her, and the shackles are in turn cuffed to the leg of the table. The table is wood. Old. Rickety. She could bust it if she has to.

But she won't have to. Not yet, anyway.

"Funny thing about lard," Tommy Grosky says, "it's got a bad rap. Demonized with all the other animal fats in the seventies. But the truth is, it's the vegetable fats that'll kill you. Crisco. Margarine. Those, eh, those trans-fatty acids will fuck you up pretty good." He squeezes a fist like he's angrily milking a goat's udder. "Closes your arteries off. Like with a clothespin."

"That is *fascinating*." She squeezes the words like a sponge, lets them drip sarcasm everywhere. "Thank you, Surgeon General Fatty McGee."

"I'm just saying, things aren't always what they appear." He pats his chest. *Boom boom boom.* "You look at me and think, *Hey, there's a blobby bastard right there. Like if Fred Flintstone ate Barney, Wilma, turned that purple dinosaur into dino burgers. Lift up one of his fat rolls, you'll see a couple Twinkies hidden away.* You think I got an expiration date coming up. That my heart's like a soup can in an old lady's pantry: sure to burst before too long. But see, here's the thing: I'm a forty-two-year-old guy who's as healthy as a sixteen-year-old. My good cholesterol is through the roof. My bad cholesterol, shit, I don't even think I *have* any. Great blood pressure. Perfect blood sugar—I don't even know how to *spell* diabetes. I eat well. I like a lot of greens. Chard. Kale. Spinach, obviously."

"Obviously."

"So maybe don't be so smug." His mouth hangs open. He waggles his tongue between the two rows of flat Chiclet teeth. It makes a wet, hollow sound. "Because maybe you don't know what you're looking at."

"Maybe you forget, I know how you're going to die."

His eyes sit tucked behind folds of flesh that look like someone is pinching the skin shut, but suddenly the eyes go wide and she sees something flash there in the dark of his pupils: anger, bright white, like light trapped in the steel of a knife blade.

"This again," he says. "Right. I'll play. So you're saying it's my health that kills me? If you can even do this thing that you say you can do."

"What time is it?" Miriam asks. Her turn to change the subject.

Here Vills looks down at a nice watch. A new watch. Movado. It hangs on her gaunt bone-knob wrist near a bandage. Miriam thinks, *We'll get to all this soon enough.*

"Five after noon," Vills says. A smoker's voice. A voice that's all rust flakes and precancerous nodes, all in the dry thatch eaves of the woman's scratchy throat. Then Vills drops a cigarette on the table between Grosky and Miriam.

Grosky gives his partner a look.

"Let her smoke," Vills says. "Let's get this over with."

"Fine," Grosky says. He flicks the cigarette over toward Miriam. It rolls and she catches it: a trap-door spider leaping upon its prey. Vills hands him a lighter but he doesn't give it over. He twirls it. Grinning.

Miriam screws the cigarette between her lips. Teeth on the filter. Tongue rimming the paper. She wants it. A nic-fit threatens to tear through her like a pack of starving dogs.

Grosky leans across. Strikes the cheap gas station lighter—*flick flick flick*. Just sparks, just empty embers, hollow promises, no flame.

He shrugs. Pulls the lighter away. "Oh well."

"Try again."

"I'm not breathing in your stink. I gotta do it with this one—" He jerks a thumb toward Vills. "But I don't gotta do it with you."

"I have had a *bad* couple of weeks," Miriam growls.

"Ooooh. Ho, ho. I know. We're gonna talk about that."

"I want my cigarette."

"You tell me some of the things I want to know, maybe you'll get that cigarette. And maybe I'll fix you a plate of greens—it's good for that sunburn. And—*and!*—maybe you'll get out of those cuffs, too. Or maybe not. Everything depends on you, Miss Black."

"Miss Black? So formal. Please. Call me *Go Fuck Yourself*."

"I want to know about this boy," Grosky says, grabbing a photo from a folder in his lap. He slides it across the table. Soon as she sees it, it's like someone yanks something vital right out of her. A child's hand jerking the fabric from a doll's chest.

The young man in the picture is dead.

Puffy green Eagles jacket spattered with blood.

Blood is black in the winter slush.

Outside the hut in the here and now, the tides rumble.

Somewhere, seabirds squawk and chatter.

Gannets, maybe, Miriam thinks.

Miriam draws a deep breath.

And she tells him the story.

PUT A RING ON IT

The engagement ring is burning a hole in Andrew's pocket. That's how it feels, like it'll burn through the fabric and drop off into the dirty snow of the sidewalk, maybe roll into the sewer grate and disappear into the slurry below. And if that were to happen, how would he feel? He'd feel horrible. He loves Sarah. He wants to marry Sarah. But he can't marry her with this ring. A ring too big for her perfect porcelain fingers. A big ring with a diamond too small. A ring he inherited from his mother.

Still. The ring's like a loaded gun. He's almost proposed five times in the last couple weeks. Part of him thinks, *Just propose, you can get the ring resized, get a new diamond later. Before the wedding. Which won't be for a year anyway. Oh, God, unless she wants to get married soon . . .*

But no. He has to do this right. Her father thinks Andrew does everything half-ass. And her father means the world to her. Andrew has to make this a good show. The ring has to impress her, but more important, it has to impress her father. The problem: Even Sarah doesn't know how bad Andrew's got it right now. He's got a good job at a brokerage here in Philly, but he's thirty thousand in credit card debt. Not to mention the car loan. And the student loans from b-school *and* from grad school. And the rent. The gas bill. The trash bill. The *this* bill. The *that* bill.

He's got a little money in his pocket but, really, he's broke.

Which is why he's out here now. In Kensington at quarter till eleven on a Wednesday night. Walking through a pissy wet snowfall—fat, clumpy flakes not drifting so much as *plopping* to the earth. His nice shoes white from the road salt. His socks wet from the slush.

Derek at work said, *You want a diamond cheap, I know a place.* Derek said, *It's in Kensington.* and Andrew said, *Oh, hell no, Kenzo? Really?* He said that if he goes down there, he'll get stabbed. Or strangled. *Isn't the Kensington Strangler still around down there?* Derek just laughed. *That's old news. Crime's down. It's fine. You want the diamond cheap, or you want to pay jewelry store prices?*

Andrew thought but did not say, *I* want *to pay jewelry store prices.*

He just can't afford to.

And so, a pawnshop. Derek said, *It's called K&P Moneyloan Pawn, except they don't speak a lot of English and they misspelled "Moneyloan" so it says "Moneylawn," so at least you'll know you have the right place.*

Andrew thought he'd get there right after work, six, maybe seven o'clock. But suddenly the team of in-house lawyers demanded a new meeting at work, and meetings are like black holes: They eat up the hours, they suck in the light, they gorge on his productivity. Next thing he knew, it was past ten o'clock and he still had to get to Kensington.

The pawnshop was still open. Thank God.

The guy behind the counter—a guy Derek said was Indian (*Curry Indian, not Wounded Knee Indian*) but that Andrew thinks is Sri Lankan—showed him the diamonds and everything looked good; the prices were low enough he almost wondered if they were real, and there he had a small panic attack because wasn't he supposed to remember something about the three Cs? Color, clarity, cut and . . . was there a fourth C?

Crap! Whatever. He's no expert. Neither is Sarah. He picked a princess-cut diamond that looked—well, it looked pretty. It caught the light. It felt heavy. Sharp, too, like it could cut a hole in the storefront window.

So there he stood in a dingy, cracked-floor pawnshop, the too-bright fluorescents above humming and clicking, neon lights trapped between the pawnshop window and the big metal grate just *inside* the windows, and finally he managed to argue the little Sri Lankan man down to a price he could afford (a price less than half of what he'd pay anywhere else), and then he whipped out his Visa and—

"No credit card," the little man said.

"I have a debit card—"

"No take, no take."

"But that's what I have."

The little man pulled back the small cloth with the diamond on it. "Cash only. No diamond. Only cash. No diamond."

So he asked, "Is there an ATM machine around?"

"Is just ATM," the little man said. "No ATM machine. ATM mean *Automated Teller Machine*. You no need to say extra *machine*."

This from a man whose store is named Moneylawn.

Andrew said fine, fine, just tell me where, and he thought—hoped—that the ATM was right across the street, but no, of course it wasn't, it was three blocks up and four blocks over and now the sky is really flinging the glops of wet snow down on his head as if to punish him for his bad money management—

So now here he is. Hurrying along. To an ATM in the middle of Kensington. A neighborhood no longer in decline because it can't decline any further—the car has already crashed, the wreck has already burned out.

Derelict storefronts. A lone pizza joint at the corner, still open. Eyes watching him from under a ratty overhang. Past an alley where a homeless guy in an overcoat sleeps in the shade of a dented Dumpster, using a blue tarp as a blanket. Someone yelling a block over—a Hispanic girl in a half-shirt and jeans, no jacket, no hat, bronze hair peppered with white flakes, and she's screaming at some little thug in a leather jacket, saying something about sucking his dick, something about someone named Rosalita. The thug's just laughing. Braying, even. Waving her off.

Andrew keeps his head down.

Turn around. Go home. The diamond will be there tomorrow.

No. Tomorrow is Saturday. He and Sarah are going to Wildwood Gardens. She loves that place. The orchid house. The Christmas lights. He's going to ask her there. Do the whole thing: down on one knee, ring up, maybe in front of a crowd so they have that story to tell.

Just walk. Hurry up. You need to do this. Man up, Andrew. What would her father say?

Her father would say nothing. He'd just stare at Andrew with those dark gray eyes, eyes like bits of driveway gravel.

Ahead—a basketball court. Tall fences. Three courts lined up next to each other. He can shortcut the block, he thinks.

But then—

Footsteps. Behind him. Crossing the street. Splashing in slush.

He casts a quick glance over his shoulder.

A shadow following. Hands in pockets. Dark camo. Hood up.

His heart starts kicking.

He hurries forward. Half a short block to the basketball courts. His foot catches on an uneven sidewalk—he falls forward, just barely catches himself, but he takes the opportunity to shift into a brisk walk, almost a jog.

But the person behind him is coming up fast now.

Faster than he is. A swift step.

The person raises a gloved hand. Points a finger-gun at him.

The thumb-hammer falls.

Andrew hurries. Grabs the pole holding up the chain link leading into the basketball courts. He ducks in through the gate—

"Hey!" calls a voice.

A woman's voice.

"Andrew!"

She knows his name?

Thud. Something hits him hard in the back.

Snow plops.

A snowball. She hit him with a snowball.

He wheels. Holds up both hands, palms forward. "I don't know who you are or what you want, but I don't want any trouble—"

The woman hooks her thumbs around the hood, flips it back. It's some white girl. She shakes free a shaggy ink-black pixie cut, the front bangs streaked with red. She stares at him from raccoon-dark eyes.

"You dumb shit," she says, baring her teeth from behind a fishhook sneer. "*What* are you doing out here?"

"Wh . . . huh?"

She sighs as snow falls. "I don't know why I'm yelling at you. I knew you'd be here. Isn't that why I'm here?" She taps a cigarette out of a rumpled pack of Natural American Spirits. Cigarette between lips. Clink of a lighter. Flame in the winter. Blue smoke.

He coughs. Fans the smoke away.

"I gotta go," he says.

"You don't remember me," she says. A statement, not a question.

"What? No I—" Wait. The way one she stares from under an arched and dubious brow. He knows that look. A look of unmitigated incredulity. A mean-girl look like she's saying, *You'd really wear those pants with that shirt?* Sarah gives him that look sometimes. Her judgey face. "Yeah. Hold up. I remember you. From the bus."

She gestures at him with the cigarette. "Got it in one."

A year ago. On the SEPTA Nite Owl route home to University City.

His stomach suddenly drops out from under him.

"You . . . told me . . ." He tries to remember. He was tired that night. No. Drunk. He was *drunk* that night. Not black-out-and-wake-up-in-Jersey drunk, but drinks with Derek and the other brokers . . . Did Sarah yell at him that night? No. They were only just together then. Not even living with each other. They'd just met.

The woman vents smoke through her teeth. "You have a ring in your pocket. Left pocket, I think."

His gaze darts down. His hand reflexively touches the pocket. There the ring is heavy. *The One Ring*, he thinks. On the way to Mordor. Absurd that he's thinking about that. He doesn't even like those books.

"How do you . . ." But then it all hits him. Ice breaking. Water rushing. The memory cold as the slap of the winter air.

On the bus. He'd seen her there before. Sitting in the back. Earbuds in. Then one day she came up to him. Sat behind him. Started talking. He'd had . . . what were they? A bunch of Long Island Iced Teas. How do they get them to taste so much like iced tea? They turned her into a smudgy blur, a Vaseline thumbprint on the lens of his life.

She just started talking. Like she couldn't stop, like someone karate-kicked the spigot right off the sink—words spraying everywhere. She was amped, jacked up in the same way he was slowed down, and she told him—

You're gonna die.

That's what she said.

She knows about the ring now because she knew about it then.

Didn't she? She told him he'd have a ring in his pocket, and he said that was absurd. At the time he hadn't even thought of marrying Sarah, but here he was, with a ring—his dead mother's own engagement ring—there in his pocket, a modest little circle of white gold, *too* modest . . .

The girl gave him a date. Told him to "mark his calendar."

Was tonight that date?

He doesn't even realize he asked the question out loud.

"Yes. It's tonight, genius. You really should've written it down. I *told* you to write it down. I said, 'Whip out your fancy smartphone and write it the fuck down.' But did you? Mmm. No. You just puked on your shoes." She suddenly pauses, as if in rumination. "Okay, maybe I should have waited till you weren't drunk to give you the news, though at the time I thought it might soften the blow. I'd been watching you for days. I brushed by you on a Monday, didn't tell you until Thursday."

"You're crazy," he says, backpedaling.

"Be that as it may, Andrew, that doesn't change what's coming."

He says it again—"You're *crazy*"—because he can't find any other words, because his brain is suddenly a snarl of sparking, rat-chewed wires, and he knows he's being played. Conned, somehow. He takes a step back, turns—starts hurrying across the basketball court.

She's after him. Like stink on a skunk.

"You're processing this poorly," she yells. "Totally normal, by the way. This was all kind of an experiment for me. I've run it again and again, and it always runs smack into the same dead end every time." She clears her throat. "No pun intended until now. Hey. Slow down. Wait up."

But he keeps hurrying.

"Get away," he says.

"You've got an appointment to keep, huh? Running right toward the reaper's bony hug. Fate, man. Fucking fate! See? I *told* you how it was going to shake out. I gave you all the details—the date, the ring, the ATM machine"—*You no need to say extra machine*—"and yet here you are, not walking but *sprinting* toward the cliff's edge. It's like people *want* to die."

"I'll call the police." He fumbles for his phone. He palms it, turns around while still walking backward, and waves the phone at her like it's a weapon. "I'll do it. I'll call 911!"

"Go ahead," she says, stopping. She sucks on the cigarette. "Call them. I'll wait. You call them, you might just save your own life, Andy."

"Andrew. It's Andrew."

"Whatever. Ringy-ringy. 911."

He holds the phone. Hand trembling.

He doesn't call.

He doesn't call because he doesn't have the time. If he calls the police, they might actually show up. Then they'll want to talk to him. Take a statement. But the pawnshop closes at midnight.

And midnight is fast approaching.

Instead, he takes out his house keys. He shoves keys through his fingers and forms a soft, clumsy fist.

He shakes the fist at her.

She laugh-snorts. "What is *that*?"

"I'll hit you. It'll . . . the keys, the keys'll cut you."

"Did you learn that in a movie?"

"In a defense class."

"In a defense class for *who*? I didn't know you were a middle-aged housewife, Andy. You cover it up well."

"Fuck you."

"*There* it is. The anger. The resentment. Nobody likes being told they're going to die. They struggle like a sparrow caught in a man's hand. Flapping and scratching and pecking. You can fix this, Andy. Turn around. Go home. Whatever you're doing out here in pissing distance of midnight, do it some other time."

He kicks stones and slush at her. Like a child. He feels stupid for doing it but there it is; it's already done.

"You're a fucking lunatic!" he shouts at her.

The woman just shakes her head.

"Fine," she says. "That's the experiment, then. I'm calling it. Time of death: fifteen minutes. Go forth, spunky housewife, and meet your maker."

She turns then. Pulls her hoodie back over her head. Flicks her cigarette off into the snow.

The woman recedes. A slow walk away.

She doesn't look back. She's done with him. Good.

He stands there for a little while. Shaking. He tells himself it's just the cold. *Sarah. The ring. The ATM. Midnight. Man up, Andy. Andrew! Andrew. Damnit.* It's like the woman's insanity is contagious. Like she's in his head, a spider spinning a web, catching flies. He lets out a plume of frozen breath.

Then he turns, hastens his step across the last two basketball courts.

Through an alley. Through puddles of dirty ice-mush.

There. Across the street, next to a small alley. Glowing bright, Superman red-and-blue: the ATM. *Almost there,* he thinks, as he darts across the empty street. Above, the sky glows Philadelphia Orange, a blasted burnt umber hue as if a chemical fire burns in the heavens.

Andrew digs out his card with cold-bitten hands, shoves it in the machine. He jumps through all the hoops. Presses all the buttons. Enters his PIN number—and suddenly he realizes it's not a PIN number, it's just a PIN, a Personal Identification Number, and the absurdity of yet another redundancy makes him laugh—

Whew.

Tension flees.

This is okay.

It's all going to be fine.

Except:

The machine won't let him take out more than two hundred dollars. He needs four times that amount. *Damnit!*

He stabs the button. Fine. It spits out two hundred.

Then he crams his card into the slot again.

It beeps. Tells him he's taken out his "allotted transaction amount."

"No no no," he says, hand balling into a fist and pounding on the machine like he's knocking on a door to be let in. "I need more than that! Please, c'mon." But the machine keeps beeping its refusal. The two hundred will have to do. He'll take it. He'll . . . offer it as a deposit to hold the diamond until tomorrow. He'll come back in the morning with more money and then it'll all be fine—

Click.

"Yo, dude, step away from that box."

His blood turns to snowmelt. His bowels to chilled vinegar.

"Come on, come on, turn around, turn around."

Andrew—ten twenty-dollar bills clutched in his left hand— pivots slowly. He can barely breathe. He's going to hyperventilate.

A lanky black kid stands there. Fifteen, sixteen years old. A gun almost too big for his hand hangs leveled at Andrew's chest. The big poofy Eagles jacket makes him look like a parade balloon. His face is half-hidden behind a purple paisley handkerchief.

"I'm gonna take that money now, son," the kid says, starting to reach.

Andrew instinctively pulls the money away—

Wham. The kid clips him across the chin with the side of the gun.

Teeth bite into tongue. He tastes blood. His neck is wet— first warm and wet, then cold.

The kid snatches the money out of Andrew's hand.

The mugger laughs loud, like he's not afraid of anyone hearing him out here. "You do *not* belong in this neighborhood, motherfucker. Shit, *shit*, look at you. Even in this fuck-ass snow your shoes still all shiny. Rich white people shoes are special shoes, I guess."

"My . . . socks are wet."

"Your socks are wet. Listen to this dude with his wet-ass socks." Suddenly the kid yells in his face, eyes wide and white, "I don't give a shit about your wet *fuckin'* socks, I care about what's in your fat *fuckin'* pockets! You got more shit in there, I know you do, rich boy. So open them up and share the wealth. Let's close the *income disparity* in America starting here, tonight, with you and me, motherfucker."

"I . . . Okay, okay," Andrew says, pulling his wallet and handing it over. He can lose that. He can even lose the two hundred. He can't lose the ring. His hand instinctively presses against the flat of his pocket, as if to protect the gold, the diamond, Sarah's love, the whole future.

"Whoa-whoa-whoa, what else you got there, rich boy? Hiding something in that pretty pocket? A present? For me?"

"Hey-hey-hey, no, it's nothing, really—"

Wham. The kid lashes out again. This time Andrew holds his arms up, so the gun cracks him in the side of his hand. He pulls it away, crying out, and when he does, the kid nails him in the temple—

Next thing he knows, the sidewalk is rushing up to meet him—

Red freckles on white snow—

The world is lost in a screaming whine—

The gun in his face, the kid screaming.

He can't even hear what the mugger is saying. He thinks suddenly, *I can reason with this kid, I can make him understand,* and he starts babbling about how he's got a ring in his pocket, an engagement ring, and he needs it or Sarah won't marry him, and his eyes are closed and he's pleading, praying, spit and blood making his words sound sticky—

The gun barrel presses against his head.

The mugger yells, "Gimme that fuckin' ring!"

Andrew thinks, *It's over. That crazy woman was right. I'm a dead man.*

He tilts his head.

Sees the blur of the gun. The length of the kid's arm. The madness in the mugger's eyes.

Then: movement in a whorl of snow.

An avenging angel. A knife-slash of black hair. Ends dyed in blood.

The girl from before, she steps out from the alley.

Her own gun up—

The kid never had a chance—

Bang.

Blood mists from the side of the kid's head.

He drops into the empty street. Blood pumping.

AN EXCERPT FROM
MIRIAM BLACK:
BOOK FOUR:
THUNDERBIRD
CHUCK WENDIG

THE QUITTER

Miriam runs.

Her feet pound asphalt. Ahead, Old Highway 60 cuts a knife line through red rock and broken earth, the highway shot through with hairline fractures. Big clouds hang, clouds like the stuffing pulled out of a doll and left scattered across the sky. The side of the highway lined with gnarly green scrub-brush, plants like hands reaching for the road, hoping to unzip it, rip it, ruin it. Beyond, it's just the wide open nowhere of Arizona: posts forming electric fences that don't contain anything, craggy rocks, dusty trails, distant peaks.

Run, she thinks. Sweat coming off her hair, into her eyes. *Fucking hair dye. Fucking hair spray. Fucking suntan lotion.* She blinks back sweat carrying all those chemicals, sweat that burns her eyes. *Don't pay attention to that. Just run.*

Then her foot catches something—a rock, a lip of cratered asphalt; she doesn't know, and it doesn't matter, because suddenly she pitches forward. Hands out. Palms catching the macadam, bracing herself so her head doesn't snap forward and crack in half like a tossed brick. A hard pain jars up her arms, through her elbows like a flicker of lightning. Her hands sting and throb.

She gets up on her knees and then starts coughing.

The coughing jag isn't brief. She plants her hands on her knees and hacks hard, and between hacks she wheezes, and between wheezes she just hacks harder. It's a dry cough of broken sticks and dead leaves until it's not—then it's wet, rheumy, and angry, like her lungs have gone liquid and have decided to disperse themselves up and out of her mouth.

A mouth that wants a cigarette right now. Lips that would plant around the filter and suck smoke deep. Her whole *body* wants a cigarette, and the nic-fit tears over and through her like a plague of starving locusts. She shudders and bleats and laughs and cries and then, once again, coughs.

Her palms pulse with her hummingbird heartbeat. The skin abraded.

Footsteps behind her.

Heavy. Boots hitting hard.

Sweat pours off her, now—spattering on the road.

"It's hot," she gasps. "It's fucking hot. It's *Hell* hot. It's wearing-the-Devil's-humid-scrotum-as-a-hat hot."

"They say it's a dry heat."

Louis clomps up alongside her like a Clydesdale horse.

She looks up at him. The sun is behind him, so he's just a shape, a shadow, a black monolith speaking to her. *Oh, Louis,* she thinks, and then he turns just so, and her eyes adjust. And she can see the black electrical tape crisscrossing his eyes. She can see his pale face, his wormy lips, a tongue that traipses over broken teeth. And when he moves, she hears the rustle of feathers, the clacking of beaks.

Not-Louis. The Trespasser. Her companion who only she can see—a hallucination, a ghost, a fellow traveler to wherever it is she's going.

"You know what else is a dry heat?" she asks. "Fire."

"It's only April."

"It's, like, almost ninety degrees. I should've come in December."

The Trespasser stands over her. Like an executioner ready to drop the head-chopper ax down on the kneeling sinner.

"Why are we out here, Miriam?"

She rocks back on her knees, cranes her head back, eyes closed. She paws at the water bottle hanging at her hip. With her teeth, she uncaps it (and even there that small movement, that tiny moment, she thinks, *My teeth want a cigarette too, want to bite into the nicotine like it's a cancerous Slim Jim god. I want it so bad I'd kick a baby seal just to get one taste*), then drinks deeply, drinks sloppily. Water over her lips, down her chin.

Up in the sky, vultures spin on an invisible axis.

"*We* are not out here," she says, wiping her wet mouth with the back of her hand. "I am out here alone. You are—well, we still don't know what you are, do we? Let's go with *demon*. Invisible, asshole demon. You're not here. You're *here*." She taps her temple, then drinks more water.

"If I'm up there, then I'm with you, and we are still *we*," he says. A loose, muddy chuckle in the well of his chest. "Why are you jogging, Miriam?"

"It's not jogging. It's jogging when rich, limp-noodle assholes do it. When I do it, it's called *running*, motherfucker." She sniffs. Coughs again. "I do it because I need to get better. Get stronger. Faster. All that."

"What are you running from?"

You, she thinks. But instead she says, "It's funny. Anyone who sees me running asks me that. *Hur hur, is something chasing you?* Yeah. Death. Death is chasing me, and chasing everyone else, too. That's what I'm running from. My own clock spinning down. The sweep of the Reaper's scythe."

"Not like you to run from death."

"Things have changed."

Another damp, diseased chuckle. "Oh, we know. You're trying to get away from us. From you. From the gift you have been given."

"It's no gift," she says, finally starting to stand up. The sun is punishing enough it feels like a fist trying to punch her back down to the ground. "But you know that. And you don't care." She thinks, but does not say: *As soon as I find the woman I'm looking for, you're outta here, pal. No more trespassing for you.*

"You're not done yet," the Trespasser says. As she stands, she sees Not-Louis's eyes have become black, glossy circles—crow eyes, rimmed with puckered gray skin and the start of oily feathers that disappear underneath the skin like stitches. "Not by a country mile, little girl."

She sucks in a bit of sweat from above her lip and spits a mist of it back at him. The Trespasser doesn't even flinch. Instead, he just points.

Miriam follows the crooked finger.

There, way down the highway, she sees the glint of light off a vehicle. Her vehicle—it's where she parked it. A rust-red, rat-trap pickup truck. A *literal* rattrap, actually—when she bought it, rats had made a nest in the engine, chewed up the belts and wires pretty good.

But then:

Another car.

This one coming from the opposite direction. Hard to make out what it is—the sun catches in it like a pool of liquid magma. Despite that, Miriam can see the back of the car fart out a noxious black cloud. She can hear the bang of the engine, and she can see something roll across the road—a hubcap?—that hits the tire of her Ford truck and drops. The car stops across from her truck.

Then all is still.

"What is that?" she asks. "Who is that?"

She turns toward the Trespasser, but he's gone.

And yet his voice still reaches her: "Go and see."

Shit.

NOT DONE YET

Miriam runs. Again. Because apparently she is a glutton for punishment. She tells herself that the quarter mile or so between her and the two vehicles is *psssh*, *pffft*, no problem at all, but three steps in and her feet feel like they're encased in cement and her calves feel like sausages about to split and spill their meat. Still, she runs. She tells herself it's because she has to.

Ahead, the truck and the car roam into view. Past the flinty, flashing sun. There, on her side of the road, the pickup: Ford F-250 from 1980. Rust has taken over most of the cherry-red paint. Across the highway: a Subaru station wagon. An Outback. Also old—maybe ten years, maybe more.

She hears the engines tinking and clicking. A smell hits her— bitter, acrid, sweet. A charred fan belt, cooked antifreeze.

A hundred yards away now. The driver-side door to the Subaru pops open. A black woman steps out. She's got the ragged edge of a survivor about her—a bumpy stick whittled down to a sharpened point. She's got a feral stare going on, and as Miriam slows to a jog and then to a walk, the woman points.

"Stay back!"

The woman's hand moves behind her, to the belt of her jeans—she turns just so, and Miriam sees something back there. A gun. Tucked. The driver doesn't pull it. Not yet.

Miriam holds up her hands, slows her walk. "Hey. Yo. Relax.

That's my truck right there. No harm no foul. Just gonna skootch on past, get in the truck, and go." Fifty yards now separate them. Maybe less.

The woman's eyes flash from Miriam to the truck and then back again.

Inside the Subaru station wagon: movement.

And that's when Miriam gets it. Because she sees a small face, round and wide-eyed, peer over the dashboard. A boy. Young, maybe ten years old. Blue T-shirt with some red on it—the Superman logo, she realizes. Just the top of it. She's a mother protecting her kid. Right?

Miriam thinks to ask if everything's okay, but her gut clenches: *Just let it go. Don't get involved.* This is a trap. The Trespasser put her here—she doesn't even know if it works like that, but whatever gets her out of this situation and back at the motel where she can crack one of those little vodka bottles . . . But then her dumb mouth starts forming words, and those words somehow escape like parakeets from open cages, and she says, "Do you need help?"

"You got a cell phone?"

"I . . . do. You want me to call somebody?"

The woman leans forward like she's about to pounce. "I want you to give it here. I want that phone."

Miriam arches an eyebrow. "Yeah, no."

"I want the phone and the keys to the truck."

"I will make a call for you and I will drive you somewhere."

"Oh, I know where you'll drive me. You ain't taking my boy back." And then the gun comes out—a little thumb-dicked .380 revolver. Snubby, priggish nose pointed right at Miriam. The woman's thumb cranes forward, clicks back the hammer. "Keys. Phone. Throw them over."

"If I throw the phone, I'll break it."

That seems to stun the woman, like she's too panicked to

think clearly and this tiny little hangnail has snagged the whole damn sweater.

"Fine," the woman barks, irritated. *"Fine.* Just . . . just come over, and you can hand them to me. No nonsense. Don't mess with me or I'll put this in you." She thrusts the gun forward, as if to demonstrate. The woman doesn't look like a killer, but she looks desperate—pushed to the edge. Miriam knows that people at the edge will do anything. Any dog trapped in any corner is likely to bite.

Miriam creeps forward. Her body throbs. Even in the heat she represses a chill. No idea what's happening here. What's driven this woman to this? She tries not to care. But the carapace she's carefully crafted is cracked—makes Miriam weak. Her hand ducks into her pocket, pulls out the little burner phone and the pickup's key ring. She jingles them like she's trying to distract a cat.

Thirty yards.

Twenty.

"C'mon, c'mon," the woman says, impatient.

Miriam knows she's not going to give over the keys or the phone.

That's all she knows, though. What happens next, she's not sure.

Ten yards now, and Miriam slows her walk, tries to buy herself some time. "You don't have to do this. We can be pals." *You take my truck and my phone, and I might have to feed you to the coyotes, lady.* "I don't know who you think I am or why I'd want to take your son—"

The woman waves the gun. "You people need to leave us alone."

Five yards. She starts to hand over the keys and the phone—

Two minutes ago, Miriam's whole body ached, but now, every cell is awake and alive and without any pain at all, juicing on the natural narcotic of hard-charging adrenalin. With her free hand the woman reaches across—

Miriam flings the keys. Not enough to hurt—or, at least, to do damage—but enough where a jingly-jangly projectile launched at the woman's face will offer up the interference Miriam needs. Her gut check is right: This lady isn't combat ready, and while desperate, she's not trained to deal with distraction. The gun goes wide, the woman makes a sound—"Nuhhh!"—and Miriam grabs the gun wrist and slams it back—

There the two of them stand. Wrestling back and forth with the revolver. The key ring hits the ground with a cymbal crash. The strange lady's cell phone takes a tumble too—spinning corner to corner until it hits the asphalt, cracking the outer case. Gracie throws a punch, tries to piston it into the woman's side, but the crazy white bitch bends her body—the fist misses, and the woman catches it, twists it, pins Gracie's hand like she pins the other one. But Gracie isn't done. She won't be taken again. She won't let her son be taken again. Everyone is an enemy, and she has to get free, so she drives a hard knee up into the lady's middle. Her finger does this involuntary squeeze and . . . The gun in her hand bucks, firing up at the sky, up at the gods—bang— gun smoke plume and brimstone stink. Inside the car, Abe is screaming, pounding on the dashboard, face a mess of tears—

And then there's another gunshot—